I0762946

DEATH
ON THE
LANAI
A Golden Girls Cozy Mystery

Golden Girls Cozy Mysteries

By Rachel Ekstrom Courage

Murder by Cheesecake

DEATH ON THE LANAI

RACHEL EKSTROM COURAGE

NEW YORK TIMES BESTSELLING AUTHOR OF *MURDER BY CHEESECAKE*

A Golden Girls Cozy Mystery

HYPERION AVENUE
LOS ANGELES NEW YORK

Death on the Lanai is an original novel inspired by the television show *The Golden Girls*. Any similarities to actual persons, places, and events are purely coincidental.

For information address Hyperion Avenue, 7 Hudson Square, New York, New York 10013.

First Paperback Edition, June 2026
1 3 5 7 9 10 8 6 4 2
FAC-004510-26078
Printed in the United States of America

Library of Congress Control Number: 2025951593
ISBN 978-1-36811787-6

The authorized representative in the EU for product safety and compliance is Disney Trading B.V., Asterweg 15S, 1031 HL, Amsterdam, The Netherlands
email: DCP.DL-EU.bookscontact@disney.com

www.HyperionAvenueBooks.com

Logo Applies to Text Stock Only

FOR NICK

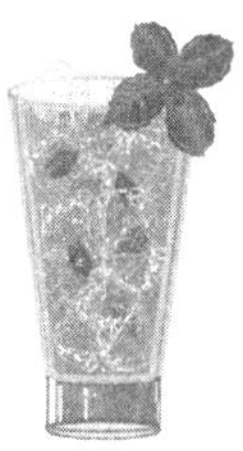

THE GUESS LIST

1

Dorothy padded through the kitchen door into the living room holding a freshly brewed mug of coffee and wearing her comfy floor-length baseball jersey nightgown. She sat on one end of the coral rattan couch, savoring the steaming aroma before she tasted the velvety Cuban blend. On the other end of the couch, Blanche paged through her slim leather-bound day planner with a scowl on her face. Dorothy took a few fortifying sips as she pretended not to notice her roommate's increasingly animated display. Then she finally turned to Blanche.

"Good morning," she said in her gravelly voice.

Instead of responding, Blanche bit her lip and flipped to the telephone number section of her planner, then back to the calendar. Frowning, she pushed up the sleeves of her aquamarine silk robe and held her head in her hands.

Dorothy put down her coffee and placed a hand on Blanche's knee.

"Do you want to talk about it?" she asked.

Blanche looked up through her fingers, her caramel curls only slightly mussed. "I'm madder than a fox in an empty henhouse, Dorothy. Something just awful has happened."

Dorothy's mind quickly came up with several reasons for why Blanche would be upset while paging through her calendar. A missed doctor's appointment? At their age, they had to watch every bump, lump, and mole, and any waiting could be agony. Or maybe she'd forgotten someone's birthday—one of her children's, perhaps? Blanche was the youngest of the four women sharing a house in Miami, but she wasn't immune to the occasional bout of forgetfulness that plagued each of them from time to time. Dorothy glanced at Blanche's planner, giving in to her curiosity, as Rose emerged from her bedroom and Sophia sidled up behind them, completing the foursome.

"Good morning, everyone!" Rose beamed, settling down

in the armchair next to the sofa in her fluffy pink robe. "Isn't it a lovely day? I awoke to the sound of a rooster crowing, just like back on the farm in St. Olaf!"

"That was our next-door neighbor passing a gallstone. Kept me up since five a.m.," Sophia grumbled.

Dorothy stifled a laugh, and her lips pursed with worry as she clocked the look of despair on Blanche's face. "Blanche was just about to tell me an awful realization, weren't you, doll? Is it anything any of us can help you with?" She nodded encouragingly as Sophia joined them on the couch and studied Blanche through her large circular bifocals.

"I've checked and double-checked." Blanche sighed, her face a grimace of confusion as she flapped her day planner in the air. "And this stupid thing doesn't have any plans for this weekend in it! No dinner dates, no lunch dates, no blind dates . . . not even a *coffee* date!"

Sophia raised her wrinkled hands to her face in mock horror. "An empty social calendar with no dates? Should we lower the flag? Wear all black? I'll pray the rosary for you. . . ."

Blanche slapped the planner on her silken lap in a huff. "You don't understand," she began. "Every weekend is a golden opportunity to find romance, to explore new worlds in the universe of love. I'm not going to waste one here, sitting around with a bunch of old biddies!"

Dorothy raised her eyebrows, and leaned against the back of the sofa, absorbing the insult. Because Blanche was the youngest of the four, her digs about age stung more than she realized.

"We're not *old*!" Rose said. She dangled a partially finished set of baby-size pajamas in front of their faces, knitted with love and featuring three tiny legs with the feet sewn in. "Could an old person do all *this* during just one episode of *Matlock*?"

"We could play gin rummy," Sophia suggested. "That's always a good time."

"Because you always win," Dorothy pointed out. "I'd go for Trivial Pursuit, if we make popcorn."

Blanche looked skyward and shook her head. "You're all proving my point," she said in her Southern drawl.

Dorothy chuckled. "It's not a big deal, Blanche. *I* don't have any dates lined up for this weekend either."

Blanche pouted at Dorothy. "Exactly."

"You walked right into that one," Sophia said with a grin. "I'll refrain from further comment."

"What I mean is, that's no surprise," Blanche continued. "But for a woman like me, who has always had suitors lined up around the block and never lacked for the attention of men . . . well, it's not something I'm equipped to handle. At least you all are used to it."

Dorothy clenched her teeth, stood, and headed toward the kitchen. She'd heard numerous comments over the years from Blanche—and her mother—about her long-standing lack of romance. "I don't need this kind of treatment first thing in the morning. I'm going to drink more coffee and get on with my boring, spinster life. Would anyone *other* than Blanche like to join me?"

Rose opened her mouth to speak just as the doorbell rang.

All four women paused, then all four rushed to answer it. Rose, who was the closest to the door, narrowly beat Blanche to the handle. She batted her friend's hand away and opened the door to find a young man in an ill-fitting red suit and cap. He held a small parcel in both hands and offered a nervous smile.

"Greetings!" he said "Is this 6151 Richmond Street?"

"Yes," the four women said in unison.

The delivery man looked at each of the girls in turn, taking in their sleepwear and expectant expressions.

"This is for you—er, for one of you, I guess," he said.

Sophia elbowed her way to the front of the pack, so the young man handed the parcel to her. She looked at it suspiciously, turning it in her hands.

"Who's it from?" she asked.

"I, uh—I don't know. All's I know is I'm supposed to bring it to this address."

Dorothy peered over her mother's shoulder at the parcel. It was wrapped in brown paper, tied with a string, and had no return address. "Is there anything else you can tell us about it—such as who hired you to deliver this?" she asked, always practical.

The nervous young man wiped his sweaty hands on the front of his uniform. "I—I can't say. But, oh! I'm supposed to give you this, too. . . ."

He dug in his satchel and handed a large cream-colored envelope to Dorothy. He waited for a few moments as if expecting a tip before realizing that the girls had forgotten all about him in their excitement over the mysterious package. He checked his watch, then hustled back down the walkway to his bike. Dorothy examined the envelope as he cycled away; meanwhile, Blanche plucked the package out of Sophia's hands and carried it over to the rattan coffee table.

The four women squeezed onto the sofa and stared at the package. They stared at it for a while, almost like they expected it to move, or explain itself.

"Let's see who this is from," Dorothy said, sliding a finger under the flap of the heavy envelope. She had to admit, her curiosity was piqued. They hadn't gotten any mail other than coupon circulars and utility bills in weeks—and over the past few months, Dorothy had gotten exactly two postcards from a man she'd had a brief and ill-fated connection with. He'd apparently made it to Puerto Rico, then Curaçao, with plans to continue on to South America, and Dorothy didn't know when—or if—she'd ever see him again.

After neatly tearing the envelope open, she pulled out a thick piece of card stock. The front was decorated with an elaborate woodcut print in a deep red pigment, depicting a Mediterranean-style building surrounded by a border of orchids, birds, palm trees, and paintbrushes. The phrase *You're Invited* took over the top fourth of the card.

Dorothy traced the details with her finger, noticing a tiny crocodile peeking out from behind one of the palm trees. "This is really intricate work. I wonder where this was printed."

Blanche impatiently snatched the invitation from Dorothy's hand and flipped it over. "'You're invited to a gala event celebrating the life and work of our century's greatest artist,'" she read. "'This Friday'—that's today—'at seven p.m., the Villa Velado on Isla Sosiega. You will be met at the parking lot at the end of Orange Blossom Road. Dress to kill.'"

At the bottom of the card was a handwritten postscript in thick black lines: *Wear this—ET.*

"Dress to kill what?" Rose asked. "If it's anything larger than a chicken, I don't think I can participate."

"I doubt they're referring to slaughtering livestock, dear," said Dorothy.

"*It means*, Rose, dress up and look fabulous," Blanche explained with a little shiver of delight. "An art in which I'm expertly skilled."

"It's an art all right," Sophia quipped. "You slap more paint on your face than Michelangelo used for the entire Sistine Chapel!"

"It's more than makeup, it's a skill, Sophia, as I'm sure you know. It doesn't just happen. Even in your day, you must have had some"—Blanche wiggled her fingers in the older woman's direction—"rudimentary techniques to highlight your assets and hide your flaws."

"It was easier to do back then," Sophia said with a shrug. "We didn't have electricity in my village in Sicily. Even my cousin Georgio looked pretty good on a moonless night."

"Oh, Ma, stop," Dorothy said, shaking her head.

"But who is this addressed to?" Sophia asked. "It doesn't say on the envelope."

"And there's nothing on the package," Rose pointed out.

"And who's ET, I wonder," Dorothy said.

"Oh, it's from that little alien!" Rose said. "You know, the one whose finger lights up? Everyone always said he looked just a *little too much* like my cousin Lars."

Dorothy leveled an incredulous look at Rose. Sometimes she couldn't tell if her airheaded friend was pulling her leg. "Rose, are you telling me you actually believe that a fictional alien from a Spielberg picture is inviting us to a dinner party on a Friday night?"

"Well, now that you put it like that, it does sound a little silly," Rose said. She looked intently at the invitation. "Why would he be hosting a gala when he just wants to get home to his own planet? Especially when he has all those sinister government types after him."

"Dear, those are *initials*," Blanche said, making her Southern drawl even slower so Rose would understand. "They stand for someone whose first name starts with *E*, and their last name starts with *T*. Now, who do we know with those initials?"

The women sat in silence for a long moment.

Relative silence, anyway, as Sophia mumbled to herself all the *E* and *T* names she could think of. Dorothy ran through her mental Rolodex. She could tell that Blanche was doing the same. Rose appeared lost in thought, a pleasant smile on her face. Dorothy wasn't sure what was going on there, but she didn't want to ask.

Suddenly, Sophia stood up from the sofa.

"Ernest Tinkelbaum!" she shouted. "Oh, wait a minute, he passed last year. He died doing what he loved: cheating at canasta."

She sat back down and frowned.

"Well, we've ruled out the extraterrestrial and Ernest Tinkelbaum," Dorothy said. "Maybe I'll flip through my address book for some ideas."

"But we haven't opened the box yet!" said Blanche. "Maybe there's a clue about who it's from—or for—inside."

The girls all simultaneously grabbed for the box. Rose politely let go first and Dorothy reluctantly relented, leaving Blanche and Sophia gripping it with white knuckles.

"I should get to open it because I'm the oldest!" Sophia said with a grunt.

"This isn't your birthday party," Blanche retorted. "And I have a feeling this is for me. Who else would be getting an invitation to an elegant gala and be expected to dress to kill?"

"It's definitely for me," Sophia said, finally ripping the brown-paper parcel away from Blanche's hands and clutching it against her chest. "Somebody probably wants to give me a lifetime achievement award for putting up with you three all these years."

Dorothy tugged at the parcel again, but her mother didn't loosen her grip. "There's a good chance of it being for me. Maybe one of my students has grown up to be an important painter or critic. It wouldn't surprise me if one of them were hosting an event like this and remembered my interest in art."

"But what if it's for me?" Rose asked. "If the party is some kind of fundraiser, they could have heard about my work at the grief center or my volunteering at the hospital. I've been known to move in sophisticated circles."

"You certainly go in circles . . ." Sophia quipped. "But this isn't a square dance with the town elders, Rose. This is the Villa Velado."

"Velado," Dorothy repeated thoughtfully. "I knew that name rang a bell. There was a piece about it in the *Herald* a few years ago, interesting enough to catch my attention. The main house is almost as old as Miami. It was built on a private island, and no guests or press have been allowed on the grounds since the original owner died fifty years ago."

"That's extremely fascinating, Dorothy," Blanche said. "But we all know my work at the museum makes *me* the most likely one to be invited to celebrate an artist, don't you agree?"

With that, Blanche reached over and gently eased the parcel out of Sophia's arms. She tore open the paper wrapper with her frosted coral nails, revealing an elaborately carved wooden box. She picked it up carefully, rotating it at eye level to reveal the designs on each side: a butterfly, a magnolia blossom, an apple with a bite taken out of it, and the iconic point of the Chrysler Building in New York.

Blanche got a faraway look in her eye as her friends peered at the mysterious object.

Dorothy blew a fine layer of dust off the top. "It looks like it's been stored away for a while," she said.

"Maybe it's an antique," Sophia said.

"Well, don't just sit there," Rose squealed. "Open it!"

Blanche slowly opened the lid, revealing an ornate brooch in the shape of a butterfly. Golden filaments supported an array of jewels in green, pink, and white forming the pattern of the butterfly's wings. A long diamond body bisected the wings, topped by a ruby head with slender golden antennae. The women oohed and aahed as Blanche turned it around in her fingers, angling it so its jeweled facets caught the light.

"It's *beautiful*," Blanche said, practically salivating. "And since it's jewelry, it's definitely for me."

She held it up to the lapel of her silk robe, craning her neck to admire herself.

"It certainly is stunning," Dorothy said. "Is there anything inscribed on the back of the box? Perhaps we can figure out who it's from that way."

"I'd be nervous wearing anything that fancy," Rose said.

"What if it falls off? Or attracts a dangerous element? You can't be too careful these days," she cautioned, gently shaking a finger at Blanche.

Dorothy put a comforting hand on Rose's shoulder. Her friends had been a little shaken since their last adventure had brought them into close contact with a few bad apples. "It does attract attention, but it might just be costume jewelry. We really don't know."

"It's not costume jewelry," Sophia said, snatching the brooch from Blanche and weighing it in her small, wrinkled hands. "It's too heavy. These are real stones and real gold. Must be worth a fortune!"

Blanche rubbed her hands together with a knowing smile on her face. "When a man sends jewelry, serious jewelry, he only wants one thing."

"With something this nice he probably wants it twice!" said Sophia, waggling her eyebrows.

"I don't mean that! Get your mind out of the gutter, Sophia," Blanche said. "I mean he wants to give it to a woman who's worthy of wearing it. Someone . . . *special*." Blanche grinned to herself, clearly convinced that meant her.

"What makes you so sure that a man sent it?" Rose asked. "Isn't that making an assumption?"

"It *is*," Blanche purred, her eyes glued to where the brooch shimmered, reflecting pinpoints of light across their coffee table. "But I'm willing to bet money that it's from a man.

Most likely a very rich, very handsome man, with exquisite taste. And there's only one way to find out."

"Call the police, fingerprint the letter, and track down who sent this package?" Rose said, her eyes alight with adventure.

"No, honey," Blanche said. "We're all going to get dressed to kill—and we're going to this party."

ALL DRESSED UP WITH SOMEWHERE TO GO

2

Blanche stood in her pink and palm frond bedroom, staring at the contents of her closet. What should she wear to meet the mysterious person who'd sent the extravagant brooch? Something about the carved wooden box and the jewelry inside made her think she must know the sender, but she couldn't put her finger on who. She'd find out soon enough, she thought with a delicious quiver of anticipation. She pressed a hand to her lips, considering the row of silk, chiffon, brocade, lace, and sequins on the rack in front of her.

She needed something eye-catching, of course.

To be fair, she didn't have anything in her closet that *wasn't* eye-catching. So the trick was to find the right thing. She didn't want to wear something too revealing. She could hear her mother's voice in her head after all these years, dripping with honey to hide the vinegar beneath it as Blanche dressed for a date in high school. She'd wanted to wear hot pink lipstick—something bright and fun, to frame her dazzling white smile—and her mama had made her wipe it off and wear a paler shade.

"You don't want to look cheap, Blanche," she'd said. "Boys won't treat you right if you do."

Blanche shook her mother's voice out of her head and pulled out a satin pantsuit, a sheath dress with a matching jacket, a long evening gown, and a short coral-toned cocktail dress. She grabbed the short cocktail dress first, holding it over herself and modeling it in her full-length mirror. Lately, she had grown a little self-conscious about her knees, which had disconcertingly begun to look the teensiest bit droopy, and this—and the sheath—hit just above the knee.

But Blanche also knew she had great calves, which were still as shapely as ever, plus a perfectly glowing tan from the Florida sun. She had plenty of assets to distract from her knees, and she'd simply draw the eye upward to showcase her shoulders, her clavicle, her face, her lips, her dainty ears, and her sparkling eyes—the eyes that her late husband, George, used to call "limpid pools of seduction."

Blanche's shoulders dropped, thinking of George.

She missed him every day.

Of course she put up a brave facade in front of her roommates, and she tried to keep a busy calendar of events: her part-time work at the museum, and of course, dating a variety of men in the Miami metro area. But what her good friends didn't know was that she was only chasing after a scintilla of the feeling she'd had with George. It wasn't just a healthy sex drive or her voracious need for male approval—though those were certainly part of it. Their marriage had been far from perfect, but she missed the way he looked at her. She missed their quiet nights when their children were asleep, the scent of magnolia blossoms drifting across their porch as they kissed on the swing, with George's Sazerac and her mint julep sitting forgotten on a nearby table. Oh, to be able to go back and relive a night like that again—if only just for a moment.

Blanche felt her eyes prick with tears, and she shoved the painful feeling back down and grabbed another dress from the rack. This one was a long-sleeved shorter number with a champagne lining overlaid with black lace, and she held it against her body to appraise herself in her mirror. Her reflection looked powerful and sexy—without a trace of sadness or grief. The dress also showed her knees, but no one would be looking down that far. Not with the way the low, curved neckline framed her face and still-pert décolletage.

She'd wear this one tonight. It was perfect.

Blanche carefully rolled the coral dress in tissue and placed it in a floral embroidered weekend bag passed down to her by her mother. She tossed in a few lacy undergarments, a satin robe, and a few negligees. She added an extra pair of low-heeled slingbacks (in case her higher heels started to hurt), a makeup bag for touch-ups, a jar of night cream, and a tiny travel toothbrush and mini toothpaste. Of course, she also had to have a shoulder bag that matched her outfit, in which she placed a tiny bottle of perfume and a few other necessities.

A lady is always prepared, she told herself.

After all, a mysterious man had sent her the beautiful brooch—and she couldn't wait to find out who he was. He clearly had excellent taste in jewelry—*and women*, she thought. And if for some reason he didn't turn out to be a total dreamboat—if he had halitosis, for example, or turned out to be like her ex-fiancé Harry, the bigamist—then hopefully there would be plenty of other eligible men at the gala.

Even if there were only a few—or even just one—Blanche wanted to be ready in case she happened to get swept off her feet. After all, Big Daddy always said you had to plan ahead if you wanted to be spontaneous, which is why he kept a roll of fifty-dollar bills in the glove compartment of his Buick and a bottle of champagne chilling in the family's icebox.

The only thing missing from this outfit—preventing it from becoming truly stunning—was jewelry. And Blanche knew that the butterfly brooch sitting in the living room would give her just the pop of color and glitz she needed. But first, she'd have to convince the others to let her wear it. She figured that Sophia was her stiffest competition, based on everyone's reactions during the unboxing. Maybe she could butter up the older woman with some sweet talk—or a well-timed snack. That always worked on the men in her life.

Still, Sophia was a tougher cookie than any man.

Blanche left her bedroom and peeked into the living room, looking for the old gal. But she wasn't on the sofa, nor was she in the kitchen or out on the lanai. Finally, Blanche knocked on Sophia's bedroom door and was greeted with a grumpy "Go away!"

"Sophia, honey, it's me," Blanche said, putting a few extra dollops of sugar into her voice. "I just wanted to see if you needed any help picking out an outfit for tonight. You know I have a knack for it!"

The door opened a crack and Sophia regarded her with one suspicious eye.

"That's true," Sophia admitted at last. "How did you know I was having trouble picking out something to wear?"

"I was having the same problem," Blanche confessed. "It's been a while since any of us were invited to an elegant soiree, and we don't have time to run out and shop for anything new."

Sophia opened the door the rest of the way and waved Blanche into her dove-gray-and-baby-blue bedroom, which smelled faintly of Bengay and lavender. Sophia's bed was neatly made, with a black suit, a black dress, and yet another black dress laid out over the cream-colored duvet.

"What's with all the black?" Blanche asked. "We're not going to a funeral."

"I realize that, Einstein. But that's what most of my social occasions are these days." Sophia sat on the edge of her bed. "That and meeting the Shady Pines girls at their all-you-can-eat buffet on Sundays. I hate that place, but the waffle station *is* fantastic. And if I'm feeling frisky, I can go play chess with the geezers at Moore Park. But they're so old, they wouldn't notice if I wore a ballgown or a bikini, so I keep it simple—"

"You must have something more colorful *somewhere*," Blanche said, heading to Sophia's small closet. "Or you can borrow something from me, like you did for that bachelorette party we had for Rose's niece."

Sophia tilted her head, remembering. "That *was* a fun night. But no offense, Blanche, I'm not trying to look like the senior madam of some two-bit whorehouse. This is supposed to be a classy event."

Blanche shot a glare at Sophia but shook off the insult. They were par for the course with the older woman, who seemed to have no internal filter, and Blanche tried not to take it personally as she pawed through Sophia's wardrobe, finding styles that were more fashionable in the sixties and seventies than now. Still, there were a few pieces she could work with. There was a long mulberry gown adorned with sequins, though it needed to be dry-cleaned. A brocade suit in a lovely green looked chic, but it was far too heavy for the late Florida spring. Finally Blanche grabbed a high-necked ivory silk number and held it up to Sophia's small frame. *This could work*, she thought. It just needed something. A pop of color.

A touch of sparkle.

Her heart sank.

"Sophia, I think you should wear the brooch tonight," Blanche said. "I really wanted to, but you need something to jazz this up."

"What's the catch?" Sophia said, giving Blanche a suspicious once-over. "Are you angling to be my plus-one at the Barry Manilow concert?"

"Of course not, Sophia!" Blanche exclaimed. "I'm offering out of the goodness of my heart."

"A moment ago you were ready to wrestle me for it!" Sophia said. "I thought I'd have to dust off my Hulk Hogan moves."

"No need for all that," Blanche said, trying to erase the mental image of Sophia wearing a bleach-blond goatee and a spandex singlet. "Anyway, an older woman needs statement jewelry, otherwise she just fades into the scenery. I'll just have to make do with my supple skin, glowing complexion, youthful curves, and exceptional animal magnetism to keep me at the center of attention."

"Keep telling yourself that, sweetheart," Sophia said.

But Blanche had already swept out of the room, preoccupied by mentally patting herself on the back for letting Sophia wear the brooch. In addition to her striking good looks, she really was a selfless and generous woman, she thought.

By six o'clock Rose, Dorothy, and Blanche had congregated in the living room sporting fresh layers of powder, lipstick, and mascara, their hair freshly curled. The air was heavy with a mix of perfume and hairspray, a familiar scent that always reminded Blanche of her first debutante ball. She had similar butterflies in her stomach tonight, too, though she didn't fully understand why. She was going out to a party on a private island with her three closest friends, which was sure to be entertaining. Perhaps it was the air of mystery around the event—the secretive host, the expensive gift, the question of who the invitation was really for.

Rose twirled, showing off her tea-length gown in a dusty rose, which matched the color in her cheeks. Dorothy flicked a speck of lint from her elegantly draped pantsuit with midnight blue sequins and billowy sleeves just as Sophia stepped from her room in the outfit Blanche had picked out, with the stunning butterfly brooch pinned prominently to her collar. The gemstones reflected multicolored sparkles onto Sophia's chin and bounced off her bifocals. Blanche felt a twinge of regret at having given up her chance to wear the brooch, but she tamped down the feeling, seeing how proud Sophia looked to be wearing it.

In lieu of the brooch, Blanche had chosen oversize crystal

earrings. They added light to her face and distracted from her jawline, which seemed a touch softer today than it had looked yesterday. She knew she was fit as a fiddle, but she had a birthday coming up that she didn't want to think about. Maybe she'd go on that new chardonnay-and-egg diet that she'd been hearing so much about. And do some neck exercises. Maybe she'd get regular massages from that handsome male masseuse who worked out of the Carlyle Hotel.

That would surely get the blood flowing to all the right places, Blanche told herself as she ushered her friends to the door. She'd taken longer than planned in deciding what to wear, and she was eager to meet her mysterious admirer.

Just as she and her friends were about to leave the house, the doorbell rang.

"Who could that be?" asked Rose. "We didn't order any pizza."

"Maybe it's another jewelry delivery!" Blanche giggled.

Dorothy opened the door a crack, then quickly shut it. She closed her eyes and brought one hand to her forehead as if she had a migraine. The doorbell rang again, followed by an insistent knock.

Dorothy shot a *Can you believe this?* look to her friends.

She sighed, then opened the door the whole way, revealing a tall, balding man in a yellow sweater and gray windbreaker.

"Hi, it's me, Stan," Dorothy's ex-husband said.

No sooner had he gotten the words out than his jaw dropped as he took in the four girls in all of their finery.

"What are you doing here, *Stan*?" Dorothy said.

"I was in the neighborhood," Stan said. "I figured it's Friday night, so you'd probably be home. I thought I'd see if you wanted to go for a ride in my Studebaker, just like old times."

"No, thank you," Dorothy said. "The old times didn't age so well." She moved to close the door again.

Stan gripped the doorframe, weaseling his way into the house a few more inches. "How about we go bowling or something?"

"Do I look like I want to go bowling?" Dorothy deadpanned as she gestured to her sequined outfit.

"Maybe." Stan shrugged and offered a nervous smile. "Do you?"

"Excuse me, but we are on our way to a very exclusive VIP event," Blanche said. She didn't want to be late, and her Southern manners prevented her from shoving him out of their way.

"That's right," Dorothy said. "As you can see, I have much more exciting plans."

"You look fantastic," Stan said, looking her up and down. "Seriously stunning. Do you need an escort? I could be your date to wherever you're going."

"We are going to a *gala*," Blanche said firmly. "You're not dressed for it."

This party was Dorothy's chance to mingle with an entirely new dating pool—hopefully much better specimens than

Stan—and Blanche was determined to not let him ruin the evening.

"Then let me be your bodyguard and keep the riffraff away," Stan joked.

Sophia laughed. "You *are* the riffraff!"

Dorothy looked from Stan to her friends, hesitating. Blanche knew that it had been weeks—or maybe months—since Dorothy had gone on a date, and she worried for a moment that her friend would cave. Blanche knew from experience that sometimes it only took one well-timed compliment during a moment of weakness to catapult back into the arms of Mr. Wrong.

"I'm sorry, Stan," Dorothy finally said. "But I'm going out with my friends."

She allowed him a chaste peck on the cheek, then she shooed him out the door.

"That was a close one!" Sophia muttered.

"Oh, he's not that bad," said Rose.

"Then you date him," Blanche said. "Dorothy's got better fish to fry this evening. Isn't that right, Dorothy?"

Piled into Dorothy's car, the four friends drove off into the early evening. As they rolled down Richmond Street, passing ranch houses dwarfed by soaring palm trees, Blanche wished

Dorothy would drive faster, since Stan had delayed them. She wondered what her mystery man would look like, how many guests would be at the gala, and if she'd be the best-dressed woman there. She hoped there were enough good-looking, eligible men in attendance to keep her and Dorothy busy.

"Any more guesses on who the host is?" Dorothy said, turning onto another street.

"Maybe it's a celebrity!" Rose said, clapping her hands. "Oh, I hope it's Don Johnson."

"Why would Don Johnson be inviting one of us to a gala?" Sophia asked.

"Because I've written over two dozen letters to his fan club," Rose said. "Maybe he read them and thought I sounded nice."

"But the invitation said one of the world's greatest *artists*, Rose," Blanche said. "What does Don Johnson have to do with art?"

"Television acting is an art," Rose said. "Perhaps the most important art of this century."

"Fine," Blanche said, assuming that Rose was probably thinking of *Miami Vice*, or even *Mork & Mindy*, rather than anything on *Masterpiece Theatre*.

Dorothy made eye contact with Rose in the rearview mirror. "But don't you think it's more likely that it's a painter or a sculptor or something like that?"

"You and your merciless logic," Rose huffed.

"Oh no," Blanche said, realizing just who the mysterious host might be—someone who *would* have invited all four of them. "What if it's that sculptor, you know, the Hungarian one?"

Sophia, Rose, and Dorothy groaned, remembering the time they had all posed nude for the artist Lazlo, unbeknownst to each other.

"But his initials weren't ET!" Dorothy said, turning onto a darkened, sandy road.

"Thank goodness," Blanche said, relieved that Dorothy had such a strong eye and memory for detail. Blanche was much better at reading body language, innuendo, and a man's intentions—usually based on his eye contact, tone of voice, and the type of cologne he was wearing—but when it came to more boring minutiae, it was helpful to have a friend like Dorothy.

No matter who their mysterious host was, or what adventures the evening would bring, she was delighted they were all in it together.

STRANGER DANGER

3

Dorothy drove through downtown Miami, then turned onto Biscayne Boulevard. Stan's voice echoed in her head as she braked behind a line of cars that were waiting at a red light. *Seriously stunning*, he'd said.

Dorothy smiled to herself, luxuriating in the way those words made her feel. Once again she wrestled with the familiar pull Stan had over her. *It's not chemistry—it's just our history*, she told herself. *He's not what you need right now.*

Thankfully, the feeling lessened the farther she drove.

As she turned onto a smaller road, she glimpsed the bay shimmering in the early twilight, and Dorothy was glad she'd decided to do something different tonight instead of fall into old habits. It wasn't long before they reached a turnoff marked SEMI-PRIVATE, and Dorothy followed the road to a sandy parking lot near Morningside Park.

"This is the address," Dorothy said, putting the car in park and engaging the emergency brake even though they were on a level surface.

There were a few other cars in the lot, as well as a large iguana soaking up the last few rays of sunshine. As the women stepped out of the old, reliable sedan, Dorothy looked around for a sign or a person to point them in the right direction. She took a few steps to the edge of the lot and peeked at the bay through a line of palm trees. She could make out the distant shape of an island a couple of miles away from shore.

That must be Isla Sosiega, she thought.

Suddenly, someone behind her cleared their throat.

Turning, Dorothy saw a middle-aged man in a stained bucket hat that was decorated with fishhooks and lures.

"Well, hello," Dorothy said. "Are you taking us to the gala?"

As soon as the words left her mouth, she felt a little ridiculous. Based on the man's clothing, he was probably a fisherman heading home after a hard day's work. But the man surprised her by grunting and gesturing for Dorothy and the others to follow him. Rose shot her a concerned look, Sophia simply raised her eyebrows, and Blanche sashayed after the man. Dorothy thought, not for the first time, she'd better keep an eye on her friend.

The man led them to a metal stairway, where a weather-beaten rowboat bobbed against a wooden dock. Then with another grunt, he gestured for the ladies to get in.

"Oh, no, I'm not doing that again," Rose said, taking a step back.

"Me neither." Sophia looked dubiously at the little boat.

Ever since the girls had had a dangerous encounter on an inflatable dinghy, they'd avoided boats of all kinds. It was more than understandable, Dorothy knew. She felt apprehensive, too, about the prospect of getting on a tiny watercraft with a man they didn't know. She'd recently learned that you can never be too careful.

"Excuse me, sir," she asked, "but isn't there another way to the villa?"

The man shook his head, making his sunburned cheeks wobble.

"Now listen here," Blanche began. "I'm not getting on a boat with a strange man unless it's a five-star dinner cruise, do you understand me?"

Rose stood behind Blanche, crossed her arms, and nodded while Sophia eyed the meager boat with equal suspicion.

The man cleared his throat again. In a cultured transatlantic accent, he said, "This boat is the only way to make it to the villa. I've already ferried the other guests over, and you are the last ones to arrive. So the question becomes: Would you care to join them?"

The four women looked at one another, slightly stunned at the incongruity of the man's voice and his appearance.

"Never judge a fish by its scales, I suppose," Rose whispered under her breath.

Sophia turned to the three women and motioned for them to lean in to a huddle. "You're going to trust this guy, just because he talks like Cary Grant? What if, once we get on the boat, he starts talking like Donald Duck?"

Dorothy frowned, wondering what to do. Her mother could be right. But they'd come so far and gotten all dressed up. It would feel like a waste to turn around now and go back, where her only option for romance was an evening with Stan. She looked across the water at the distant island. She couldn't see the famous villa from here, but she imagined a bevy of elegant guests having sophisticated conversations without them. Dorothy could see herself in the center of it all, surrounded by cultured men vying to hear her opinions on the Belgian tapestries at the Bass Museum, like an erudite version of Marilyn Monroe encircled by male dancers as she sang "Diamonds Are a Girl's Best Friend." Getting on this boat was a risk, but it also certainly beat another night at home in her pajamas, playing cards on the lanai with her octogenarian mother or watching reruns of *Laugh-In* on their familiar coral sofa.

She wanted to be at that party. She *needed* to be at that

party, but she didn't want to force the issue if her friends weren't comfortable. So with a voice full of gusto and hope she asked, "What do you say, ladies, shall we take a vote?"

Dorothy very much believed in the democratic process, even if it was hard when the four of them were evenly split. Invariably, Sophia would bellow that she should get two votes because of her age, and Blanche usually claimed she should get an extra vote since she was the owner of their home. Still, it was worth a try. "All in favor of going to this party, considering we're ninety percent of the way there, say aye."

Blanche and Dorothy raised their hands.

"I wish there was a bridge instead of this rickety old boat—but I've got to find out who sent the brooch," Blanche said.

Although it seemed deadlocked for a few brief heartbeats, Sophia eventually raised hers, too.

Sophia shrugged. "If this guy tries any funny business, I'll make him a knuckle sandwich so good he'll forget his own name," she said, loud enough for the boatman to hear.

Dorothy grinned. Her mother was barely tall enough to see over the dashboard, but she was a spitfire.

Rose was the only one with her hands firmly at her sides. "This reminds me of the last time we played Ugel and Flugel!" she huffed.

"How's that, Rose?" Sophia said.

"Well, I'd squirreled myself away in a laundry basket and no one ever found me! When I finally crawled out from under a week's worth of dirty socks, you all were eating cheesecake together in the kitchen," she said. "I felt a little left out."

"Oh, Rose, it's just that your hiding place was so good, we were positively famished after running ourselves ragged looking for you," Blanche said in her soothing Southern drawl. Dorothy and Sophia exchanged guilty looks, then quickly nodded.

Rose considered this. "That makes sense. It was a pretty good *Ugel* spot! I don't want to miss out again, so I'll come along. But if anything bad happens, or there is any *whiff* of danger this evening at the gala, don't say I didn't warn you!"

"Deal," said Dorothy succinctly. Before anyone could change their minds, she turned to the boatman. "Let's go."

Climbing into the boat was no easy feat in their heels and finery, and it was only once they were finally settled that Dorothy started to have second thoughts. The boatman strained and grunted as he gripped the oars and pushed away from the dock, his face ripening like a plum with every stroke. Dorothy chewed her lip as the shore receded.

"Would you like me to help you row?" she asked.

She could practically set her watch by the big vein that was pulsing on the ferryman's forehead, and she didn't want the poor guy to give himself a heart attack rowing all five of them.

The boatman simply grunted in response.

"I'm sure this fine specimen of a man can handle it," Blanche said, fanning herself with the party invitation. "We're practically as light as a bundle of feathers!" She glanced at the stranger and batted her eyelashes, looking for some sort of agreement. When none came, Blanche shifted in her seat. "Well, most of us, anyway," she muttered, tossing a petty glance over at Dorothy and Rose, who were squashed together on one of the tiny boat benches.

"*You're* the one bringing luggage to a formal event!" Dorothy said as she eyed Blanche's bulging travel bag at their feet. Still, she gripped the side of the wooden boat to stop herself from saying anything further. She'd been making a concerted effort not to take the bait and acknowledge Blanche's—or anyone's—comments about a person's weight since she'd read a thought-provoking article about body image in *Ms.* magazine.

"A lady is always prepared," Blanche said with a sniff.

"A lady's probably got an inflatable mattress in there, it looks like," Sophia quipped.

The older woman shivered when some bay water splashed against the boat's hull as they made their way across the waves. Rose pointed in delight when a pelican flew low over their heads just as the first glimpse of an island came into clearer view: a strip of sand and an old wooden dock. Beyond the narrow beach a dense line of mangroves and palms and cypress shielded the rest of the estate from prying eyes as their foliage blurred into the fading twilight.

Villa Velado, Dorothy thought, vaguely remembering that *velado* meant hidden or veiled.

Eventually, the boat pulled alongside the rickety platform. Dorothy felt the word *dock* was insufficient to describe this precarious and partially rotting structure, but the boatman tried his best to make up for it by silently offering a hand to help each lady out of the boat. Dorothy was the last to disembark and couldn't help but notice that the man's fingers were rough and calloused, most likely from the oars and other manual labor. She wiped his sweat from her palms as he gestured to a path in the trees that was lined with two rows of flickering tea lights in glass votives. He remained with the boat, wrestling with a snarl of ropes to secure it to the dilapidated pilings.

"Isn't this kind of spooky?" Rose said, linking arms with Blanche. "The way the candles make the shadows move?"

"I think it's rather romantic," Blanche said. "And it's the most forgiving type of illumination." With her free hand, she smoothed her caramel hairdo back into place, allowing her crystal earrings to sparkle in the meager lighting.

"It's a fire hazard," Sophia noted as they navigated the sandy footpath.

Soon the dark tunnel of trees and Spanish moss opened to reveal an elaborate garden with fountains and statues nestled among the shadowy greenery. A line of manicured trees shrouded a walkway that disappeared off to their right, and to their left Dorothy caught a glimpse of a maze made of clipped boxwood hedges. Just ahead of them loomed a sprawling mansion in a Mediterranean Renaissance style that reminded Dorothy of the Vizcaya Estate in Miami proper. The roof was covered in red barrel tiles, and much of the building's pale brick was obscured by the dark green leaves, white blossoms, and reddish-orange bursts of bleeding-heart vines and coral honeysuckle. The open windows glowed with a warm yellow light, and the lively sounds of Cuban jazz spilled out into the humid evening air.

That could be a live band, Dorothy thought. She pictured glamorous couples mambo-ing across a dance floor and imagined trying a few moves of her own. Dorothy knew her mother didn't like loud parties, but she hoped she'd be able to find a chair on the sidelines while she, Rose, and Blanche danced together—or, hopefully, with some handsome new acquaintances. With a smile, Dorothy straightened her shoulders and led the way up the terra-cotta path to the front steps.

The mansion's wide front door was painted bloodred and featured a large brass knocker shaped like a bull's head. Dorothy glanced back at her friends, who had clustered behind her, then knocked three times.

"Ma, maybe you should get up front," she said. "You're wearing the brooch that came with the invitation."

Sophia angled in front of Dorothy, fingering the jewelry at her neck. "This party better have some good canapés," she grumbled. "I'm starving."

Dorothy sighed. "I offered you lunch, remember? You said you didn't want it."

"You call a peanut butter sandwich on whole wheat lunch? I call it elder abuse."

Dorothy rolled her eyes. It wasn't her fault they'd run out

of jelly and the fluffy white Italian bread Sophia preferred. Still, nothing stung like a mother's guilt trip. She should have made Sophia a bowl of soup or taken her out to Wolfie's instead of spite-eating the dry, chewy sandwich herself while pretending it actually tasted good.

Just then, the door opened with a groan. In the entryway, a handsome man in his sixties appeared, sporting a full head of silver hair, dark eyebrows, and dazzling sable eyes. He reminded Dorothy a bit of Ernest Hemingway, thanks to his robust features, barrel chest, and ivory fisherman's sweater—with a dash of Ricardo Montalbán in his smoldering gaze. His face was a deep tan adorned with crow's-feet at the corners of his eyes, indicating that he spent a lot of time outdoors. They only added to his rugged charm.

"Welcome," he bellowed warmly, with the slightest touch of an accent, "to Villa Velado, my *home*."

His voice contained an enchanting mix of inflections from New York City, Cuba, and a hint of somewhere else . . . perhaps Scotland? Dorothy tried her hardest not to imagine him in a tartan kilt and guayabera.

"Thank you," Dorothy said, taking charge. "We received your beautiful invitation, but we weren't exactly certain who you meant to invite, or who specifically the brooch was for." She gently nudged Sophia forward, and his smile faded a bit when his eyes landed upon her. "So we *all* came. We hope that's okay."

"Ah, yes," the man said, raising his eyebrows as he fixed his gaze on Sophia. "Bianca, you're a bit shorter than I remember," he purred. "And the years have been . . . long. Nevertheless, I'm thrilled to have tracked you down at last."

Dorothy widened her eyes at Sophia. Her mother made friends wherever she went, but she'd never mentioned knowing such an attractive man. Dorothy wondered why she'd never set her up with someone like this, instead of the steady stream of socially awkward misfits and white-collar criminals Sophia usually sent her way. Recent case in point: her dry cleaner's pasty son.

"Who's Bianca?" Sophia exclaimed, raising her hands in confusion. "I'm Sophia Petrillo. I presume I was invited because of my very important charity wo—"

"I think he's talking about me," Blanche interrupted.

Dorothy, Sophia, and Rose all turned to stare at Blanche as she stepped out from behind them.

"But your name is *Blanche*," Rose said, furrowing her brow. "Not Bianca!"

Dorothy looked from Blanche to their mysterious host. He seemed entranced, drinking Blanche's face and body in as if she were a saucer of milk and he was a very thirsty cat. Meanwhile, Blanche seemed to be enjoying every morsel of his attention, flashing a dazzling white smile and subtly posing with one long leg crossed in front of the other, her hand strategically placed at her hip to draw attention to her curves. A saxophone howled from somewhere inside the villa, underscoring the moment.

Flicking her eyes between the two of them, Dorothy shoved aside the desire for someone other than Stan to look at her like that. As she opened her mouth to ask for an explanation, Blanche took another step forward, her eyes wide and sparkling.

"Declan, is it *really* you?" she breathed, placing a hand on her heaving chest.

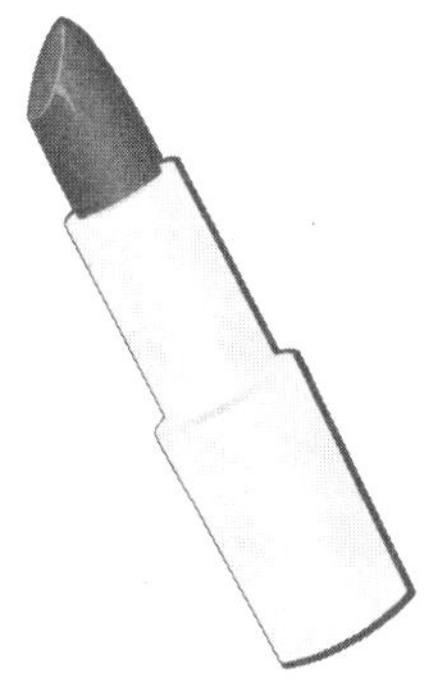

AN OLD(ER) FLAME

4

She tried to keep her smile steady, but inside Blanche was melting like a scoop of butter pecan in an Atlanta heat wave. It *was* him, she was sure of it. He was undoubtably a touch more weathered and a tad thicker around the middle than when she'd last seen him. But that was decades ago, and he'd been practically a boy then—and boy, oh boy, had he grown into a genuine, bona fide *man*.

One thing, at least, hadn't changed a bit. His curious deep brown eyes, always with a glint of mischief, hungrily taking in every detail of the world around him—that was pure Declan. She wondered how she looked to him now. Was he thinking the same thing, that she looked a little weathered, or—God forbid!—a little thicker around the middle? She'd been a young woman in those days, just out of girlhood, speeding toward an adventure up North that she hadn't been prepared for. Back then she'd felt like a brand-new Barbie doll, ready to try on different lives as easily as slipping on a new outfit. So much had happened to Blanche since Declan had briefly entered her life that it was no wonder she'd mostly forgotten about him until now. She'd gotten married, borne several children, and become a widow, for goodness' sake. She hoped the mileage didn't show.

Blanche sucked in her stomach a teeny bit and lifted her chin a centimeter. And from the fire in Declan's eyes, she had a feeling he liked what he saw.

Maybe she wasn't so weathered after all.

Declan stepped forward, extending his hand, and Blanche lifted hers to grasp it. His hands were exactly as she remembered—warm and soft in places, calloused at the edges of his palm.

"It took me a while, but I finally found you," he said. "That brooch is yours."

Blanche glanced at Sophia, who was openly staring at her, along with Rose and Dorothy, their mouths agape.

"I—I just don't know what to say," Blanche started.

Her head positively swam with questions. Where had he

been all these years, and why had he tried to find her now, after all this time? And then there was the issue of the note: If this truly was Declan—*her* Declan—standing in front of her, why had he signed his invitation *ET*? Blanche looked down at her delicate hand, still clenched in his strong one, and noticed a few flecks of orange and red paint at the edges of his thumbnail. A faint memory from years ago arose in her mind, like mist from a bayou at the end of a languid summer.

Thirty-some years ago in New York, Blanche had been struggling with her keys at the entrance to a small brick building in the West Village, her bulky laundry bag hanging from a strap across her back as rain poured down from a heavy gray sky. Her friend Maxine, who she'd met at finishing school in Atlanta, had not only offered Blanche the extra bedroom in her apartment; she'd also made Blanche copies of her keys, given her a foldable map of New York City's subway system, told her the best places to get groceries, and shown her how to do her own laundry at the coin-operated laundromat around the corner.

The only problem was, Blanche's shiny new key kept getting stuck in the lock.

Doing her own laundry had seemed kind of fun at first—dropping coins and soap powder into the machines, watching her bright clothing swirl around in those round little windows. But after her very first attempt, in which she'd accidentally shrunk a mohair sweater, she realized how much she missed the staff at her family's home in Georgia. Before she'd gone off on her own, Blanche had just thrown her dirty clothes across the foot of her bed. Or more frequently, onto the floor. But they always appeared clean and pressed in the morning, hanging in her closet or folded neatly in her chifforobe. It must have been so much work for her nanny, Viola, to do all her laundry, let alone the whole family's, Blanche realized. Her shoulders had sagged under the combined weight of her guilt and the heavy laundry slung over her shoulder.

As she pressed into the shallow alcove of the doorway to avoid the worst of the rain, she thought about how her first few weeks in New York weren't quite what she'd imagined.

She had assumed that she'd simply tap-dance into a well-paying Broadway role with her flawless figure, natural talent, and enviable youth. That she'd be up and running in a day or two, with a fat New York paycheck to cover a picture-perfect apartment on the Upper East Side, far away from her controlling Southern family. She'd fill her apartment with fresh flowers, stroll in Central Park every day, and meet a handsome man—maybe someone in advertising, in a sharp suit and a snappy fedora. He'd smile at her, enchanted by her lithesome beauty and honeyed accent, and whisk her off to places like the Stork Club or to Long Island for Gatsbyesque parties.

But there were a million girls in the city almost as pretty and talented as her—and they were quite a bit pushier. Acting and singing gigs didn't grow on trees, and Blanche found it exhausting to run to auditions, dance her heart out, then haul laundry or groceries up four flights of stairs, without Mama, Big Daddy, or Viola to handle the business of life for her. Her feet constantly hurt, and, to her horror, she'd even had to switch to flats instead of heels—except for nights when she went out on the town. The subway was loud and screechy, and Blanche found herself washing off a fine layer of grit every night in the cramped, mildewed bathroom she shared with Maxine.

She liked to call it "stardust" to keep her spirits up.

But she knew in her heart that it was really just dirt.

All those struggles faded away when she met *him* on the stoop that fateful day. He'd given her a sunny smile, popped open the front door, then carried her overstuffed bag of laundry up the four flights of stairs like it was nothing. He'd introduced himself as Declan Toro, fresh off the bus from Pittsburgh and ready to find inspiration and make his name as a great artist.

That chance meeting was the moment Blanche's New York experience transformed from a gritty black-and-white film to a Technicolor musical.

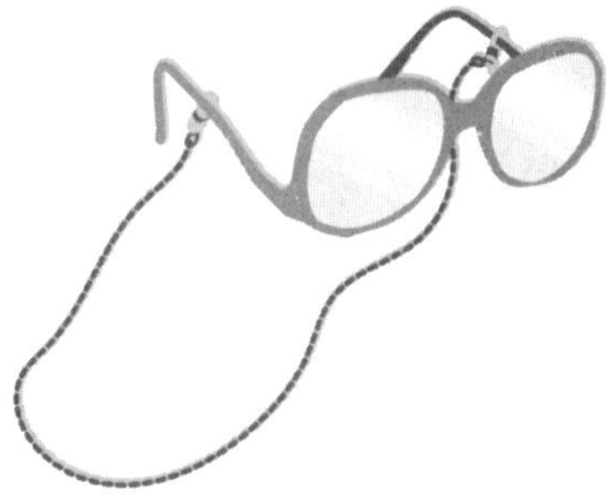

THIRD, FOURTH, AND FIFTH WHEELS

5

After watching the two heart-struck ex-lovers visually devour each other for what felt like an eternity, Dorothy cleared her throat—but Blanche and their mysterious host didn't break eye contact.

She coughed again, to no avail, then looked at the others.

"It's getting chilly out here," Sophia said sharply. "Wanna let an old lady in out of the cold before she becomes a popsicle?"

Still, neither Declan nor Blanche seemed to hear.

Dorothy cleared her throat a third time.

Rose looked at her with concern, then quickly caught on and began doing some fake coughs of her own. They were so loud and guttural that they reminded Dorothy of the hog-calls Rose had practiced when they'd briefly cared for Baby, Rose's uncle's elderly pig. But they needed all the help they could get.

Sophia coughed too, but soon raised her voice. "Don't let my appearance fool you! I may be old, but I'm not a vampire. You can let me over the threshold!"

Declan blinked, the spell cast by Blanche momentarily broken. Blanche chuckled to herself and smiled as if waking up from a particularly delicious dream.

"Of course, my apologies!" Declan exclaimed. "Please, come in! I don't want you all eaten by mosquitoes, or"—his dark eyes twinkled—"the endangered American crocodiles that are known to roam the grounds at night."

"I hope you don't mind that I brought a few extra guests," Blanche said as Declan plucked her travel bag from her hand and led her inside. "Like we said, we weren't sure who the invitation was for. Dorothy, Rose, and Sophia are my dear friends—and roommates."

"Friends of yours are friends of mine," he said. "I'm delighted to meet you all."

The other ladies hustled in behind them, with Rose casting a nervous glance behind her.

"I don't like the idea of crocodiles—or alligators," Rose whispered to Dorothy. "But I suppose we're practically in the wilds out here."

"I don't think this is their normal habitat," Dorothy said. "We're more likely to see a manatee in these waters. I'm sure he's just trying to add a little drama to the evening. It must be his sense of artistic flair."

"I'm not risking it," Sophia said, making sure the front door closed firmly behind them. "I didn't survive two world wars, the Great Depression, and Dorothy's teenage years to get taken down by some reptile."

"A gator would be no match for you, Ma," Dorothy said. "One bite of your tough old hide and he'd spit you out."

"Very funny," Sophia said. She opened her mouth to deliver another wisecrack, but paused as she took in the splendid foyer of the mansion. Dorothy followed Sophia's gaze to the heavy brass chandelier above their heads, the rounded lines of Spanish-style arches, the sculptural marble-and-brass wall sconces, the terra-cotta tile overlaid with a plush carpet that led to a sweeping staircase bearing an elaborate wrought iron railing. Entering this mansion felt like stepping back in time a hundred years. The only exception was the walls. Lined with undeniably modern artwork, they framed an explosion of unbridled expression in the otherwise more stately historic space. Dorothy was drawn to a series of small-to-medium-size cubist works, most set in wooden frames.

Is that a sketch by Picasso? Dorothy wondered.

She'd have to take a closer look.

At a sudden burst of laughter from somewhere deeper in

the house, and the sound of guests talking over music, Declan dropped Blanche's travel bag in the foyer and motioned for the three women to follow Blanche and him.

"Is this *really* your home?" Blanche asked, resting a hand on his arm.

"I bought it about ten years ago," he said, leading them down a hallway. "The original owner's heirs had let it fall into disrepair, and I've been slowly restoring it and filling it with art."

Dorothy leaned forward, trying to hear their conversation. "So you're a collector, then?" she said.

Declan turned around, smiled, and with a flourish, gestured to a large canvas hanging on the wall, a saturated, abstract painting of a bull's head surrounded by roses, in deep tones of teal and red and ocher. "I am *El Toro*," he said. "Some say the greatest painter of the twentieth century. Some say the most underrated. Some say the most overrated. What do you say?"

Dorothy knew that name. It was famous, and often listed alongside names like Jackson Pollock, Andy Warhol, and Frida Kahlo. "ET," Dorothy said triumphantly, remembering the mysterious initials on the card. "For El Toro. *Now* it makes sense."

"So, we're not going to meet the alien?" Rose asked, her shoulders slumping.

"It'll be okay, dear," Sophia said, patting Rose on the back. "I'm sure you'll be reunited with your kind one day."

Rose nodded glumly, pulling out a half-eaten packet of Reese's Pieces from her purse and popping a few in her mouth. "I guess we won't be needing these. . . ."

"You didn't tell us you knew one of the most illustrious artists alive today," Dorothy said to Blanche. "You might have mentioned that small detail."

Blanche opened her mouth to answer just as Declan swept them around the corner, into a spacious dining room only sparsely populated with guests. The verdigris-painted room was dominated by a massive dining table laden with platters of appetizers, bowls of tropical fruits, and unruly floral bouquets in shades of red, hot pink, and yellow, all illuminated by a curving glass chandelier that looked vaguely like a sea creature. Dorothy glanced around and wondered where the rest of the party was as the small group paused in their chatter, leaving only the sounds of jazz emanating from an ancient Victrola on a side table. With a sinking feeling, Dorothy realized that this was the source of the music she'd heard, and that there was no live band or dance floor.

"My friends and associates!" El Toro roared, commanding the room. "My last guests have arrived! Please, everyone, meet *Blanche Devereaux*, whom I knew years ago as Bianca Holloway. And please also welcome her charming companions Dorothy, Sophia, and Rose."

Dorothy forced a smile and nodded to the assembled guests. If they were the last ones to show up, that meant that this was the entire party. Not quite the elegant throng she'd imagined, full of dozens of potential suitors. Rather than a bustling gala, this appeared to be an intimate dinner party of strangers.

A striking Black woman in a draped metallic sheath and short haircut—with cheekbones that gave Grace Jones and Cindy Crawford a run for their money—nodded back at Dorothy. Next to her stood a balding, mustachioed man in his sixties or early seventies who was hanging on the woman's every word. He was exactly her opposite, in a tweed suit, a bow tie, and a rumpled pocket square—and he was twirling a an old-fashioned fountain pen in one hand. Dorothy momentarily considered him as a potential dating prospect, but then she realized how short he was. Even though she tried not to judge a man by his height, there was the practical matter of getting a crick in her neck looking down at him. Would they have to use a booster seat at restaurants so they could see eye to eye? Or perhaps he could stand on an apple crate when kissing her good night, or she could hunch over like Strega Nona. Either option was less than romantic.

On the other side of the room, a petite East Asian woman about Dorothy's age—give or take a few years—stood near the record player. Her black leather trousers and jacket, blunt bob, and dramatic red glasses gave her an intimidating, almost punk air. She held a half-empty martini glass in one hand as she spoke to a thirtyish man to her left, who was scribbling down the older woman's words in a wire-bound notebook. He had a boyishly handsome face and wore glasses, making

Dorothy think of Clark Kent, if he were played by Jimmy Smits. Dorothy didn't even consider him as a potential love interest. He was certainly attractive, but far too young for her.

"How do you do," Dorothy said, suddenly feeling a bit awkward in this group full of artsy and accomplished-looking people without being able to get lost in the crowd. She'd have to decide if she was going to mingle or stick with her friends and mother in a corner.

After a couple of polite, noncommittal replies, chatter in the room recommenced, and Rose and Sophia made a beeline for the table laden with hors d'oeuvres. Declan poured a glass of champagne for Blanche, which she accepted with a blissful smile. Rose interrupted Dorothy's focus on the couple by bringing her a plate loaded with cheese puffs, fresh pineapple, and chicken croquettes replete with a Cuban mojo dipping sauce.

"I thought there'd be more people at a gala," Rose said. Then her eyes lit up. "But that means more food for us!" She turned back to the table and filled another plate.

Dorothy took a bite of a croquette, which was perfectly savory and sweet when dipped in the bright green sauce. It was delicious, but that didn't stop the vague feeling of disappointment about the evening from descending on her like a cloud of gnats. Irritating, but not the end of the world. She determined to try to make the most of the evening, as she so often did. At least Blanche was enjoying herself, she thought.

After taking a moment to hand champagne flutes to

Dorothy, Rose, and Sophia. Declan tapped a fork against the side of his glass, capturing the room's attention. A young woman with a golden-brown complexion and a chic black jumpsuit entered the room and stood with her hands clasped behind her back. Her curly hair was pulled into an updo, and her eyebrows quirked, as if she were already bored by whatever El Toro was about to say.

"My esteemed guests," he began, pacing in a small circle. "You're probably all wondering why I gathered you here tonight. Especially those of you I haven't spoken to in years." Here he raised his glass toward Blanche, and to a couple of the other guests in another corner of the room. Dorothy couldn't tell who he was gesturing to there—was it the tall woman in the metallic dress? "*And* those I've never met before tonight," he added, nodding at Sophia, Rose, and Dorothy. "It's special for me, seeing you here together. So many pieces of my life in one place make a strange and beautiful mosaic, don't you think?"

He strode over to Dorothy, Blanche, Rose, and Sophia.

"I'd like to propose a series of toasts," he continued, gesturing to the young woman in the jumpsuit. "Misia, make sure everyone's glasses are full!"

The woman let out the tiniest of sighs but obediently grabbed a bottle of champagne and circled the room, topping off glasses as she went.

"My first muse," Declan said, slinging his arm around Blanche. "My Bianca, the Southern belle, icon of beauty and charm, who inspired me in my earliest student years: now Blanche, still as lovely and enchanting as ever."

Blanche lifted her chin as the room lifted a toast in her honor. She beamed so widely that Dorothy could've sworn she saw the crowns at the back of Blanche's dazzling smile. This was the type of attention her friend craved, Dorothy knew, and Blanche was clearly relishing every second.

Declan then strode over to the woman in the shimmering silver sheath dress. "And my dear Vee, my first true love." Here Blanche's smile faltered. "My greatest cheerleader, and my toughest critic. The woman who pushed me to great heights and pulled me from the deepest abyss. A creative genius in her own right, whose artistic installations—particularly her seminal work with that ventriloquist dummy; yes, who could forget that?—should have earned her a cover story in *Artforum*." Vee didn't smile, but serenely regarded Declan as he spoke. "To the whetstone against which my paintbrush was sharpened over the years."

"I hope he mixes martinis better than he mixes his metaphors," Sophia stage-whispered as the room toasted to Vee.

Dorothy noticed that Vee didn't sip her drink but rather held the champagne flute steady in a fierce grip, bejeweled rings on nearly every finger.

Next Declan crossed the room to the woman in the black leather pants and red glasses. He dinged his champagne flute against her refilled martini. "The incomparable Akiko Kakutani," he said in a low, reverent tone. "The woman who discovered me and brought me to fame. Did you know her empire started with just one gallery in New York? Now she dominates the global art scene with her unrivaled eye for talent, her fearsome negotiation skills"—here his voice took on a snide, nasally tone—"and of course, her exorbitant commission percentages!"

The crowd raised their glasses again, a bit uncertain if that last comment was meant to be cheered for, or not. Akiko nonchalantly sipped her drink and raised her eyebrows at the room, as if daring anyone to challenge her worth.

"She must be rolling in it," Sophia muttered. "She probably bought that outfit straight off David Bowie's back."

"I'm running out of champagne in my glass," Rose whispered. "And it's making me feel like dancing! Back in St. Olaf, we only had sparkling wine after the Festival of the Dancing Sturgeons—"

"Take smaller sips, honey," Blanche whispered. "We've still got a few more to go."

"I'd like to honor the whip-smart Luis Cabrera from the *Miami Herald*," Declan continued, pointing across the room to the thirty-something man in a gray suit, blue tie, and white button-down shirt. His dark wavy hair was parted neatly on one side, and his silver aviator frames sparkled in the light from the chandelier. "A wunderkind reporter and rising journalistic talent worthy of describing my humble backstory and impending comeback with the world." The man ducked his head as more toasts were raised. He looked like he'd rather sink into the marble flooring than have the attention on himself, Dorothy noticed.

Then Declan whirled around to clap the older gentleman in tweed's shoulder. "And finally, the impeccable Herman Price, here to properly evaluate and inspect my latest masterpiece for the insurance company, as he has done with my life's work for years. A man of precision, keen perception, and of course, dollars and cents. Everything must have a price, eh, Herman?" Declan shook the man's shoulder, though not lightly.

Herman coughed, then recovered with a meek smile. "My impossible task is to put a price on the priceless. I can only trust I am equal to the challenge," he said, in a thick accent that was hard to place above the jazz and the murmurs in the room.

Possibly French, Dorothy thought. *Or maybe Belgian*.

Declan threw his head back and shook with laughter. "You old goat, flattery will get you everywhere." He planted a kiss on the top of Herman's bald head. "You know I adore you."

Looking up from Herman Price's shining forehead, Declan scanned the room, his eyes passing over Misia as she filled Rose's glass again to the laconic boatman who lurked in the doorway, watching the room like a bouncer. "Over there is Ralph, the estate's caretaker, groundskeeper, and chef. He doesn't talk much, but he's a whiz with cilantro."

Ralph grunted to the room, then stepped back into the shadows of the hall.

"And, yes, Bianc—I mean Blanche's friends. I'm so sorry,

I don't know you as well to give each of you a proper introduction, but I hope you all will speak with Rose, Dorothy, and Sophia and get to know them. Because tonight I will be revealing something I've kept hidden from the people in this room." Declan's smiled faded and his voice dropped an octave. "It has been a hard road for me lately, but this group will be bonded forever after my secret is revealed, and you will all play a role in my triumphant return to the pinnacle of the art world."

He erupted in thunderous laughter, and Dorothy wondered what the rest of the room made of it. But as she observed them she saw that the assorted guests mostly stared into their beverages quietly with varying levels of confusion and worry on their faces. It was clear that each one was trying to guess at the artist's secret—and at what their respective roles in it might possibly be.

Taking a moment to check on her friends, Dorothy noticed that Blanche was slightly frowning, while Rose bounced on her heels.

"I love a surprise!" she said, rubbing her hands together. "What do you think it will be?"

"Mark my words," Sophia said sagely, "he's selling Tupperware, and we're not getting off this island until we all pony up."

"It must be something to do with art," Dorothy said. "Don't you agree, Blanche?"

Blanche looked up from her champagne flute. "Hmmm?"

"Don't you think he's going to tell us something about his painting? A new artistic direction, perhaps?"

Blanche shrugged and shook her head. "I don't know what that handsome man has up his sleeves. I'm still trying to figure out how he tracked me down, and how come I didn't *know* that I knew *the* El Toro—and that he's been living in Miami for a *decade*." She quickly downed the rest of her champagne. "Because, if I had, you can bet we'd have reconnected sooner. Can you imagine what the staff back at the museum would say? I certainly wouldn't still be xeroxing the director's mind-numbing memos if they knew I had a connection to El Toro. Why, I could spearhead a retrospective of Declan's work. I could single-handedly raise millions for the museum and get myself—I mean, *the museum*—featured in magazines and on the national news. Of course, I'd have to get a new gown for the opening. . . ."

Blanche bit her lip, clearly imagining her future glory, as a smattering of rain began to fall outside the open windows of the dining room. A warm breeze picked up, blowing out a few of the candles in the room and fluttering the napkins.

"Oooh, I wonder if that's why he invited me," Blanche said. "So that I could help make him famous."

"Isn't he already world-famous?" Dorothy said, gesturing to their extravagant surroundings.

"Well, yes," Blanche admitted, pushing her shoulders back. "But don't you think having a beautiful woman on his arm would make him even *more* famous?"

"It could help," Sophia chimed in. "Maybe you can give him Christie Brinkley's phone number."

"Oh, *Sophia*," Blanche tutted. "I meant *me*. He needs more than just a pretty face. We have a shared history, you see." Blanche played with her crystal earring, a faraway look on her face.

Dorothy gazed at her friend, who was clearly lost in a romantic reverie, and wondered about that shared history. Why, exactly, had El Toro invited Blanche to this intimate event? And what secrets would the artist reveal?

A DARK AND ARTY NIGHT

6

Blanche's head swam with questions as the gentle patter of raindrops outside the windows grew more percussive and a gust of wind whipped the curtains into sails. Misia and Ralph scurried around the dining room, closing the windows against the sudden storm.

Blanche had recognized a few of the names Declan mentioned earlier from the art magazines she'd page through on her lunch break at the museum. Thank goodness she was dressed to the nines to make a good impression. Big Daddy had always told her she was destined for great things, and it was important to look the part. Ever since she was a little girl, he'd also told her she was special and to be ready when the luck came. That's why Big Daddy always had a couple of bucks in his pocket for a wager and carried a rabbit's foot, and why Blanche always wore silk underwear and kept breath mints in her purse.

She couldn't deny that there was something electric in the air this evening—a crackling energy that zipped around the room as the artsy crowd and her three best friends conversed over the mouthwatering spread of food and drink in a dining room that looked like it had been plucked straight out of Versailles. Maybe this was the rarefied milieu in which she truly belonged. Sure, the party was a lot smaller than she'd assumed from the invitation, but perhaps that gave her more of an opportunity to rub shoulders with the movers and shakers of the art world. Of course she felt a little bad for Dorothy, who'd been hoping to meet someone new this evening, but she would try to not let her friend's ongoing romantic disappointments interfere with having a good time.

Blanche cast her eyes around the room, hoping to strike up a conversation with some of the other guests. Akiko was deep in conversation with Vee, and the reporter, Luis, had disappeared, perhaps to visit the men's room. After a moment, though, it was Herman Price, the understated insurance appraiser, who caught her gaze with his baby blues behind thick lenses. He sidled up to their group, tucking his fountain pen into the breast pocket of his suit.

"Good evening, ladies," he said in his hard-to-place accent. "It's so refreshing to meet new people—very stimulating to the little gray cells, as they say." He tapped his bald pate. "One hardly gets to socialize outside of the art scene these days."

Blanche straightened her shoulders. "Well, I happen to work at the Center for the Fine Arts," she said. "Unlike my friends here, I *am* a part of the art world. On top of being the muse that inspired El Toro's whole career, of course."

"Of course," Herman said, peering at Blanche intently over the tops of his horn-rimmed glasses.

Dorothy stepped forward and offered her hand to Herman. "And I'm actually quite knowledgeable about art and art history myself," she said.

"*But* you don't work in the field," Blanche said in a corrective tone. "You're a teacher. A substitute." She hissed the last sentence as if it were something less than, when she knew it wasn't. But darn it—even though she felt guilty about it, she wasn't going to let Dorothy overshadow her art-world credentials, as slender as they might be.

"And you think educating today's youth is less important than your *part-time* assistant job at the museum?" Dorothy intoned. "The one where your main responsibility is ordering donuts for the security guards?"

Herman swiveled his head, watching the two trade barbs

like he had a front-row seat to an Olympic Ping-Pong match.

Rose placed a placating hand on Dorothy and Blanche's arms. "Why don't we change the subject?" she said in a cheery voice. "How about we all share our favorite artist, or type of art?"

Blanche snatched her arm away and pasted a smile on her face, choosing to go along with Rose's attempt to steer the conversation to smoother waters. *This should be easy*, she thought. She'd pick some trendy, up-and-coming artist that Dorothy wouldn't know about, but one that might impress Herman.

But now her head was suddenly only full of Declan's work, like the three large abstract canvases hanging in the Center for the Fine Arts. She'd walked beneath them nearly every day, completely unaware that they were by the same man whom she'd had a fling with all those years ago in New York.

"I like the old Italian masters," Sophia said. "Michelangelo, da Vinci, Sinatra."

"Sinatra, Ma? Really?" Dorothy said, raising her eyebrows.

"I dare you to listen to 'Polka Dots and Moonbeams' and tell me it's not a masterpiece!"

"I prefer ice sculpture to paintings," Rose declared. "They're so pretty, and they taste better when you lick them."

"You know what? I'm not even going to ask," Sophia said.

"We're trying to have a conversation about *real art*," Blanche said. "Works by Rothko and Picasso and Matisse, for example."

"I'm not as familiar with those artists," Rose admitted. "But do you know about St. Olaf's Norman Rockhard?"

Dorothy chuckled. "You mean Norman Rockwell. The chronicler of Americana who had a distinctive, almost illustrative style."

Blanche narrowed her eyes at Dorothy, who was clearly showing off in front of Herman.

"No, I mean Norman Rockhard. He's famous for his paintings of brawny ship captains and handsome, shirtless fishermen battling stormy seas," Rose said. "There's an entire wall of the museum in St. Olaf dedicated to him, and he's got quite a following. He even has a thriving mail-order business where you can get prints of his work in magazine format, mailed out in a discreet envelope. Oh, and don't forget St. Olaf's Georgia O'Klingelhoffen, whose paintings of kringle look just like— Well, I probably shouldn't say in mixed company."

Rose blushed, then looked down at her toes.

Herman's eyes sparkled as he listened to Rose. "How delightful you are! It's so rare to find an unpretentious woman these days."

Rose beamed back at him. "Thank you," she said. "I think."

Just then, a crack of thunder rocked the room.

Rose shrieked as rain lashed against the windows so hard it sounded like volleys of nails thrown against the glass. Lightning illuminated the dripping greenery outside in strobe-like flashes, and the four women and Herman instinctively inched closer together.

Blanche searched for a way to bring the conversation back to more interesting topics—such as Declan's artwork, or herself.

"Mr. Price," she began, fluttering her lashes. "What do you think Declan's announcement will be? You know, I used to model for him years ago. I wonder . . . perhaps he wants me to sit for something new?"

"Ah, one wonders," Herman said, patting his mustache Then he lowered his voice, causing all four women to lean even closer to hear him over the sound of the rain. "I thought perhaps it would have something to do with some mysterious messages El Toro has been receiving."

Blanche's eyes sparkled with curiosity under the now-flickering chandelier. "Mysterious messages? What did they say?"

Herman started to answer, but another crack of thunder drowned out his words just as a streak of lightning lit up the windows. It had struck dangerously close, so close that the sweet scent of crackling ozone filled the room.

The last thing Blanche saw was her friends' startled faces frozen in the ghastly white light right before the entire villa went completely dark.

THE LIGHTS ARE OFF AND EVERYBODY'S HOME

7

The sudden darkness was heavy and all-encompassing as the music on the Victrola slowed to an eerie, elongated groan before coming to a reluctant stop. Dorothy's heart rate shot up and she reached for Sophia—whether to reassure her mother or herself, she couldn't say. She felt the older woman's small, bony shoulder just as it jerked away from her. From somewhere in the room, she heard a garbled cry and the sounds of a scuffle.

And her mother's unmistakable voice.

"Maledizione!" Sophia spat into the night.

Dorothy waved her arms, feeling for her mother—her eyes still adjusting to the fuzzy blackness—and bumped into someone's bosom. It was too soft to be Sophia's.

"Hey, watch it!" Rose cried.

"Sorry!" Dorothy muttered. "Ma! Where are you?"

Dorothy wondered if the power had gone out all over Miami—or just on this tiny island. With the room as black as the inside of a coffin, it was hard to tell anything at all. Dorothy could hear a chair being knocked over and glass shattering as the guests struggled to get their bearings in the inky darkness. Finally, she heard the sound of a striking match. A billowing flame briefly illuminated Herman's face and added a small amount of light to the gloom.

"We need to find some candles," he shouted. "Here are more matches!"

Dorothy took a lit match from his hands and scanned the room for her mother before the flame sputtered out. A moment later, more matches were struck, and Dorothy could see Misia holding a brass candelabra filled with flickering candles. Misia placed it on a small corner table, before quickly lighting a second candelabra and handing individual tapers to the guests. The room slowly brightened—at least, enough to see one another.

Fitful light danced across worried faces, and strange shadows cast by the floral arrangements seemed to creep across the walls. Dorothy spotted Rose and Blanche clinging to each other, but there was no sign of her mother. El Toro leaned against a wall holding a candle, his face ashen. Misia, Herman, the groundskeeper Ralph, the journalist Luis, and Vee were all clustered near the light of the largest candelabra. Only Akiko—the leather-clad gallerist—and Dorothy's own mother were nowhere to be seen.

"Please, I need your attention!" Dorothy boomed. At moments like this, she was thankful for her height, her strong vocal cords, and her sonorous and commanding voice. "Has anyone seen my mother? She's an older woman with glasses, about the size of a child."

"Hey!" A shock of white hair poked out from beneath the large dining table at the center of the room. Sophia's wrinkled face, draped in the fringed tablecloth, squinted up at Dorothy. "I prefer the term 'petite,'" she said. "Or fun-size, if you want to get cute about it."

Sophia slowly emerged from under the table as Dorothy let out a deep sigh of relief.

Thank goodness she's not hurt, Dorothy thought.

Her second thought was that on all fours, with her ivory-colored dress and cropped, curled hairdo, Sophia looked a bit like an arthritic poodle.

Declan joined the girls in rushing to Sophia's aid, but she shook them off and stood up without help. Sophia straightened her dress and dusted off her shoulders, just as Akiko appeared from beneath the table, too, her leather-encased knees squeaking against the marble floor.

El Toro offered her a hand and helped her up as well.

"Ma, what were you doing under there?" Dorothy asked.

"I felt someone grab at me, and I got knocked around a bit in the commotion, so I dove for cover." Sophia shrugged. "I wasn't the only smart one, eh?" She turned to Akiko, who quickly smoothed her bob and bangs back into perfect symmetry.

"I thought that the house had been struck by lightning, or that a tree would crash on us, so I felt my way to the table," Akiko said. "But somewhere along the way I dropped my martini. Can I get another?"

She motioned impatiently to Misia. Misia rolled her eyes but headed to the sideboard to mix the drink.

"Knocked around?" Dorothy gasped, frantically examining her mother for injuries. Now in her ninth decade, Sophia was as spry as ever, yet Dorothy couldn't help but worry. *And what if she'd hit her head?*

"Are you sure you're okay?"

Sophia tugged at her collar. "I felt someone yank my dress, here," she said. "But don't worry, I kicked them in the shins."

That's when Dorothy noticed that the butterfly brooch that her mother had been wearing—the same one that had been sent to them by El Toro for Blanche—was missing.

"The brooch is *gone*!" Dorothy shouted, whirling around the room.

Her analytical mind worked quickly: Whoever was holding the brooch must have ripped it off her mother's collar. But no one was holding anything, except for candles and martini glasses. But someone in this room must have snatched it, she knew. Dorothy scanned the room for a glint of gold peeking out from a pocket or sleeve. This group of shadowy faces now seemed more like a rogue's gallery than an artistic salon. Dorothy glanced at everyone's shins, looking for some sort of mark, for an expression of pain on one of the faces in the low lighting.

But it was impossible to tell who had recently been kicked.

El Toro's eyes went wide.

He stalked around the room, eyeing each of his guests with suspicion, his face rigid with anger.

Dorothy sympathized with his reaction—how could this happen among people who were supposed to be his friends?

"That brooch was special to me," he began. "*Priceless. Historical*. It was given to me by Queen Elizabeth on my first international tour, in honor of my artistic contributions to the National Gallery. The first time I felt that I had really 'made it' as an artist. There was a reason I wanted Blanche to have it."

He paused, seeming to work to get his temper under control.

"I'm sorry I wore it," Sophia said. "If I had known how valuable it was, I would've hired a bodyguard."

"Ma, could you tell anything about the person who grabbed it?" Dorothy asked, trying to decide who in the room might've had the gall to steal the brooch. "Were they tall or short? Did they smell of perfume, or have bad breath, or anything?"

"Pussycat, it was pitch-black. I just felt someone fumble at my neck, then a quick tug. No time to pick up any other details." She paused for a moment as if to think. "You know, back in the old country, we'd call that a good time."

Dorothy bit her lip, thinking.

"I'd like everyone to empty their pockets and purses," El Toro commanded. "Right now."

Dorothy was the only one of her friends lucky enough to have pockets in her formal pantsuit, which she dutifully turned inside out. Then Rose, Sophia, Blanche, and Dorothy opened their purses for El Toro's inspection. He scanned the inside of their pocketbooks, which held similar contents: wallets, tubes of lipstick, Kleenex, loose coins. Blanche's had a tiny travel perfume, some wintergreen Certs, an old matchbook, and a prophylactic, which made El Toro raise his eyebrows. Sophia's purse held a rosary, a key chain, a few pill containers, some crumpled papers, and a small penknife, while Rose's held a powder compact, a small tin of herring, and a piece of cheese wrapped in plastic.

"You know what they say about dairy," Rose said. "Don't leave home without it."

"I think that's American Express," Dorothy corrected.

"No, I'm pretty sure it's Norwegian Jarlsberg," Rose said, unwrapping a corner and taking a small nibble.

El Toro smiled at the girls. "I know it wasn't you four,"

he said softly. "But I must appear fair and check everyone."

He strode over to Herman, who began rummaging in his pockets. Dorothy craned her neck to see the list of items he laid on the dining table among the plates of half-eaten chicken croquettes and browning pineapple chunks: a wallet, a book of matches, his shiny fountain pen, a small notebook, a pencil stub, a jeweler's loupe, a tiny eyeglass repair kit, and mini versions of a magnifying glass and tape measure.

"Tools of the trade," Herman said, smiling up at El Toro. "Which I hope to employ on your latest work very soon."

El Toro grunted, proceeding to Luis.

Like Herman, Luis also had a small notebook, in addition to a laminated press ID, a wallet, keys, a mini tape recorder, and an unopened roll of Now and Later candy.

Next was Akiko, who struggled to access the tiny front pockets of her tight leather pants. "You know I can barely fit myself in these, right?" she said. "Anyway, what do I need your old brooch for? Get serious."

From her back pockets, she produced a crushed pink packet of Bubble Yum gum.

Their host moved on to Ralph, the closest person to Akiko. He'd been working to light some of the blown-out candles but paused his efforts to reach into his pockets.

"I know you don't have it," El Toro said. "You couldn't care less about that stuff."

Ralph nodded, but still turned his pockets inside out to reveal a few fishing lures, a crowded key ring, and a tiny flask.

"Now you," El Toro said.

He gestured to Misia, who had been prying fresh dribbles of wax off the antique table with her fingernails. The wax was already starting to pool next to the candlesticks and candelabra, and she gave El Toro a look that Dorothy had seen in her daughter Kate's eyes many a time when she was a teenager.

Boredom with a soupçon of disdain.

In a reluctant show of obedience, Misia reached into the pockets of her black jumpsuit, of which there were many. She placed the contents onto the table with a series of thunks: a few artist's pastel sticks, a painter's scraper tool, a bunch of rubber bands, a small key ring, a tube of Dr Pepper Lip Smackers, and finally, a small flask similar to the one from Ralph's pocket.

"*Really?*" El Toro growled.

Misia snatched the item back up and shoved it into a hip pocket. "It's okay for Ralph to have one, but not me? Nice double standard," she said coolly. "Here's a thought: How about not driving your staff to drink?"

Dorothy and Blanche caught each other's eyes, noting the obvious tension between the artist and his assistant.

Vee stepped forward.

"I don't have any pockets," she purred. "And my purse is in the hall closet." She opened her hands, showing her empty palms.

"I'm sure you have other places you could tuck something away," El Toro suggested, a touch of flirtation in his deep voice.

Vee smiled and leaned forward, letting the draped neckline of her metallic dress swing open. El Toro took a discreet peek down her décolletage and Blanche let out a small huff, her eyes narrowed.

"Nothing out of the ordinary there," El Toro said, his voice hoarse.

"And you would know," Vee said, straightening back up with a satisfied smirk. The rest of the room clearly felt uncomfortable witnessing their intimate moment, Dorothy noted. Luis buried his nose in his notebook, Misia looked like she was going to throw up, and Akiko rolled her eyes.

"Well, we need to report the brooch missing," Blanche said. "Especially if it's as priceless as you say."

"Maybe the phone lines are still working?" Dorothy asked, looking at El Toro.

"This island has stood for one hundred years and weathered many storms. I'm sure things will be back to normal soon," he said. Then he turned to Ralph and roared: "What are you waiting for? Get out there and check the telephones, assess the grounds, and haul out the generator we have in the shed!"

Ralph grunted in agreement and turned to go.

"It still seems pretty dangerous out there," Misia muttered to El Toro. "Are you sure that's a good idea?"

"Wait, Ralph!" El Toro said. "It's still raining, and it's dark. It's too dangerous."

Dorothy let out an incredulous snort and quickly covered it by pretending to sneeze. She marveled at El Toro's ability to switch gears so quickly yet still sound effortlessly commanding. Perhaps if he weren't a famous artist, his capricious moods wouldn't be heeded so assiduously.

Ralph turned back, relief spreading across his sunburned face. Though the wind had died down, the rain still fell in sheets, creating a soft roar beyond the windows.

"Let's see if we can call out first," Misia said with crisp efficiency. "And Ralph and I will make sure all the windows are shut, and check for any leaks inside."

"I was just about to say that," El Toro said, dismissing Misia with a flick of his hand. "But what are we to do with our guests?"

Misia looked around the room at the well-dressed dinner party, and Dorothy did the same. Though they'd been amply fed and plied with champagne, everyone's faces were strained with worry. Some seemed rumpled from the commotion, and when Dorothy traded glances with Rose, Blanche, and Sophia, all she could do was wonder if they would even be able to get home that night. Her car was parked back on the mainland, and she couldn't imagine Ralph rowing them to it now. Dorothy thought of her comfortable bed and longed to take off her high-waisted dress pants and heels, both of which were starting to pinch. All she wanted in this world was to wash her face and curl up with the Dorothy L. Sayers novel she'd recently started.

"Perhaps another round of drinks—or dessert—until we know more?" Misia suggested.

El Toro looked helplessly around the dining room, as if its contents were all new to him. An hour ago he was the Bull, a titan of the art world, so confident it was nearly off-putting. And now he looked completely unmoored at the prospect of serving dessert.

"Fine." Misia sighed. "I'll take care of that, too."

She nodded to Ralph. He grabbed a candelabra and left the room to make his rounds as Dorothy exchanged a knowing look with Sophia. Stan had acted the same way when anything went wrong during their marriage: leaving Dorothy to take charge and do all the work when things got hard, whether it was a kid with a fever or their Pontiac breaking down.

Misia disappeared into the kitchen and reappeared with a key lime pie on a tray decorated with fluffy rosettes of whipped cream. She expertly cut the cake and plated it, then passed servings around to the guests. "Please pour yourselves more to drink," she said, angling her shoulder toward the sideboard. "I'm going to help Ralph."

Blanche leaned over to Dorothy. "She sure seems to run the place, doesn't she?"

"I'll say," Dorothy said. "I bet El Toro would be lost without her, but he doesn't seem like the most appreciative boss."

"Well, he's a great artist! His mind is probably focused on his next masterpiece, not on where the dessert forks are," Blanche said.

Rose licked a dollop of whipped cream from the corner of her mouth. "Take a bite of the pie. It's delicious!"

"Is food all you can think about at a time like this? We might be stuck here with a jewel thief!" Sophia gestured at Vee, who sniffed at the pie with disdain, then at Akiko, Luis, and Herman, who were busy pouring themselves heavy-handed cocktails. At the rate this crowd drank, Dorothy doubted the rum would last the night.

"They all look suspicious to me," Sophia continued. "Even Sal Magluta knew better than to steal from an old woman."

"Hush," Blanche said, glancing around to make sure El Toro hadn't heard. "These are artsy, sophisticated types."

"One of whom ripped that brooch right off my neck!" Sophia shook her finger in Blanche's face.

"That's right," Rose said. "Something here stinks like yesterday's herring!"

Dorothy brought the other girls into a tight circle to shield their conversations from the prying eyes of the other guests. "Did any of you see anything suspicious?"

"I wish I had," Sophia grumbled. "Whoever took it must have hidden it real good, since it didn't turn up in El Toro's search. Sneaky."

"Which means they stashed it somewhere," Dorothy mused, looking around the ornate dining room. With all of the furniture, flowers, platters of food, and works of art, there were lots of hidden nooks and crannies that could conceal a piece of jewelry that size.

"Or they hid it on their person," Blanche said, narrowing her eyes. "Just because it wasn't in anyone's pockets or, *ahem* . . . tucked into somewhat paltry cleavage . . . that doesn't mean it's not stuffed away somewhere else."

"You didn't like El Toro sneaking a peek down Vee's dress? Just how close were the two of you, anyway?" Sophia said. "You never told us how you met."

Blanche pressed her lips together, as if about to offer a tasty morsel of gossip. "Do you remember when I told you about how I ran away when I was young—I mean, slightly younger than I am now?"

The girls nodded.

"You mean the time you ran off to Mexico?" Rose said. "Or when you faked your own death?"

"No, no. This was *after* that," Blanche said in a conspiratorial tone. "I was mad at Mama and Big Daddy for pulling me out of cheerleading senior year. Never mind why. I felt so confined in that big ol' house, not even able to do my routines and splits in my little pleated skirt at the football games anymore."

"The horror!" Sophia said with mock dismay.

"It certainly *was*," Blanche said, with a tilt of her head. "So that summer, I took a few bucks out of Big Daddy's wallet, packed a bag, and took off for the Great White Way to find fame and fortune."

"I thought you had to have a lot of training to be an astronaut." Rose frowned.

"*Broad*way, Rose. Not the *Milky* Way," Dorothy said, and groaned.

"One sultry summer night I climbed out my bedroom window, and took the midnight train from Georgia," Blanche said, wiggling her shoulders as she savored the memory.

"All by yourself?" Rose gasped. "That's dangerous!"

"Well, I was technically an adult by then," Blanche said. "And I was just suffocating in my parent's house. I felt like a bird of paradise, trapped in a tiny cage. I had urges, you see. A song of passion in my heart that I just had to sing, and a fire in my loins that couldn't be quenched. I needed to break free and spread my luxuriant wings."

"I'm sure that's not all she spr—" Sophia started.

Dorothy squeezed Sophia's arm lightly to silence her.

"So, then what happened?" Rose asked, polishing off the last of her pie.

"Well, I bunked with my friend in the Big Apple and tried to find work in the theater. Declan lived in the same building. Of course, no one knew he was going to become El Toro then! He was just another poor art student, trying to make ends meet."

"How romantic," Dorothy said. "A starving artist! So very *La Bohéme*."

"There's nothing romantic about starving," Sophia said, shaking her head sagely. "It's much easier to fall in love if your stomach isn't growling. That's why I say carbonara is the first ingredient in a healthy relationship."

As if on cue, El Toro returned and handed Blanche a slice of the pie on a dainty dessert plate.

"I asked Ralph to make this tonight," El Toro purred. "I hope I remembered the recipe correctly."

"'Off-Key' Lime Pie." Blanche chuckled. "How could I forget?"

Dorothy raised her eyebrows at Blanche. Blanche's eyes sparkled as she took a bite. Then she closed her eyes as she chewed in what Dorothy felt was a slightly overdramatic display of gustatory ecstasy.

"He got it right," she said as El Toro beamed next to her. "I made this one chilly night in New York. We'd been out singing at this piano bar downtown and we were famished. I wanted to bake a special treat for Declan—but our local bodega didn't have any key limes that time of year. So I whipped up a version with regular limes instead."

"This flavor always reminds me of her." El Toro grinned.

"Because it's a little tart?" Sophia joked.

He chuckled. "Because it's as sweet as a sunny Southern afternoon."

Just then, the dining room door banged open and Ralph entered, his face flushed and his hair and clothes dripping with rain.

"House is fine," he grunted. "No leaks. But a tree fell on

the shed, smashing the generator. And I couldn't make it far enough to check the dinghy."

"And the phone line is dead," Misia added, right on his heels. "Not even a dial tone."

"Great, we're stuck here! And I have a suite at the Deauville—the same one the Beatles stayed in," Akiko complained. She popped a piece of bubblegum into her mouth and chewed angrily.

"So what happens now? Are we all supposed to stay the night?" Vee raised her beringed hands to her shoulders, looking around at the other guests with widening eyes as Luis glanced up from scribbling in his notebook.

"If the storm's as bad as it sounds, the whole city might be affected," he said. "I wish I could call my colleagues at the paper and find out."

"This is a big house," Vee said. "But are there enough rooms?" She directed her question to Misia rather than Declan, who was pacing back and forth, his hands clasped behind his back. Misia counted on her fingers, scanning each member of the group.

"Some of you will have to share," she said.

"I'll pass, thanks," Akiko muttered. "No offense to anyone, but I'm a very private person."

"Same here," said Vee. Her bracelets glittered in the dwindling candlelight as she pinned her arms firmly to her sides. "I need my own space."

Blanche, Dorothy, Sophia, and Rose looked at one another with a mix of resignation and annoyance. Dorothy knew for a fact that her mother snored. And she hoped Rose didn't talk in her sleep; she didn't think she could take any rambling St. Olaf stories at three a.m. As for Blanche—who knew what Blanche might get up to in the middle of the night?

But still, it made the most sense for them to share a room. "We can double up," Dorothy said wearily. "We've done it before."

"Anyone else?" Misia asked, cocking her head toward Herman and Luis, who hadn't said anything yet.

"I don't know any of you," Luis said. "I don't think it would be appropriate."

"I could stay with one of the ladies," Herman suggested with a smile. His eyes lingered on Rose and he moved closer to the four women. "And serve as protector throughout the night, of course."

"Who ever heard of a coed sleepover?" Rose giggled, looking down at her now-empty dessert plate.

"We're quite capable of protecting ourselves," Sophia said. She had a streetwise edge to her voice and crossed her arms like Mr. T. "The brooch-thief may have had the element of surprise, but now I'm on guard. No one wants to mess with a Sicilian."

Herman cleared his throat and stepped back from the group. "Of course, I didn't mean to imply any impropriety.

It's just that I, as a certified art insurance appraiser, am the closest thing to an officer of the law in this house. I'm simply offering my assistance."

"Thanks," Sophia said. "I'll be sure to call you if someone uses the wrong shade of burnt sienna."

"If you four can share, there's a room with a king-size bed, and we can set up a cot," Misia said. "It's up on the third floor by itself, but it's the largest."

The girls turned to one another and grimaced in unison. "We'll make do," Dorothy said, trying not to sound as grouchy as she felt. "It's just for one night."

"My apologies, I know this isn't ideal," Declan said, turning to address the whole room. "I had such plans for this evening! I wanted to speak with you all and reveal my new work in progress before you left. But without power and light, perhaps it's best if we go to bed. The sun will come out tomorrow, as they say. And Ralph and Misia will get you all settled."

The once-boastful El Toro dropped his broad shoulders, and his barrel chest seemed somewhat deflated as he shook hands with the men and kissed the women on the cheek. "Things will look brighter in the light of day," he said. "I bid you good night."

THE GARDEN OF BLANCHELY DELIGHTS

8

An intoxicating scent of sandalwood, paint, Paco Rabanne cologne, and testosterone lingered in Blanche's hair after Declan kissed her cheek. As she breathed it in, it reminded her of the time the two of them had sat on an iron fire escape, splitting a pastrami on rye from Katz's and a cheap bottle of wine, waiting for the sun to rise over the roofs and treetops of Greenwich Village. Of course, Declan hadn't worn Paco Rabanne back then.

He couldn't have afforded it.

"Would you escort us to our room?" Blanche asked in a tone she knew would work.

It wasn't that she necessarily wanted or expected alone time with Declan. But being near him made her feel three decades younger. She wore the same dress size—well, *almost*—as she had back then, and she was vivacious as ever, with a fulfilling life and a home full of friends . . . but Blanche had to admit that around Declan, she felt a little less achy and fatigued than she usually did at this time of night. Her mind overflowed with memories from their youth: the time they ice-skated at Rockefeller Center, drank vodka gimlets until the wee hours at Marie's Crisis, and strolled hand in hand through the Museum of Modern Art, pointing out their favorite works. Blanche realized that when she stood next to him, her feet didn't hurt anymore despite having worn pointy-toed slingbacks all day.

"Of course," Declan said. "Follow me."

He led the four women into the hall and back to the foyer, where Blanche picked up her travel bag, then up the dramatic staircase framed by the ornate wrought iron railing. Each woman carried a candle, angled away from their bodies to avoid dripping wax on their evening wear, and cupped their hands around the flames to prevent them from going out.

"Please be careful on those stairs, ladies!" Herman shouted from below in his breathy, slightly nasal accent. Blanche still couldn't quite place it and would have to ask him where he was from. Half the time he reminded her of Monsieur Zahler, her high school French teacher; the rest of the time he sounded like the Danish Olympian yachtsman who'd taught her to navigate some particularly breathtaking swells.

Sophia rolled her eyes. "He's probably just trying to look up Rose's skirt," she muttered.

"Well, joke's on him," Rose said with a twinkle in her eye. "I wore my Tuesday panties today, even though it's Friday."

As they climbed to the second floor, Declan pointed out the framed artwork on the walls from names Blanche recognized, and some newer Florida artists that she wasn't familiar with.

"I need to be surrounded by beauty," Declan declared. Blanche smiled to herself, certain that he was referring to her. "This house was built by Edmund Pilfur, the wealthy orange magnate. He was a ruthless businessman, a contemporary—and rival—of James Deering. It's said he modeled Villa Velado after Deering's Vizcaya mansion, and that he was so obsessed with money and distrustful of others that after construction on the island was complete, he had the access bridge demolished."

"Can we take a breather?" Sophia said as they reached a wide landing. "I haven't climbed this many stairs since I landed at Ellis Island."

Blanche didn't mind having a little rest herself. After all, every Southern woman knew it was a slippery slope from a dewy complexion to sweating like a hog at a barbecue. As they took a moment for everyone to recuperate, Declan continued his story.

"His heirs were as greedy as he was, but none of them had

his head for business. Soon they drank, gambled, and blew their fortune away as the house fell into disrepair. Which was fantastic." He tapped his nose. "Because it meant I was able to snap up this property after I'd made a sale to the Guggenheim. I found a local woman who burned precious herbs to cleanse it of any dark and lingering energy before I moved in. This is my haven, a temple to art, not craven business."

Blanche nodded, hanging on Declan's every word. Once everyone had caught their breath, he led the girls the rest of the way up to the second floor, where hallways of closed doors stretched out from both sides of the stairway. Next, they mounted a second set of stairs, climbing up to the third floor. Blanche's candle went out along the way, making their ascent slightly darker. She used it as an excuse to huddle close to Declan as he took them down a tiled hallway. The lack of plush carpeting or art on the walls up on this level made Blanche wonder if they were being banished to the servants' quarters. But when Declan opened the door at the end of the hall, Blanche was relieved to see a spacious and elegant room.

The five of them placed their candlesticks by the mirror on the bureau, which seemed to increase the available light. The warm glow illuminated a large, canopied bed draped with mosquito netting against one wall. The windows were covered in thick drapes that tried, but failed, to block the sound of heavy rain pounding down outside.

"There's an adjoining bath," Declan said. "And I'll have Misia bring you clean towels and anything else you may need.

I have some extra clothing should you wish to wear it instead of your party attire. Again, I apologize to you all; this was not my vision for the evening."

"Don't you worry your pretty head," Blanche said, rubbing Declan's arm, noticing how firm his biceps still were. "This is a lovely room, and the storm is not your fault! We'll be cozy up here, like a gaggle of sorority sisters, isn't that right, girls?"

Rose and Dorothy made weak attempts to nod politely, but Sophia piped up quickly.

"The last time I had to bunk with this many other single women, I was visiting my friend Vittoria at Our Lady of Perpetual Heartburn!"

"Perpetual Heartache, Ma," Dorothy corrected.

"I'm telling you, it was heartburn from all the peppers the sisters grew in the convent courtyard. My throat was burning so bad, it felt like I'd swallowed a cherry bomb."

"Well, the last time *I* had an all-girls sleepover, it was at Camp Catchahootchie, just across the lake from St. Olaf," Rose interjected. "Oh, we had so much fun singing songs, making friendship bracelets, and learning wilderness skills." She shook her head wistfully, lost in the memory, then added, "I'll never forget the time I caught and deboned a seventeen-pound carp with my bare hands."

"*That* was one of the wilderness skills?" Blanche asked, placing a horrified hand to her neck.

"Oh no, that was independent study. I'd already mastered

archery and basketmaking, so the counselors let me do whatever I wanted. And that night, I wanted *carp*," Rose said proudly.

"Bian—I mean Blanche," Declan said with a raise of his eyebrows. "You have such a colorful collection of friends. And I'm glad you're all here. However, perhaps I should let you all get settled in and we can find some time alone together tomorrow?"

"I'd like that," Blanche said, feeling a little thrill zip up her spine as she wondered what he had in mind. A romantic walk through the villa's gardens? Or perhaps he wanted her to pose for his latest masterpiece? She imagined herself reclining on a daybed in a sun-drenched studio, her softer parts strategically concealed by 500-thread-count sheets. Or maybe she'd pose regally in a stately armchair—an iconic modern-day queen on an antique throne. She was so lost in thought she almost missed Declan leaving, until she heard the door shut behind him.

Finally on their own, the girls explored the guest room in the flickering light: the paneled walls with palm tree–shaped brass sconces, beautiful but useless without power, an overstuffed armchair and ottoman, and two polished wooden bureaus. A faint mustiness pervaded the room, as if it were rarely used.

A few minutes later, Misia entered, dragging a metal cot that she left unceremoniously in the middle of the room with a pile of linens and an assortment of men's pajamas before exiting with one of her patented sighs.

"I think I should get the cot, since I'm the tallest," Dorothy said, claiming her territory by tossing her sequined blazer onto the narrow bed.

"But you and Sophia are family, so you two should share the bed. And so should Blanche, who's the reason we're in this mess," Rose said. "I'll take the cot."

Blanche pouted. She couldn't think of a good reason why she should get the cot instead of having to share the big bed with two other women, other than the fact that she just didn't want to. She much preferred to have her own space unless there was a man to keep her warm.

"Fine. Let's do rock, paper, scissors," she suggested. "Like Dorothy said, it's only for one night. We'll be up and out of here in the morning."

After three nail-biting rounds of rock, paper, scissors, Sophia finally won.

"Never bet against a Sicilian," she cackled.

Dorothy and Rose tried on T-shirts and drawstring pants from the pile Misia had brought, grumbling as they bumped into each other in the darkened room. The sleepwear turned out to be comically large on the girls, but serviceable, and one of their host's button-down pajama tops was long enough for Sophia to wear as a nightgown.

Then Sophia locked the bedroom door and asked Dorothy to help her drag one of the chairs to prop under the handle.

"Don't forget, someone in this house is a thief," she cautioned.

Blanche stepped into the bathroom, carrying one candle for light. She slipped into the black lace and white silk nightie and robe she'd packed, relishing the cool feel of the fabric as the delicate garments cascaded over her skin. Too bad only her roommates were going to see her in them tonight, she thought. She winked at her reflection in the antique mirror over the sink. Turning side to side, she admired herself from all angles in the glow from the solitary candle, thinking she looked almost twenty again, before she rejoined her friends.

"Where'd you get that?" Sophia said.

"I brought a little overnight bag, remember?" Blanche said. "Though shacking up with you three wasn't exactly what I had in mind. Now, if you're all nice to me, and you promise not to snore, I'll share some of my toothpaste with you."

"You're not the only one who came prepared," Rose said with a delighted grin. "I have a tin of herring in my pocketbook, should anyone want a midnight snack."

"Tempting, Rose," Dorothy said. "But I'll pass on your generous offer." Turning to Sophia, she said, "Do you have anything in that purse that could knock me out?" She gestured to Rose.

"Sorry, pussycat, I wish I did," Sophia said, tucking herself into the cot.

Blanche and Dorothy settled on either side of Rose in the big bed, tugging the covers from side to side until everyone was equally annoyed. From the way Dorothy rolled to one side without even saying good night, Blanche had to assume she was frustrated about ending the evening in bed with her and Rose instead of with a new paramour. Well, one couldn't help that Mother Nature had decided to send a tropical storm their way, or that sometimes there weren't enough handsome, brooding artists to go around.

Blanche shut her eyes and tried to sleep, allowing herself to get lost in soft-focus memories of New York and the soothing sound of rain against the windowpane—when a loud groan from outside shocked everyone.

"What was *that*?" Rose cried, clutching the bedsheets to her chest.

"Probably that crocodile Declan was talking about," Blanche said, rubbing her eyes. "Don't worry, it can't get up here. We barely could."

But the sound came again, a prehistoric screech that finished in a hair-raising growl. The women all grabbed at one another and Sophia jumped into the king-size bed, forcing the others to squish even closer together.

"It's just nature, red in tooth and claw," Dorothy said.

"Nothing to be scared of . . ." quavered Sophia, clearly trying to convince herself.

Rose gulped, pulling the sheets over her head—and everyone else's. They clung together under the covers until all four of them finally fell asleep.

It wasn't long before Blanche found herself in the muscular arms of a handsome stranger who whisked her away from crocodile-infested waters to a pristine island, where white curtains billowed through the windows of a fairy-tale castle and the air smelled of honeysuckle. Blanche daintily stepped onto a veranda, where a quartet of faceless violinists played a swelling, romantic melody and doves wheeled in the cloudless sky above. A chiffon dress swirled around her knees as the stranger expertly twirled her, dipped her, then clutched her tightly in his manly embrace, squeezing her as if he wanted to possess her, body and soul. He was just about to kiss her when she awoke in bed with three other women.

Sophia's arm was flung across her chest, and the air smelled more like morning breath and tinned herring than honeysuckle. Gone were the violins, replaced by a cacophony of whistling snores. With a disgusted huff, Blanche shook herself free from Sophia's errant limb and hopped out of bed. She threw open the drapes, allowing the bright morning sunshine to pour into the room, illuminating the pools of candle wax that had burned overnight, the evening clothes hanging over the back of the armchair, and the unused cot in the middle of the room. Blanche peered out the window, looking for crocodiles. But all she saw were wet leaves and shrubbery below, an empty terra-cotta lanai one floor down, and some broken tree limbs.

The casualties of last night's storm.

"Good morning, sunshine!" Rose called as she crawled out of bed and proceeded to do some vigorous calisthenics.

Dorothy awoke next, pulling herself up to a seated position with a slight groan.

"I can't wait to go home," she said. "I need a hot cup of coffee and my own bed. Ma was poking me all night."

Sophia sat up and fumbled for her glasses. "Consider it payback for those nine months in the womb. You should've been the next Pelé, the way you kicked."

Blanche hurried to get ready as the others dressed themselves. She wished she had her full suite of beauty enhancements: curling iron, hairspray, mousse, and a few other items that helped lift and tuck and smooth and plump just about everything that needed it. She'd have to make do with her overnight bag, and soap and water in the guest bathroom. Even without the comforts of home, she didn't really want to go back quite yet. She'd just gotten reacquainted with Declan, and they had so much to catch up on.

Finally, the four women were zippered back into their outfits from the night before, albeit with cleaner faces and slightly flattened hair. They descended to the first floor, following the sounds of disembodied voices to the patio, where a breakfast buffet was arranged on a long wooden table. A light breeze ruffled the flowers and leaves of the nearby gardens, and the grounds appeared to be a muddy mess, shrouded in mist and scattered with fallen branches and the shards of a flowerpot that must have fallen in the storm.

"We have to use up everything perishable from the fridge since the power's out," Misia said. "Though the gas stove seems to be working—for now. Help yourselves."

Sophia took a plate, adding cut fruit, some scrambled eggs, and two scoops of ice cream. Rose followed suit, selecting ice cream with a sprinkling of granola, while Dorothy opted for a sensible breakfast of untoasted whole wheat and scrambled eggs. Blanche was too busy looking for Declan to make herself a plate.

"Is there coffee?" Dorothy asked Misia.

"Only instant," the young woman said apologetically.

Dorothy grimaced, but gamely poured boiled water into four mugs, and each woman sprinkled little packets of Maxwell House inside. Akiko appeared on the patio in her leather pants from the night before and took the kettle of boiled water from Dorothy without a word. Blanche found her silence a little rude, but clearly the art dealer needed caffeine as badly as the rest of them.

Blanche glanced around, zeroing in on Vee, who sat on a wrought iron chair sipping juice next to Luis. She wore an artist's smock as a tunic with men's striped pajama pants beneath, looking effortless in a Katharine Hepburn kind of way. Blanche choked down a bitter sip of coffee, thinking that it was unfair for the other woman to look so good in a strange house at eight in the morning. And Blanche couldn't help but notice that Luis looked particularly handsome in his clothes from the night before, with the collar popped on his blazer to keep off the morning chill as he paged through his spiral-bound notebook.

"Good morning," he said to Blanche. "Did you hear those noises last night?"

"I most certainly did," said Blanche. "What do you think it was?"

"So far, I have two votes for an endangered American crocodile, one vote for a coyote, and Ralph said it was a skunk ape," Luis said, reading from his notes.

"Which is most illogical," Herman said, joining the conversation. He looked extra rumpled this morning with the fabric of his shirt bunched up under this tweed blazer as if it were too big.

That man needs an iron, Blanche thought, *and a lint roller.*

Herman placed his teacup on the table next to Luis's notebook. "A skunk ape is a puerile legend, invented to frighten schoolchildren. And a coyote couldn't make it to this island, unless someone transported one over. By the power of deduction, it *must* have been a crocodile—a fearsome beast, to be sure. We'd do well to avoid it at all costs."

He paused, as if waiting for someone to congratulate him on his obvious conclusion.

"It might have been something else," Rose said. "Isn't there any other creature that could make a noise like that?"

"My dear, innocent Rose, what do you imagine it could be?" Herman said, his eyes twinkling behind his horn-rimmed glasses.

Blanche smiled to herself, recognizing a man with a crush. Although his interested gaze was aimed at Rose, Blanche didn't mind that someone other than herself was getting a smidgen of masculine attention. Herman was far too short and tweedy for her taste—why, he practically faded into the wallpaper when a real man like Declan was around.

"Well, maybe it was a panther, or something less exotic," Rose said. "In St. Olaf, you'd be surprised at the sounds regular cows could make, when it was mating season. And what about iguanas? Do they make any noise?" Rose furrowed her brow, thinking hard, as Declan swept onto the patio, looking a bit more haggard than he had the night before.

But still as handsome as ever, Blanche thought. In the watery daylight she noticed the glint of his silver hair, which gave him a distinguished air, and his rugged blue sweater brought out the rich dark brown of his eyes.

"My esteemed guests, my dearest friends, it appears you all have made it through the night." He let out a loud, throaty laugh, as if trying to banish the terrifying storm from their minds. "I'd like to meet with you individually in my studio today after breakfast, as I have much to discuss with each of you, and share my plans to reveal my new work, which will lead to fame beyond the grave! But first"—he clapped his hands together with gusto—"Blanche, I have something to show you and your friends."

Blanche stood up a little straighter, enjoying being singled out by Declan.

She hoped she looked as good as he did in the unforgiving morning light when he took her hand. As he led the four women back into the house and through a maze of hallways, Blanche felt a quiver of excitement at being by Declan's side and getting to explore his unique home by the light of day. They entered a small library lined with mahogany shelves that were filled with books and objets d'art.

"What an interesting collection!" Dorothy said, trailing her fingers along the shelves, which had been impeccably dusted and polished, presumably by Ralph or Misia. Blanche peered at the spines, seeing tomes of art and Florida history, biographies of famous artists, along with a few hardcovers by Don DeLillo, Tama Janowitz, and Gabriel García Márquez.

Declan grinned at her reaction.

"Watch this," he said. He pulled at an ancient-looking book entitled *How to Succeed in Business by Trying Really Really Hard* and a mechanism behind the bookshelf made a muffled clicking sound. Its series of levers and pulleys whirred, and the entire bookshelf swung open in front of him, revealing a hidden passageway. "My secret sanctum."

Blanche raised her eyebrows, and followed Declan into

the dusty passage, her roommates close behind. After about twenty feet, they reached a door, which Declan unlocked with a brass key.

"Blanche, I've wanted to share this with you for years," Declan purred. "Remember, as Bianca, you changed my life."

The three women glanced at one another warily, but Blanche felt her heart beat a little faster. Many men had declared their love for her over the years—but to have one say that she changed his life? And one *so famous*? That made her feel as effervescent as a bottle of Dom Pérignon.

"We don't think this is a Bluebeard's castle situation, do we?" Sophia whispered.

"Hush your mouth," Blanche snapped. "I'm sure it's something nice."

"Prepare yourselves," Declan said, sweeping the heavy door open. "Some of it is quite rough. After all, it's my earliest work."

Through the door they entered a plain white gallery illuminated by sun streaming through skylights cut in the stucco ceiling. Artwork covered nearly every inch of the walls: paintings, sketches in charcoals, pastels, and ink—some framed, and some on raw-edged canvas. Statues in stone and wood filled the center of the room.

"My heavens," Blanche whispered as she placed her hand over her mouth and glanced around the gallery. "I'm as confused as a virgin at a key party."

Sophia made the sign of the cross, her eyes wide.

"Holy smokes, Blanche," Rose exclaimed, as her eyes focused on a Leonardoesque painting. "Is that . . . *you*?"

Dorothy took in a sharp breath as she recognized the main subject of the artwork. Rose was right.

Blanche whirled openmouthed as she looked around the room. Every single portrait contained an unmistakable face: hers. Rose stood transfixed in front of a *Mona Lisa* that had Blanche's eyes and nose and a sphinxlike smile on her lips. Next to it was a chalky, saturated painting of a topless Blanche seated near a tree, in the style of Gauguin, from which Dorothy and the others politely averted their eyes.

"*The Birth of Bianca*!" Declan whispered, pointing to a youthful-looking Blanche emerging from a clamshell that floated over a rippling body of water, her more personal feminine aspects tastefully concealed under waves of long golden hair.

"And here, *Madame B*."

Blanche took in a portrait of herself in a dramatic black dress with a plunging neckline, her head turned to the side.

"I was still copying the greats," Declan explained, without a hint of self-consciousness. "I didn't have my own style yet." He turned to Blanche. "But I found inspiration in your beauty."

Dorothy and Rose paused in front of a painting crafted in dark, murky colors. In the image, Blanche's face had been transposed onto the body of a hideous monster that was biting the arm of a headless human figure clutched in a pair of feminine hands boasting a bloodred manicure.

"You painted a *Goya* . . . of *Blanche?*" Dorothy said in disbelief.

"One of my favorites," Declan said with pride. "So powerful."

Blanche shuddered, turning her back on the Goya and focusing on an abstract portrait composed completely of triangles.

"I don't think I'm in this one," she said.

"But of course you are! See your cheekbones?" Declan pointed to two blue triangles. "And here, the unmistakable line of your impeccable breast?" He pointed to a red triangle. Blanche squinted, failing to recognize herself in the slashes of paint but not wanting to hurt Declan's feelings. As she well knew, men's egos were often as delicate as camellia petals.

"See how I captured your vibrance, your joie de vivre?"

Blanche studied the riot of primary colors. "I think so," she said. "Though I confess, I always thought of myself as a jewel-tone type of gal."

Blanche circled the gallery, marveling at paintings in Renaissance and Impressionist styles, as well as the sculptures, including an armless and headless female form with wings, whose shoulders and figure were unmistakably Blanche's. Her favorite, she decided, was herself as a bronze ballerina, reminiscent of Degas. She wondered briefly if she could get one of these placed prominently in the lobby of the Center for the Fine Arts.

"Now this one's just funny," Dorothy said, pointing to

a Giotto-style painting on a wood panel. It was a vision of Blanche draped in blue robes and cradling an oddly adult-looking baby, both crowned with shining halos applied with delicate gold leaf.

Sophia clapped a hand over her eyes. "Truly, El Toro is the greatest artist of the century if he can make Madam Shore Leave here look virginal."

As she considered every piece, Blanche felt like she was viewing herself through a fun-house mirror: a kaleidoscope of lives she never lived, her own face looking back at her from various historical eras, distorted by different angles and artistic styles. Her head grew light, and dark spots appeared at the corners of her vision. What had driven Declan to do this? Was he obsessed with her? What was the line between simple infatuation and artistic inspiration? Blanche certainly enjoyed being admired, but *this* . . . this was almost too much for her. She wished she had her silk fan to cool her face, or a tall glass of lemonade to sip.

Suddenly, she couldn't breathe.

She needed air.

"My dear Blanche, what's wrong?" Declan asked, gently clutching her elbow.

"I'm just feeling a little warm is all. Did it get hotter than a firecracker on the Fourth of July in here?" Blanche looked around for a window to crack open, her eyes settling on Declan's worried gaze as her voice grew serious. "And I didn't know you felt this way about me."

"You are my *inspiration*, my dear. You always have been. It doesn't mean I demand anything more from you. Once I was able to explore your form in different styles, I was able to develop my own. Now, even though my skills have evolved, there's always a trace of Blanche infusing my work. See here?" He pointed to an abstract work, with dribbles of silver paint forming rough constellations on a black background.

Blanche saw nothing of her likeness—or any woman's— in the streaks and blotches.

"I painted this during a dark night of the soul. I had no money—and no Daddy Warbucks to save me. I was going to drop out of the academy, return to Pittsburgh, and seek work at the ketchup factory, but you were the one who told me ketchup was not my future, that I should not give up on my talent. These are the tears I cried, and see this splotch of yellow—"

"You worked at the mustard factory instead?" Rose began.

"—*that* is the sun dawning on a new day, when I sold my first sketch the very next morning at a stoop sale on Greenwich Avenue."

"That's a beautiful story." Rose sighed. "It reminds me of back in St. Olaf—"

"Shhh," Sophia said. "Don't ruin the moment. This is better than *All My Children*."

Declan gripped both of Blanche's hands in his paint-stained fingers.

"Your beauty exists on the levels of sunsets, the Fibonacci

sequence, the elegant proportions of da Vinci's *Vitruvian Man*. Though I'm certain I was in love with you then, please understand that to me, my feelings for you are beyond mortal attraction or bourgeois ideas of love. You are a symbol, a shining ideal. As an artist, my job is to chase the sublime—ever elusive, ever changing—and re-create it on canvas."

Blanche blinked back tears. She'd gotten many compliments in her life, but being called sublime and immortalized in all this artwork was sweeter than buttercream frosting on a slice of hummingbird cake. It was certainly better than being some fleeting crush, or simply an object of desire. If only she could cast this moment in bronze and experience it forever.

"That's why I wanted you to have the brooch as a symbol of my undying appreciation," Declan said. "To me, your essence is as beautiful and natural as a butterfly's wings. Delicate, yet strong enough to migrate across continents."

"I don't need a symbol," Blanche breathed. "Your words—and this gallery—are enough."

"But someone still took the brooch!" Sophia broke in. "Mark my words: There's a snake hiding in Villa Velado."

"That's right," Rose added. "And didn't Herman say last night that you were getting mysterious messages? Do you think that has anything to do with the theft?"

Declan's face darkened, and his dark brown eyes flashed with something Blanche couldn't place.

"One of my hopes in gathering everyone here was to expose

certain half-truths in my circle as I prepare for my artistic renaissance," he said evenly. "And also to reveal some secrets of my own."

"What secrets?" Blanche asked breathlessly. Her friends leaned forward, curious to hear as well.

But Declan shook his finger and grinned mysteriously. "All in good time, ladies. I must retreat to my studio. It is my private refuge, my temple to the muse, which I always keep locked. But today, I will unlock it, and then will reveal all!"

After thanking them for allowing him to share his inspiration gallery with them all, the artist ushered Rose, Sophia, and Dorothy through the gallery door. Blanche lingered to cast one last moist-eyed glance around the artistic shrine to her image.

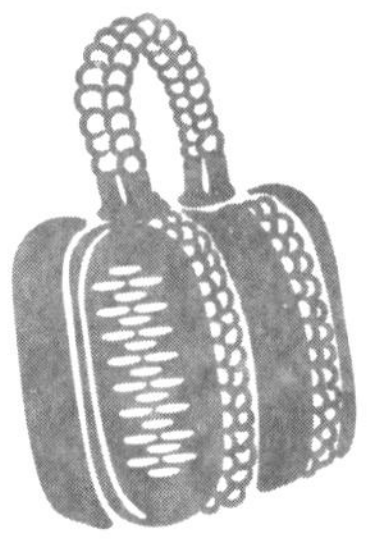

ROGUES' ART GALLERY

9

As the fivesome stepped through the secret door and back into the library, they found Misia tapping the toe of her black Doc Martens.

"I'm going to my studio," El Toro instructed. "Give me some time to get set up. Please bring in my guests one by one, starting with Bian—I mean Blanche. And I'll take a fresh coffee. Don't forget the milk this time."

"We only have instant," Misia reminded him as they walked to the hallway. "And we're out of milk."

El Toro glared at her. "Unacceptable," he roared.

Dorothy grimaced. Shouting at Misia seemed uncalled for, though she could understand overreacting when it came to a lack of caffeine. After a mostly sleepless night, she craved a second cup—but couldn't stomach another dose of tasteless powdered crystals.

"The storm, remember?" Misia said. "We used up what we had in the fridge, and we have no electricity."

El Toro opened his mouth as if he were about to yell at Misia, but then his expression grew gentle. He turned to Blanche. "Fame and fortune has made me soft, but I can handle hardship. Remember the blackout that summer in New York? We all shared the simple food we had with our neighbors and watched the stars from the rooftop together, not knowing it would take a full week for our building to have power again."

Blanche nodded. "I do remember," she said. "Your roommates played jazz while we ate up all the ice cream in your freezer so it wouldn't go to waste."

"The good old days," El Toro said. Then he turned on his heel, heading up the stairs to his studio. "Instant is fine," he shouted over his shoulder.

"Please join the other guests in the courtyard. I'll let you know when it's time to go up," Misia said. "In the meantime, I better get started on that coffee."

But when the four women reached the courtyard, it was deserted except for Vee, who leaned nonchalantly against the patio wall next to a plate of strawberries, looking like a *Mademoiselle* photo shoot.

"Where is everybody?" Rose asked her.

"Luis went to explore the grounds," Vee said. "He said he wanted to assess the storm damage and take notes for his story. Herman was here a moment ago. I assumed he went looking for you."

"Why me?" said Rose, plucking a mini croissant from a platter on an antique side table.

"He said something about 'tracking down that Norwegian cream puff,' I think. It was hard to tell with his accent," Vee said airily.

"I'm sure he was talking about one of these delicious pastries," Rose said as she wiped crumbs from her mouth.

Dorothy suppressed a grin. That officious little man did seem to be interested in Rose. At least someone other than Blanche was getting some romantic attention, she thought wryly, then wondered when it would be her turn. The way this weekend was going, her eighty-something mother would have a new boyfriend before she did.

"Where have you four been for the past half hour? And where is Declan? Did you all already go up to his studio?" Vee said, turning to Blanche. "I'm sick of waiting here. I should have been first. But I'm already familiar with what he's working on, since he runs everything by me. He won't even start a new canvas without hearing my opinion. I'm the one who told him his work needed to be more trapezoidal in '72, which as everyone knows, was a breakthrough for him."

"Well, he showed us something . . . special," Blanche said, smiling smugly. "But not in his studio. He said he wants to meet with me first."

Blanche and Vee stared at each other with narrowed eyes.

"Maybe he's going in alphabetical order," Dorothy added, trying to interrupt the tension between the two women, who each clearly felt threatened by the other.

Vee let out a little huff as Luis appeared, tucking his notebook into the pocket of his blazer.

"The island's a mess," he said. "Lots of trees down, and it looks like the dock has completely washed away. I found pieces of the rowboat on the sand—the waves from the storm must have demolished it. We're going to be stuck here for a while."

The entire group exploded in expressions of dismay and worry as Ralph wrung his meaty hands.

"How will we get home?" Rose asked.

"You'll just have to wait until we can use the phone, or figure out another way to signal to the mainland for a boat to come get you," Misia said. "Last time we had a storm like this, it only took a day or two."

Sophia groaned. "A day or two! There goes bingo at the community center. I was hoping to win a boom box!"

"What do you need a boom box for?" Dorothy asked. "We have a record player and a radio at home."

"So I can blast music at Haulover Beach! You know, a little Bobby Darin, a little LL Cool J." Sophia shook her finger. "And I'm missing my chance, stuck out here!"

"I'm sorry, Ma, but it can't be helped," Dorothy said, trying to soothe her mother's mood. After all, Sophia wasn't supposed to let her blood pressure get above eighty-five. And neither was Dorothy, according to her doctor. Unfortunately, both women seemed to raise each other's daily.

"I'll try. It's just at my age, there are only so many adventures left," Sophia said. "I'd like to decide what they'll be, you know?"

Dorothy, Blanche, and Rose nodded. Life had thrown curveballs to all of them over the years. Dorothy thought back to her own ups and downs during her marriage to Stan, and how hard it had been trying to find love since then, often facing disappointment and rejection. Though she'd certainly grown from those experiences, there were many she wouldn't choose to go through again.

Dorothy shook the negative thoughts from her mind and looked around the lush greenery surrounding the terra-cotta patio, focusing on the song from a nearby mourning dove. The misty air smelled fresh, as if it had been scrubbed clean by the rain. This particular adventure wasn't so bad, she thought. Though it wasn't what anyone had planned for, being stranded at Villa Velado meant delicious food, world-class art, and interesting company, even if she did have to share a bed with her roommates and wear yesterday's clothes. It made her feel a little bohemian in the way El Toro and Blanche had described their time in New York.

After a while, Herman Price appeared, sans fedora, followed by Akiko.

"What do you think El Toro is going to reveal at *your* meeting?" Luis asked Akiko, his notebook at the ready. "Can you give a statement for the paper about what's next for him?"

Akiko took a sip of coffee before answering. "I think the art world should brace themselves for El Toro's new piece, for which I'll be hosting a record-setting auction."

"How can you say that if you haven't even seen it yet?" Vee said.

Akiko rolled her eyes. "The world *needs* a new El Toro piece to excite and inspire them. Once he finally unlocks his studio and shows us his new work, I'm sure we'll all be impressed."

Dorothy raised her eyebrows and looked at Blanche. Her friend returned the expression, clearly just as curious as Dorothy to see El Toro's last painting. She wondered if Blanche would feature in it somehow, if only in an abstract way. Dorothy tamped down a tiny surge of jealousy that she'd never inspired such artistic devotion herself. Though she loved her friend, Dorothy didn't exactly feel that Blanche—of all people—really needed more ego-boosting.

Meanwhile, Herman had moved next to Rose at the patio table. He spread a generous portion of butter across a croissant, which he then offered to her. Rose hesitated, then took a small, polite bite.

"What do *you* think he's going to say?" Akiko asked Luis. "Are you going to give him front-page coverage, like we discussed?"

Luis coughed into his fist. "I'm not in charge of story placement," he said. "But I think the information I've gotten so far from El Toro—and some of you—is certainly front page–worthy." His dark eyes gleamed behind his aviators.

Everyone on the patio leaned toward Luis, eager to hear more. But he simply patted the mini tape recorder sticking out of his blazer pocket. "I can't wait to get to the office to file my story."

"I'm eager to read it," said Vee, taking an elegant bite from a ripe strawberry. "But I'm also curious what Herman thinks of all this. Do you think Declan's comeback will be as epic as *he* hopes it will be?"

Herman was busy watching Rose finish the croissant. "Oh yes," he said, snapping to attention. "His new work is, of course, brilliant . . . I assume. How could it not be? He is El Toro, after all. A visionary. It will get people talking, which as the esteemed Ms. Kakutani knows, is good for business."

"As long as he finishes it," Akiko muttered.

"It's true, he was creatively blocked for a long time," Vee added. "Though I suspect this weekend has reignited his spark." She dabbed the strawberry juice from her lips with a linen napkin and smiled mysteriously, as if sharing a private joke with herself.

Dorothy saw Blanche's shoulders visibly stiffen, but she didn't say anything.

"He and I have much to discuss," Herman continued, eyeing other guests with a suspicious, narrowed-eyed gaze. "About his work—and about all of you."

Dorothy glanced at her friends. Herman's ominous tone echoed El Toro's earlier statements, and she wondered what secrets would be revealed.

After about an hour of strained small talk, Misia stepped onto the patio and waved to Blanche. "Declan would like to meet everyone one by one in his studio. Except for my weekly dusting, he never lets anyone else inside, and usually has it locked. So I have to ask that you all not to touch anything—not a single paintbrush. And don't ask about his work in progress until he shows it to you."

"Why's that?" Blanche said.

"He's been increasingly secretive these days, and quite fastidious about his art supplies," Misia said. "He won't even open the lanai doors, as he claims the breeze would disturb his materials."

"Oh, please take me with you," Rose whispered as Blanche turned to leave the patio. "That Mr. Price keeps staring at me while I eat. I can't be stuck down here with him any longer."

"Me too," said Sophia. "These artsy types are so up their own *culos* about how important they are. We're coming along."

Dorothy put a hand on her mother's frail arm. "Don't you think Blanche should have a bit of privacy with El Toro, considering their history?" She honestly did want to give Blanche and El Toro some alone time—she also didn't need a front-row seat to more of their flirtation.

"He already showed us their history. All eight hundred years of it in oil paint. And all of Blanche, too," Sophia said, waggling her eyebrows.

"Please," Rose whispered as Herman approached her with a flaky palmier in his hand and an eager glint in his eye.

"Oh, fine," said Blanche. "You three can at least walk me up and lurk outside the door."

"Works for me," Sophia said.

Rose grabbed another croissant as the four friends filed off the patio and into the mansion.

"Where are you going, my dear? Why not have a seat next to me?" Herman called.

Rose quickly stuffed the croissant into her mouth and pointed to it to indicate she couldn't talk. Then she hurried after her friends.

Once inside she pulled it out of her mouth again. "I shouldn't have taken that last croissant," Rose whispered. "Mr. Price was staring at me! I think he wanted it for himself."

"He was looking at you, not at the pastry," Dorothy said.

"He was looking at her like *she's* a pastry," Sophia added. "I'm sure he wants a little nibble."

Rose's big blue eyes widened in surprise; then her brow furrowed with worry.

Dorothy placed a comforting hand on Rose's arm. "She

means that he likes you, not that he's going to bite you!"

"Well, he might a little bit," purred Blanche. "But they're right. I can always tell when a man is interested in a woman." She winked at Rose, who still had flakes of croissant on her chin and on the shelf of her bosom.

Misia led the group up the stairs. "Last door on your left," she said.

Blanche led the way down the long hallway, which felt shadowy and airless compared to the bright patio.

She knocked on the door, then turned to her friends. "You all wait here." After a moment, she knocked again. "If I'm gone longer than, say, fifteen minutes . . . why don't you all go downstairs and I'll come find you?" Her eyes sparkled.

"Fifteen minutes? I know you've made better time than that," Sophia quipped.

"He and I are going to have a *conversation*," Blanche insisted, placing her hands on her hips. "Not every connection has to be a carnal one, you know."

"I know that," Sophia said. "I just didn't know that *you* knew that."

Blanche rolled her eyes, and pushed open the studio door, closing it quickly behind her. Dorothy looked around the hall for a chair for her mother to sit in. *This is silly*, she thought. *We should just go downstairs and wait in the living room.* At least then they could sit down.

She was just about to voice this thought when she heard a bloodcurdling scream from behind the closed door.

PORTRAIT OF THE ARTIST AS A DEAD MAN

10

Blanche froze in her kitten heels, her hands clapped over her mouth. The first scream that had erupted from her throat was from shock. The next scream was in horror as her mind made sense of what her eyes were seeing.

She'd entered the studio and looked around for Declan through the cavernous room filled with canvases, easels, racks of paint, and other artist's tools. It was eerily quiet, and a breeze ruffled some papers next to a full cup of coffee on a weathered worktable. As she stepped farther into the room, she noticed the sliding glass doors to the attached lanai were open. As she approached the entryway, she realized something was very, very wrong.

A man in a blue sweater and linen pants lay across the threshold of the lanai, face down in a pool of dark liquid. His body was motionless, and what she could see of the side of his face looked waxy and pale.

It was Declan. Her Declan. A man so vibrant, so full of passion, now oddly still.

Blanche didn't know how long she stood there screaming, but soon she was surrounded by the gentle arms of Rose, Dorothy, and Sophia, hugging her and whispering soothing words into her ears. After a few minutes, Dorothy pulled Blanche a few steps back from Declan's body.

"Oh, honey," Dorothy said, wiping a tear from Blanche's cheek. "What happened?"

Blanche gulped, trying to catch her breath enough to speak. "He was lying there when I walked in! I just can't believe it!" Blanche thought back to how healthy, how alive he seemed when they'd last seen him. A flicker of hope caught fire in her heart. "Maybe he just hit his head and is in a coma or something? Perhaps we can get him to a hospital, and he'll be okay. Dorothy, can you check?"

Dorothy shook her head sadly. "Sweetie—"

"We know how much you cared for him," said Rose. She

offered a lace handkerchief to Blanche. Blanche took it and dabbed at her eyes, her mascara leaving little black smudges on the fabric.

"It's not fair. God always takes the good-looking ones first, like my Sal," Sophia said, wrapping Blanche in a fresh hug.

As Blanche allowed herself to be enveloped in Sophia's comforting scent of rosewater and baby powder, she thought back to when Big Daddy had fallen ill. She'd felt so certain then that nothing could stop such a strong, willful man that she hadn't even canceled her appearance as Queen of the Citrus Festival to go see him when he'd called for her. Once he'd died at their family home in Atlanta, she found out the hard way how wrong she had been.

But this . . . this just didn't compute, Blanche thought, as she buried her face against Sophia's shoulder. Declan was younger than Big Daddy, and there were no signs that he'd been sick, or even slowed by age. How could Declan be taken so soon? Surely Blanche had already faced her fair share of heartache and grief in losing her husband, George, and her beloved Big Daddy. She couldn't face any more.

"Please check," Blanche said, stepping back from Sophia's hug. "I need to be sure. Remember what we did at that murder mystery party?"

Dorothy grimaced and nodded at Rose. Rose opened her purse and pulled out a green Clinique compact, clicking it open to reveal a tiny mirror. She offered it to Blanche, who shook her head, and then Sophia, who also refused it.

"Fine," said Dorothy, "I'll do it."

"No way!" cried Sophia. "Remember what happened last time we found a dead body? I don't want you getting too close—you might incriminate yourself!"

Dorothy hesitated, heeding her mother's words.

Blanche found herself reaching for the compact, thinking, *I can do this.* She flipped open the case, though she'd much rather one of her friends do it. Whether it was handling all of the Hollingsworth family's cooking and cleaning, as Viola had, or paying all their household bills, as George had—Blanche had always been more than happy to let other people take care of difficult things for her.

She took a few steps toward Declan's motionless form. Her breath grew rapid, and suddenly oxygen would not reach her lungs, even with fresh air blowing through the open lanai doors. She tried to take a deep breath and another step forward, but she faltered. She just couldn't do it. She turned to Dorothy, pleading with her eyes. Dorothy was just so much more practical than her. She wasn't as close to Declan as Blanche had been; therefore, it would be easier for her friend to do it, she told herself.

Dorothy reluctantly took the compact, pressing her lips together in a determined frown. She crept over to Declan, careful not to step into the congealing liquid surrounding his legs and feet. She held the mirror over his mouth. The shiny surface didn't change; no breath condensed on the glass. Blanche peeked over at Rose.

Rose shook her head. "I promise, I didn't put any defogger on it," she said sadly, referencing the time she'd tricked Blanche at that murder mystery party. "I think he's gone."

The edges of Blanche's vision grew shadowy. Her head felt light, and she slumped in a nearby armchair, which had been draped with paint-stained drop cloths.

Her three friends surrounded her, their familiar faces creased with concern.

"Stay with us, Blanche," Rose urged. "We can't lose you, too."

"You need to snap out of it," Sophia said sternly. "My condolences to you—but we've just stumbled upon a dead body . . . *again*!"

The four women stared at each other, clearly all picturing what they'd discovered in a hotel freezer not that long ago. Blanche shivered at the thought.

"But that was totally different," Rose said. "That was a murder scene!"

"Well, what do you think this is?" Sophia said, gesturing to the man on the floor.

Blanche bolted upright in the armchair, now fully alert. "Are you saying that this handsome man was *murdered*?"

Dorothy paced back and forth across the studio, stealing glances at the body. She tapped an index finger against her lips, thinking. "Well, he might have fallen," she mused. "Or had a heart attack or stroke . . . That wouldn't be out of the question for a man his age."

"But what's all that red stuff around him? Is it paint, or is it . . . blood?" Rose asked, her voice quivering on the last word.

"No matter what it is, we shouldn't touch it," Dorothy cautioned. "It could be evidence."

"It all seems pretty suspicious to me," Sophia said. She lifted her hands in a gesture of exasperation. "But what do I know? I lived next door to the Cosa Nostra for years, and have decades more life experience than the rest of you."

"All this talk of blood and evidence is making me nervous," Rose said, wringing her hands. "I knew I had a funny feeling in my gut about coming here."

"You've just been spooked since Nettie's wedding," Dorothy said. "That doesn't mean we're dealing with foul play here."

"I disagree. Though there was something off about that egg salad Rose made yesterday. Maybe that's what she was feeling deep in her gut," Sophia added.

"Either way, something isn't right," Rose said. "Our host has gone to the great green cornfield in the sky! Oh, why did we have to be the ones to find him? Unless . . ."

Blanche's eyes widened. "What exactly are you saying, Rose?"

"This must have happened after we saw him go upstairs. But when exactly? So how can we be sure that we're the first people to have seen him . . ." Rose lowered her voice to a whisper. "Like *this*?"

Blanche shook her head, which was spinning faster than a pinwheel in a Lowcountry hurricane. Had there even been time between him showing them his gallery and their meeting for him to have had a medical emergency—or for someone to have killed him? Had anyone else noticed any signs of illness? Just as she was about to give voice to her questions, Rose clapped her hands, as if struck with a realization.

Rose bit her lip, then continued. "I'm saying that if anyone else interacted with him in the time between when he saw him on the stairs and when Blanche found him, then that person was either the last person to have seen him alive—"

"Or was the person who killed him!" Sophia interrupted. "You're not as dumb as you look, you know. And even if they didn't kill him, someone else could have gone up there in the meantime, and not said anything."

"That's a big *if*. Do you really think that's a possibility?" Dorothy said. Her deep voice was skeptical. "Why wouldn't they say something?"

"To protect someone! To cover it up! To buy time! To make us look guilty!" Sophia said, pacing in small circles, being careful not to get too close to the corpse. "I don't know—I'm just trying to think like someone with something to hide."

Blanche tried to clear her head and visualize all the other people in the house. There were the guests, and the staff. She didn't really know any of them, beyond the conversations she'd had and superficial observations she'd made about them over the course of the previous night and this morning. Those conversations had either been about art, or simple dinner-party small talk, revealing nothing of substance about their lives or relationship to Declan. Any one of them could have something to hide, she realized with a chill. Maybe, just maybe, they were trapped on the island with a murderer.

SEEN NO EVIL

11

Dorothy stared at Sophia with one eyebrow raised. Her mother had gone all in on the theory that El Toro had been murdered—or at least, that there was something suspicious about his death. Yet while Dorothy's mind grasped for other rational explanations, a sinking feeling materialized beneath the band of her Olga underwire. A sudden heart attack or stroke probably wouldn't be accompanied by a pool of mysterious liquid. A liquid that she and her friends had studiously avoided looking at too closely.

She didn't want to touch it, just in case it *was* blood. Though Dorothy wasn't quite sure what a pool of blood would smell like, she hadn't detected the corporal, coppery smell she'd expect when she sniffed the air. Rather, a light chemical smell permeated the room from all of the paint, turpentine, and other artistic substances El Toro used in his work.

Dorothy's sinking feeling deepened as she realized that the four of them could easily be blamed for his death. After having been investigated for another recent fatality, she wasn't keen on trying to clear her name a second time. Dorothy took a step back from the body and bit her lip.

"We have to be smart about this," she told her friends. "What are we going to tell the others?"

"Do we have to tell them anything?" Blanche said, waving her hands nervously at her sides. "Perhaps we can sneak back downstairs and let this be somebody else's problem."

"They'll probably pin it on us anyway, knowing we had just gone up to his studio," Sophia said. "Maybe we can hide the body, buy ourselves a little more time. Then we can figure out a way off this island and make for the southern border. I'll get in touch with my cousin Jimmy and get us new IDs."

"Ma, we are not destroying potential evidence by moving this man!" Dorothy scolded. "And we're not changing our names or running away to Mexico. There's got to be a better way."

"Why don't we just tell everyone the truth?" Rose said. "You know, once in St. Olaf, there was a little farm boy called Edgar Allan Hoe. He tripped and spilled an entire pail of milk in their family's parlor. He was too busy to clean it up and didn't tell anyone. But that day was a scorcher, and that spoiled-milk smell started emanating from the floorboards—and his overalls. Even though he pretended nothing had happened, he heard the drip, drip, drip of the milk beneath the floorboards so loud that it drove him crazy, and he turned to a life of petty crime. He's still babbling in the St. Olaf County Jail and Deli to this day!"

"I hate to say it, but the Blond Wonder here *is* right," Sophia said. "Sometimes it's better to come clean."

"All right, we'll simply explain that we found him like this," Blanche said. "I mean, how could anyone suspect *us* of doing anything untoward? After all, it's obvious that Declan and I adored each other, and you all are too elderly to hurt anyone."

Dorothy crossed her arms as a flush of anger heated her cheeks. She certainly wasn't too old to smack Blanche right in the mouth.

But she controlled herself, as usual. Blanche was hurt and grieving, and she could be forgiven for speaking out of turn. It was a burden, Dorothy thought, always being the most rational and responsible one of their little group.

"Of course no one should blame us for anything," Dorothy said. "But that doesn't mean they won't. We'll have to tell everyone what happened—and fast. The longer we wait here, the guiltier we look."

"Good point," Sophia said. "I say that we watch everyone's reactions when you tell them the news. See who looks surprised, or sad—and who doesn't."

"I can do that," Rose said, clasping her hands together. "Just like Jessica Fletcher!"

Blanche sniffed, dabbing at the last of the tear tracks on her cheeks and patting her hair into place. "Can I just pull myself together first? I'm such a wreck," she whimpered.

Dorothy led an ashen-faced Blanche, Rose, and Sophia down the stairs.

"Try to act normal," she said under her breath, just before they entered the living room, where the other guests had congregated.

"There's a first time for everything," Sophia said, jerking a thumb at Rose.

The spacious room was painted a brilliant azure and hung with antique-looking botanical canvases patterned with palm fronds, vines, alligators, and pelicans. As Dorothy stepped across the ornate parquet floor, the other guests fell silent. Luis sat in a green leather club chair, paging through a day-old newspaper as Akiko and Vee sipped liquid from highball glasses. Dorothy couldn't tell if it was water or something stronger. Herman appeared from a side entrance, patting his mustache with a plaid handkerchief.

"Ah! The lovely Rose," he said. "May I pour you some more coffee? The chill of this foggy afternoon reminds me of Switzerland's fresh breezes."

"Thank you, but I'm fine," Rose said, stepping behind her friends.

"I'll take a lemonade," Blanche added. She stared haughtily at him until he scurried toward the kitchen.

She has a gift for getting men to do whatever she wants, Dorothy thought. That power would have been helpful during her own marriage when she'd needed Stan to take out the garbage—or at least put the toilet seat down.

"Well, now we know he's Swiss," Blanche said. "It explains the accent."

"Maybe not Swiss," Rose said. "He smells more like Havarti."

"Wait, Herman," Dorothy said, reminding herself of the solemn task at hand. "Everyone, we have something to share with all of you." She glanced around the room. "Does anyone know where Misia and Ralph are?"

Wordlessly, Akiko stood and pulled a heavy tassel that hung next to a carved marble fireplace. A gong-like bellow rang throughout the house, and soon Misia and Ralph appeared in the living room, both of their faces glistening with a sheen of perspiration.

"You rang?" Misia said sourly.

Akiko nodded toward Dorothy.

"Thank you for rushing over," Dorothy began. "I don't know how to say this—I imagine it's going to be quite a shock." She paused, shifting from one foot to the other. The fact that they were some of the last people to have seen El Toro alive--and the first ones to have found him dead—made them look pretty suspicious, she had to admit.

"We went up to meet with El Toro in his studio . . ." Rose interjected, motioning for Dorothy to continue.

"Right," Dorothy said. "But when we walked in . . ."

Suddenly Blanche erupted into loud sobs. "He had gone to a better place."

"No, he hadn't!" Rose cried. "He was lying *right there!*"

Blanche shot Rose a look cold enough to turn romaine lettuce into iceberg. Everyone in the room froze, their eyes locked on Rose.

"What Rose is trying to say," Sophia said, "is that our host is dead as a doornail."

Vee choked on her beverage, coughing loudly, as Akiko dropped her glass, which rolled onto the thick carpet without breaking. Dorothy quickly scanned the room, trying to catch everyone's reactions to the news. Luis's jaw dropped, and he squinted at Sophia through his aviators. Herman gulped, his eyes widening in surprise. Dorothy flicked her eyes to Misia, who'd gasped and gone pale, and to Ralph, who furrowed his brow in dismay. Misia looked up at him and grasped his meaty arm.

"Excuse me," Herman said, clearing his throat. "I think I speak for all of us when I ask: Are you quite sure?" His piercing blue eyes connected with Rose, Sophia, and Dorothy, then lingered on Blanche.

Blanche slumped down on an empty velvet love seat. Everything about her seemed to droop like a silk blouse with the shoulder pads ripped out. She nodded sadly. "We don't know what happened. We just found him."

"It's too late for an ambulance, even if we could call for one," Dorothy added. "Did any of you notice anything wrong with him? Any health issues?"

Akiko shook her head in disbelief. "He was healthy as any of us, as far as I know." She picked up the glass she had dropped and frowned at it, as if answers lurked inside the crystal facets.

Vee stood up and paced around the living room, pausing by Misia and Ralph. "This can't be. I just talked with him—he was *fine*! Better than fine—he was invigorated by his new project. I don't believe it!"

"Me neither," Misia said, still gripping Ralph's arm. "This is messed up."

"Oh, how could this happen?" Blanche burst into a fresh bout of sobs, tears cascading down her cheeks.

Dorothy searched her pockets for a Kleenex to offer to her friend but paused when she saw Luis reaching into his blazer. But instead of offering a tissue or handkerchief, he pulled out his tiny flip-top notebook and started making notes with a pencil stub.

Interesting, thought Dorothy. *He's treating this like a scoop.*

She tried to make eye contact with her friends, to see if they were aware of what she'd seen, but Blanche was busy crying, and Rose had her hands full comforting Blanche. She noticed her mother was terrifying everyone in the room with a threatening Sicilian stare as she joined Blanche on the love seat, never lowering her gaze.

"Great question," Akiko said. She tore open a fresh piece of gum with shaking hands. It took her more than three tries to unwrap it, Dorothy noticed.

"I need to see for myself," Vee stated, towering over everyone in the room except Dorothy. "Anyone care to join me?"

Glances flew around the room, and everyone seated rose to their feet, including Sophia, whose knees cracked. Ralph grunted, and Misia nodded as Vee led the entire group out of the living room and up the marble stairway, with Sophia and Herman bringing up the rear.

"This can't be happening," Misia said. "It has to be some sort of joke, right?"

Ralph shook his head sadly. "It's hard to believe, though he was getting old."

Dorothy frowned. El Toro wasn't *old*, she thought. He had been close to her own age.

"Then what should we do?" Misia said on the landing. "Call a funeral home? Track down his brother in Pittsburgh?" She looked at Ralph. "That's what we should do, right?"

Dorothy expected him to grunt in response. But he spoke gently instead. "We can't call anywhere, remember? And with all the fog around the island, I'm not sure anyone could get here if we could. Perhaps in the meantime, I can carry him to his bed."

"I wouldn't touch him—or move him," Dorothy cautioned, just as the group reached the second floor.

"Why not?" Misia asked, just as Vee started to push open the studio door, making it creak.

"Because it seems this unknown foursome of women suspect that El Toro's death *might not* have been from natural causes," Herman said, putting an arm across the half-open doorway. "We don't want to disturb any evidence if something nefarious has befallen our host."

THE BLAME GAME

12

Herman's bespectacled eyes sought out Blanche, his gaze so piercing that she had to look away.

Why is that little man staring at me like that? she thought.

There was no attraction or yearning in his look—that would have been expected from someone of the opposite sex. This was something else entirely. Something cold and curious.

Surely he can't think I had anything to do with Declan's death, Blanche told herself.

"Nefarious!" she tittered nervously. "You certainly have an active imagination, Mr. Price."

"We shall see," he said, pushing ahead into the studio, slightly bumping into Vee as he did so. Everyone jostled to get a clear view of the body lying across the threshold to the lanai. Dramatic gasps and sniffles emanated from the group as they solemnly observed their motionless host on the ground. Blanche couldn't bear to see Declan like that again and instead turned toward the corner of the room, where a massive work was covered by a drop cloth.

"You'd think they were lining up to see Tony Bennett," Sophia quipped.

"Oh, hush," Blanche whispered, hoping that no one else had heard the older woman. "Show some respect for the deceased!"

"It's as if they've never seen a dead body before! When you get to be my age, you attend at least one or two funerals a week," Sophia said, gesturing with both hands. "It starts to become routine. Like brushing your teeth."

"Routine? I can't imagine facing mortality can ever be as familiar as . . . basic hygiene!" Dorothy said.

"Eh, it's more like flossing," Sophia said. "You don't want to do it, and maybe you forget some days. But it's never pretty."

"Especially after eating corn on the cob," Rose added unhelpfully.

"You didn't mention that he was surrounded by a pool

of . . . something," Vee said, and Blanche turned to find the woman glowering accusingly at Dorothy.

"Seems like a pretty important detail," Luis added. "Can we confirm if it's blood?"

At the mention of blood, Blanche began to feel lightheaded again. She took a deep breath, trying to steady herself on the soles of her Evan Picones.

"Now wait a minute," Dorothy said. "We came down to tell everyone about the situation as soon as we could. We have no idea if that's even blood—it could be paint, or varnish, or—"

"Ketchup!" Rose said.

Everyone paused and swiveled their heads toward Rose.

"What?" she said, suddenly aware that everyone was glaring at her.

"Are you being serious right now?" Misia said, her voice sharp.

Rose ducked her head apologetically. "I suppose that was a silly thing to say."

"It sure was," Vee said under her breath.

"It does look more like barbecue sauce . . ." Rose said glumly.

Sophia groaned.

"If I might make a petite suggestion?" Herman said, clapping his hands together and drawing the attention toward himself. "Of course, an innocent like Rose should not be expected to identify a mysterious substance at the scene of a sudden demise. However, a seasoned investigator, such as myself, might be allowed to make that determination."

He strode toward the center of the studio, leading the group away from the lanai.

"I shall examine the body and attempt to ascertain the cause of death," he said. "A sad duty, to be sure." He pulled a small magnifying glass from his pocket and polished it with a clean rag from Declan's worktable.

Blanche let out a slow breath, feeling some tension leave her chest. It would be such a relief to have someone else take charge. It made sense to have someone more official look into Declan's death, rather than three women of a certain age and herself, their much younger friend. She looked at Dorothy with questioning eyes, hoping that her friend would just go with the flow for once and let the expert handle things.

But Dorothy pressed her lips into a hard line. "I think none of us should touch anything until the officials arrive," she said.

"But how will we even call the officials?" Vee said. "The phone line is down!"

"And with the boat smashed, there's no way off of this island," Ralph reminded them.

"We're stuck here," Sophia muttered. "We've got to figure this out ourselves."

"So you think it *is* foul play?" Luis said, his thick eyebrows so inquisitive they looked ready to spring off his forehead. "Could you elaborate on that?"

"We're not saying that." Dorothy glowered at the young man, and Blanche realized she was getting a glimpse of what Dorothy must be like leading a classroom of unruly students. "I'm sure there's a simple, natural explanation for why he passed away so suddenly."

"Madame Dorothy is correct," Herman said. "No one should touch anything. I must make my assessment without outside interference. We wouldn't want anyone to accidentally . . . how do you say it in English? *Incriminate* yourselves."

"Now wait just a minute," Sophia said, poking a tiny finger toward Herman's chest. "I don't like this talk of 'incriminating.' As far as I'm concerned, this poor gentleman had an aneurysm or something. Just because we don't think anyone should meddle with the body doesn't mean there's anything unlawful going on here."

Blanche chewed her lip as the tension in the room grew thicker than the blackberry patch at the edge of her family's property where she'd had one of her first kisses with the boy from the farm next door. Momentarily distracted by the memory, Blanche could feel the prickly branches at her ankles and the warmth of the boy's hands on her waist. Then she shook her head, quickly snapping herself out of it.

Herman strode around the studio, gesturing in the air with his fountain pen.

"You two are quite adamant about not allowing anyone a closer look," he said, his eyes darting between Dorothy and Sophia. "I wonder why."

He cast a glance around the rest of the room. Vee raised her eyebrows, and Misia and Ralph exchanged bug-eyed glances. Akiko stopped chewing her gum and pressed her lips into a hard line. And Luis, Blanche noticed, was keeping his eyes on Dorothy.

"We've got to stop this," Rose muttered in Blanche's ear. "Or people will start suspecting them! Can't you do something?"

"You're the one he has the hots for," Blanche whispered back. "*You* do something!"

"Mr. Price," Rose said, blinking rapidly. Blanche thought Rose had something caught in her eye before she realized her friend was attempting to bat her lashes seductively. "Shouldn't we see if there's some security camera footage? That could tell us what happened."

"There are no cameras on the property," Ralph said sadly. "Declan was very private."

Rose blinked again, harder. "Then in that case, wouldn't it be better if we all discussed this downstairs? We've all had quite a shock." She gestured to Blanche and Vee. "And I think we need to find some Kleenex. . . ."

"And some liquor," Akiko added, her voice husky and strained.

"Good idea," Misia said. "Ralph and I will close off this

room until further notice." Ralph nodded. Once everyone filed into the hall, he pulled a key ring from his pocket and flipped through the keys until he found a shiny copper one.

"Wait!" Herman cried. He dashed back into the studio, returning with a roll of blue painter's tape. After Ralph locked the door, Herman stretched several long strips of tape across the frame, an art-world version of crime-scene tape. "Now no one can enter and disturb the evidence before we uncover what has happened here. And believe me, I will hunt down the person or persons responsible." He chomped on the end of his fountain pen as if it were a cigar. "Relentlessly."

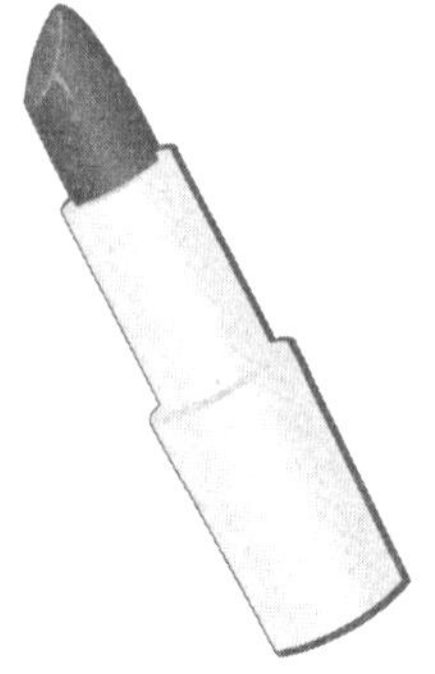

SWOON-WORTHY

13

"We've got to figure out what's going on here," Dorothy muttered as she and her friends trailed the rest of the group down the hallway.

"Can't we just sit tight until we're rescued?" Blanche asked.

"Perhaps," Dorothy said. "But we don't know how long we'll be stuck here. With the boat destroyed and no way off the island, it could be a while."

"Maybe we can ask Ralph to fix the boat," Sophia said. "Or if he has anything we can use to signal the mainland."

"Let's do that," said Rose as the rest of the group started down the stairs. "It's creepy enough to be stuck in a house with a dead body. And what if we're trapped here with a *murderer*?"

"It reminds me of being back in the old county," Sophia said. "When somebody passed, their body would be displayed in the parlor for days. Come to think of it, if the poor sap had ticked off the wrong crowd, you'd never know if the hit man was among the mourners coming to visit. A wolf among the lamb ragù, so to speak. Kind of like our situation here."

The girls paused for a moment, allowing even more space between themselves and the others before they descended the massive staircase. Blanche's stomach felt queasy, as if she'd eaten shrimp gumbo that had been left out in the sun. It wasn't easy facing Declan's death, but the thought of his life being taken on purpose was almost too much to bear.

"Where do we start?" Blanche said. "And how will we investigate his death under everyone else's noses?"

"Especially if one of those noses is the killer!" Rose said ominously.

"I'd start by taking another look at the body," Dorothy said. "With the shock of what happened, and then all those people around, I didn't take in any details that might turn out to be clues."

"We can't go back in there without looking suspicious," Rose cautioned.

"Then we'll have to create a diversion," Sophia said. The

girls instantly quieted when they met the others at the bottom of the stairs.

Misia directed them into a small sitting room filled with Victorian furniture, and the guests milled around in a combination of borrowed clothes and last night's finery, eyeing each other with thinly disguised suspicion.

"Don't you have a radio or something?" Akiko demanded as Ralph set up a few extra chairs.

"I did, but it was in the boat," he said glumly. "We're cut off until I can figure out some way for us to get off the island or someone comes to check on us."

Blanche's mood sank even further at the news about the radio, until she gazed up at the huge painting over the mantel: a large, Warhol-style square canvas, with her own face depicted in neon pink and yellow. It touched her, having her image in pride of place in this elegant room, and her eyes prickled. *Oh, Declan*, she thought. *That poor, dear man.* She closed her eyes, pressing them with the handkerchief Rose had given her, making stars appears on the back of her lids. It reminded her of when she thought she was going to faint, back in Declan's secret gallery.

That's it, she thought. *I know just what to do.* Especially since she was an expert in the art of diversion. She knew how to divert the eye away from the fine lines on her forehead with a touch of pearly shadow on the inner corners of her eyelids. How to draw focus to her tanned shoulders and exquisite décolletage—and away from her thighs—by employing shoulder pads, sweetheart necklines, and glittering necklaces. In the same way she could avert a man's attention on a date from a pretty, young waitress to bring it to herself with lively conversation and sensual eye contact.

"I have it! I'll create the diversion, and you and Dorothy can sneak off and explore the studio," Blanche whispered in Sophia's ear. Then she concentrated on the sad, lightheaded feeling that enveloped her when she thought of Declan.

"Oh heavens," she gasped, throwing a hand to her heart. "I can't believe that he's gone!"

Blanche allowed her bosom to heave dramatically as she gulped for air, angling her chest first toward Luis, then Herman, then Ralph.

"Are you all right?" Rose exclaimed, her eyes wide.

"No!" wailed Blanche. She wished she could get it through Rose's head that she had already started the diversion. Sometimes her friend was slower than molasses. "I'm simply—excruciatingly—overcome by emotion!"

She squeezed her eyes shut, forcing out more of the genuine tears she'd been shedding for Declan.

"It's all just too much!" She staggered forward, bumping into Akiko and spinning off her to tumble into Ralph's arms. As she leaned against his torso, she realized he was strong and surprisingly solid, and she relished his manly scent of cut grass, cured meats, and something slightly mechanical, motor oil perhaps. She pressed her face into his chest and pounded on it with one fist and sobbed, while slipping her other hand deftly into his pocket. She found what she was looking for and slid it up her lacy sleeve. Then she pushed herself off the handyman/chef with a dramatic flourish.

Blanche tottered toward Dorothy, slipping her the key ring with one hand while fanning herself with the other. She'd learned that trick from a very sexy magician in Coconut Grove. She remembered his skillful sleight of hand when he'd miraculously made all of her inhibitions disappear.

"Oh, I'm so embarrassed, carrying on like this," she blubbered. "It's just that we'd lost touch for so long and I'd only just found him again . . . and now he's gone!"

Out of the corner of her eye, she saw Dorothy and Sophia slowly backing toward the side door of the sitting room. Just as Vee started to turn her head in that direction, Blanche grasped at her arm.

"*You* understand, Vee," Blanche said, pulling the woman's attention away from Dorothy and Sophia. "You loved him, too. It's a terrible, terrible loss."

"Yes . . . We're all very upset," Vee said, carefully removing her elbow from Blanche's grip.

"Do you need some water or something?" Luis asked, looking around the room.

Blanche nodded, trying to make herself look devastated and frail.

"I'll get it." Misia sighed.

"Wait!" Blanche said, trying to stop Misia from turning around and noticing that Dorothy and Sophia were edging out of the room.

"Air! I need air!" she gasped, then threw herself into Luis's strong arms. She didn't need to pickpocket anything from him, but something about the set of his eyes reminded her of a much, much younger Fidel Santiago. Blanche got a delicious whiff of Davidoff Cool Water before Luis helped steady her on her feet.

"I need to lie down," Blanche moaned, staggering toward the nearest piece of furniture, which conveniently happened to be an antique fainting couch. In one graceful movement, she reclined on the sea-green brocade and let her eyelids flutter shut. She slowed her breathing and let her mouth hang slightly ajar. Not so much that she'd look like a hooked catfish, but just enough so she'd look fetchingly—and convincingly—unconscious.

"Oh no!" Rose cried theatrically. "Please help her!"

Blanche held her pose for as long as she could, letting her arm fall slack off the side of the couch. She tried to still the rising and falling of her enviable chest and imagined that her sun-kissed complexion had gone pale, channeling the heroines in the gothic novels she'd sneak out from under her mattress at night as a teenager. The ruse reminded her of the time she pretended to fall asleep on Declan's arm the night they'd stargazed in Central Park, just so she could snuggle longer on the blanket next to him. The memory made her all the sadder.

Soon, Blanche could hear the others clustering around her. "Does anyone have smelling salts?" Herman asked. Someone fanned Blanche's face and she heard Rose ask for water.

"I could try slapping her," a gravelly female voice said.

Was that Akiko? Blanche wondered. She tried not to visibly frown and ruin the illusion that she was completely passed out.

Suddenly, a splash of cold water splattered across Blanche's face, pouring down her cheeks and snaking down her neck. Her eyes flew open, just in time for her to see Vee's hand, pulling the water glass away from her face.

"You—you . . ." Blanche sputtered, finally understanding the phrase Big Daddy used to say when she or her sisters were vexed: *madder than a wet hen.*

"That was some quick thinking, Vee," Rose cut in as she patted Blanche's face with a handkerchief. "I'm so glad she was able to revive you!"

Rose held the handkerchief on Blanche's mouth an extra second or two while Blanche muffled obscenities beneath it.

"I still don't feel very good," Blanche said at last, sitting up and glaring at Vee. She yanked the handkerchief from Rose and dabbed at her eyes and cheeks, trying and failing to prevent her eyeliner from smearing.

Now she'd have to reapply her whole face, she thought with frustration.

"Maybe you should put your feet up," Rose suggested. "I'll find you a pillow."

"I think you're supposed to bend down and put your head between your knees," Luis said. "To help the blood flow."

"Is that so," Blanche purred, peeking up at Luis. "Between the knees, you said?"

Luis's cheeks flushed like ripe pomegranates.

"Such an attentive companion you are," Herman said as he sidled up to Rose, joining the circle of faces looking down at Blanche. "Is your friend prey to these types of displays often?"

"Well, no," Rose said. "She's normally fit as a fid—"

Blanche squeezed Rose's hand, trying to shut her up. She was a bit too honest and forthright sometimes.

Rose yelped. "But it's true that sometimes she can be a real pain—I mean, be *in* a lot of pain." She squeezed Blanche's hand back. "She was raised to be ornamental, you see. Not like us strong Northern girls. In St. Olaf, by six years old we had to be able to catch a cow in a pasture, lead it to the barn, milk it, and decorate it with ribbons. Before the cows, we practiced on goats. And before goats, we practiced on turtles."

"You can't milk a turtle," Misia pointed out.

Ralph widened his eyes in horror. "They're not mammals," he whispered.

"Most people don't try hard enough," Rose giggled. "It made the goat and cow seem pretty easy by comparison."

"Excuse me," Akiko said, snapping her fingers in the air. "Aren't we missing a few people?"

Herman turned away from Rose to quickly survey the group.

"Where are the really old lady and her daughter?" Akiko said, sweeping a leather-clad arm around the music room.

Herman's eyes bored into Blanche's. "Your friends seem to have disappeared."

SNEAKY CLEAN

14

When Dorothy and Sophia reached the studio door, Dorothy flipped through the keys from the ring Blanche had clandestinely passed to her. Sophia reached to unpeel a section of the blue painter's tape that crisscrossed the doorframe like a spiderweb.

"Stop!" Dorothy cautioned. "If we take it off, we might not get it back in the exact same place, and someone could notice."

"Well, we tried," Sophia said, dropping her arms to her side and quickly turning to go back down the hall.

"Wait a minute, Ma. Do you remember that episode of *Wonder Woman* where she had to evade all those laser beams?"

"I can't remember what I had for breakfast, so it's not likely," Sophia said.

Dorothy carefully reached through a gap in the tape to unlock the door. It swung inward, but the doorway itself was still blocked by the tape. "Maybe we can find a way to wriggle through this."

"Are you sure you can do it? At your age, your back must be as stiff as mine," Sophia said.

Dorothy bristled at the thought of being just as inflexible as her octogenarian mother, but unfortunately, she did have a point. Dorothy's last step aerobics class at the Y had left her gasping for breath, but she'd kept pace with most of the women decades younger than her clad in neon spandex.

"I happen to be very fit," she huffed.

"Then by all means, contort yourself!" Sophia frowned as the two of them surveyed the webbing of tape. There were only a few openings that seemed large enough to fit an arm or a leg through—maybe a set of shoulders.

Dorothy considered her long torso and even longer legs. Her statuesque proportions were all wrong for this, she realized, and she looked at Sophia with a hopeless expression on her face. Then she smiled. Her mother was a petite four foot ten with small, wiry limbs.

"You're gonna have to do it, Ma," Dorothy said. "Put your left foot in. No, your other left."

"What is this, the Hokey Pokey?" Sophia grumbled. After a few false starts, she found an opening that seemed big enough. She bent her small body to stoop through the gap.

Dorothy peered through a face-size hole in the painter's tape and watched her mother pick her way across the studio. As Sophia approached the lanai at the far end of the room, Dorothy could only see her mother's cloud of white hair in the meager light from the windows. Sophia made a semicircle around the body, pausing to look at something that Dorothy couldn't see from her vantage point. She adjusted her thick spectacles a couple of times as if examining something in greater detail.

Dorothy's curiosity got the better of her, and she lifted one leg through the largest opening in the tape, bending backward like she was playing limbo. Her spine let out an unmistakable *pop*.

I may very well regret this, she thought.

By using what felt like every single muscle in her body, Dorothy twisted herself through and then tiptoed across the studio. A languid breeze from the open lanai doors riffled loose papers and wafted the scent of paint through the room.

Dorothy patted her pockets. The last time they'd investigated a crime, she'd made detailed notes that helped them solve the case. But she had no notebook with her, and she couldn't exactly run home to get hers, or pick one up at the five-and-dime. She eyed the loose papers that had floated to the floor. *Tempting*. But what if someone caught her with the paper, matched it to something in this room, and used it to prove that she'd been in here without the others? Perhaps she was feeling a tad paranoid, but it still wasn't a good idea, she decided. She couldn't risk becoming a suspect.

Thankfully, her mother never went anywhere without her boxy bamboo wicker purse. When she reached Sophia, she gestured to her mother to open it. Dorothy pawed through a few wadded-up receipts, looking for anything she could write on. She found a dry-cleaning slip, a prescription for hemorrhoid cream, and a flyer for salsa dancing classes.

"Really, Ma? Salsa dancing?" Dorothy said. Still, the back of the flyer was blank, giving her plenty of room to jot down some notes.

"What, you think I don't have moves? I got through that crazy door first, you know," Sophia said. "Besides, it seemed like a good place to meet a good-looking guy."

"Thanks for always keeping an eye out for me, Ma, but I don't need a salsa dancer."

"Riiiight . . . For you."

When Dorothy looked askance at her, Sophia shrugged. "What? I figure a guy who's good with his feet might know what to do with his other parts."

"Ma!" Dorothy clapped her hands over her ears. Her mother had a special talent for driving her up the wall, which had only sharpened over the years they'd spent living together under Blanche's roof.

"Stop acting so shocked," Sophia scolded. "If I were as

innocent as you expect me to be, you wouldn't have been born!"

Dorothy shook her head. "Can we focus on the task at hand, *please*? Have you found any hints as to why he died?"

"What do I look like, Remington Steele? But I do think that red stuff came out of these jars." Sophia pointed to some broken containers, their insides stained with a dark liquid. Then she painstakingly lowered herself to her hands and knees and gave the liquid a sniff. "It's not blood. . . . It smells sort of chemical."

Dorothy pulled her mother to her feet, hoping that the experience wouldn't throw out either of their backs.

"Are you sure?" Her mother was sharp, but in her old age she sometimes got confused.

"You wanna get down and give it a whiff?"

"No," said Dorothy. "But if it's not blood, it still could be related to his death. And look!" She pointed toward El Toro's feet, to a deep smear in the liquid. "Do you think he could have slipped? That looks close to the width of a man's foot, wouldn't you say?"

"So he stepped in this goo, slipped, and maybe died from the fall?" Sophia said.

"It's a pretty good working theory," Dorothy said. "Unless maybe the fumes from this stuff did him in."

"But why is this stuff all over the floor in the first place?" Sophia asked.

Dorothy tapped her chin. "It must all be connected."

She tiptoed past El Toro's body and peeked through the lanai doors. She made a quick sketch of the general shape of the pool of drying liquid with rough circles and squares to indicate the various cans and jars scattered on the floor of the lanai and into the studio.

"Don't forget that twine," Sophia pointed out.

There were a few thin, rope-like strands scattered across the lanai—at least, as much of the lanai as she could see without stepping too close to the body—and inside the studio.

"Maybe he was going to paint on the lanai, trying to carry all these jars and cans and stuff, and dropped them as he went through the doorway," Sophia suggested. "He was in good shape, but it's not like he was twenty-one anymore."

"That makes the most sense so far," Dorothy said. "But then what is this twine for?"

"Maybe he was using it to fix something, or it was part of his artwork?" Sophia suggested.

Dorothy frowned. It didn't add up—at least, not yet.

But she added the filaments of twine to her drawing, and though she wanted to close the lanai doors against the elements, she left them as she'd found them. No one could know they'd been in here. On their way back through the studio, Dorothy noticed a full, presumably cold coffee mug on the table. A few feet beyond the table sat a large covered canvas, which was presumably Declan's latest work. She hadn't even looked at it when they'd discovered the body or returned with the others—she'd been too focused on comforting Blanche.

She lifted one corner of the drop cloth. The painting's proportions were large, probably six by eight feet, if Dorothy had to guess, and one corner was unfinished, with only a light undercoat of red paint with bits of pale canvas peeking through. The subject itself was a grand self-portrait of El Toro on a dark background that at first looked grayish black, but upon closer inspection was made up of countless lines of red, purple, blue, and gray, overlapping in such a way as to make the two-dimensional surface look uncannily alive.

The main figure itself was made up of tiny squares, each of them a miniature portrait of another person. Dorothy saw Blanche's face repeated multiple times, as well as Vee's and Akiko's. Others she couldn't place; perhaps they were people who Declan had met over the course of his life or career. There were even babies, animals, and birds in some of the squares, and Dorothy recognized a younger-looking Herman, as well as Misia's and Ralph's faces.

Zoomed in, the painting was a collection of a thousand portraits. But if you stepped back, it created a cohesive picture.

An interesting take on Impressionism, Dorothy thought. *This must have taken him ages to create.*

Knowing the portrait would be impossible to sketch, Dorothy jotted down a quick description instead. It was so much easier to take stock of things without Blanche screaming nearby.

"The only thing I can think of for that twine is rather . . . silly," Dorothy said.

"Spit it out," Sophia said.

"We know he and Blanche were lovers," Dorothy said. "Maybe he was planning some sort of intimate moment with the two of them in the studio, like old times? You know how Blanche likes certain . . . *unorthodox* activities."

"You've got a dirty mind, but it's a decent hypothesis," Sophia said. "If I weren't so disappointed in you, I'd be proud of you."

Suddenly, the sound of voices broke through the quiet of the hall. *Was someone coming up the stairs?* Dorothy cocked her head, listening. *Yes, that's the thump of shoes on marble*, she thought, her heart pounding.

"Psst—Ma! Hurry!" she hissed.

The voices drew closer, making Dorothy's pulse pound. "Hurry, someone's coming!" she urged. She and her mother would look especially guilty if they got caught breaking into El Toro's studio.

Sophia trotted back to the doorway and angled herself back through the opening she'd used to enter the room. Dorothy held on to her arms as Sophia threaded one support hose–clad leg through the hole, then ducked the rest of her body between the strips of tape. Then Dorothy squirmed through and reached back to pull the door shut, quickly locking it with the stolen key.

"We've got to get out of here!" she whispered as she scanned to the left and right for somewhere to hide. Dorothy and Sophia raced down the hallway, as fast as Sophia could go. For a brief moment, Dorothy wondered if she could tuck the petite Sicilian under her arm like a football.

Dorothy yanked open the first door they reached. Unfortunately, it was a linen closet, too full of shelves for them to fit inside.

They hustled to the next door as the voices drew closer. They practically tumbled through the doorway, finding themselves in a pink marble bathroom.

"Quick, Ma, take off your dress!" Dorothy said, tugging at the zipper on the back of Sophia's neck.

"What's gotten into you?" Sophia said, wriggling out of Dorothy's grasp. She batted Dorothy with her purse.

"I have a plan, all right?" Dorothy said. She pulled her mother's dress over her head, mussing her white curls and leaving Sophia shivering in her ivory slip.

"At least buy me dinner first!" Sophia protested, as Dorothy quickly but gently hefted her mother into the pink marble bathtub. "A nice porterhouse!"

"Just play along," Dorothy said, turning the taps on full blast.

"Hey, I still have my stockings on!" Sophia complained as the water gushed down over her legs, quickly filling the small tub.

Dorothy grabbed at the fluffy towels hanging on a rack and piled them up on the tub's edge, giving Sophia as much cover as she could. She grabbed a nearby bottle of Jean Naté and dumped a generous amount into the water.

Suddenly, a sharp knock came at the door.

"Just a minute!" Dorothy yelled.

The knocks came harder and Dorothy crept to the door and opened it just enough for her face to show through.

"Yes?" she said in an imperious tone.

Herman, Ralph, and Misia glared back at her. Behind them stood the rest of the guests, craning their necks to see through the crack in the door.

Blanche tried to push to the front. "Like I said, I'm sure there's a very simple explana—"

"Quiet," Misia tossed over her shoulder. Then to Dorothy, she added, "We're all very curious what you're doing up here."

"Indeed," added Herman, trying to wedge his foot through the door. "You weren't trying to destroy evidence in the studio or lanai, were you?"

"Why *on earth* would you ask me that!" Dorothy did her best to sound offended as she tucked the keys behind her back. She quickly worked them under the waistband of her slacks, giving silent thanks to the forgiving elastic panel at the back and slipping them into the top of her high-waisted briefs. She prayed no one would discover them, but to be honest no one had rooted around in there for quite a while. She shivered as the cold metal keys settled near her tailbone, and tried not to think of how many germs might be on them.

"I'm sure I don't know what you're talking about," Dorothy said haughtily, drawing upon the acting experience she'd developed playing a six-foot-tall rabbit named Harvey in a high school play. "I don't have any keys, and I certainly wasn't trying to enter the studio!"

"Then what are you doing up here?" Misia said, her eyes narrowed.

"I'd rather not say," Dorothy said. "It's none of your business."

"It *is* our business, when a murder has just occurred and then two people suddenly disappear," Herman said. "It's most unusual. One might even say suspicious."

"Fine," Dorothy said. "I'd rather not, but you'll see we have nothing to hide." She opened the door a few more inches to reveal Sophia's tiny head poking above the marble edge of the bathtub surrounded by mountains of bubbles.

"Some privacy, please! If you gawk any longer, I'm gonna have to charge you." Sophia shook a bubble-covered fist over the edge of the tub.

Dorothy moved her upper body in front of the partially open door and tried to block as much of the view as she could just as Sophia flung a wet washcloth toward the onlookers.

"You see? I didn't want to embarrass her," Dorothy said. "Sometimes older people can have . . . accidents." She bit her lip, playing the part of the dutiful but beleaguered caregiver. "My mother is in her eighties, as you know. We found ourselves in a bit of a situation. I had to get her straight to the nearest bath. Please don't make me describe it further."

"My profuse apologies," Herman said, clearly uncomfortable.

"We'll give you some privacy," Misia said hurriedly.

"That happened to my grandma at Aventura Mall," Luis said from the hallway. "She was so embarrassed. I bought her a whole new outfit at Burdines."

"You see why I was trying to be discreet," Dorothy said. "I apologize if it looked suspicious. I've got to find her some clean clothes and then we can rejoin everyone."

"I have an extra outfit in my overnight bag," Blanche chimed in from the back of the group. "I'm sure we can find something that will fit."

"What a wonderful daughter you are," Herman said evenly to Dorothy. "How conscientious. Still, in the spirit of preserving our communal safety, we must stick together."

Blanche huffed, clearly frustrated with Herman. She nudged Rose.

"Well said, Mr. Price," Rose said quickly. "A rule like that is a wonderful idea! We've got to stick together as much as we can. What if everyone went straight back to their rooms while Sophia gets changed? Then we can all rest for a few hours before dinner. You could watch the hallway if you like, to make sure no one is creeping around here." She finished with a warm, sunny smile pointed directly at Herman.

"A marvelous suggestion!" he said. His mustache twitched as he smiled back at Rose.

"If you don't mind, I need to dry her off before we all meet back up for dinner," Dorothy said, tilting her head toward Sophia, who angrily blew perfumed bubbles off her glasses. "Blanche and Rose, can you give me a hand?"

The two squeezed through the door and Dorothy closed it firmly behind them. A minute later she peeked back through it, just to make sure everyone else had dispersed to their rooms under Herman's watchful eye.

"I can't believe you said that!" Sophia hissed. "I am not incontinent!"

"It's nothing to be ashamed of," said Rose kindly.

"I know that!" Sophia huffed. "Some of my best friends are incontinent! That doesn't mean that *I* am."

"Well, it did the trick," Dorothy said, rather pleased with herself for her quick thinking.

"At the cost of my dignity!" Sophia grumbled. "You don't see me talking about the time you wet your pants on the bus."

"Ma, that was in first grade," Dorothy said. "And I'm sorry. It was a low blow, but it was the best I could come up with on short notice."

"Next time, it'll be you in the bathtub," Sophia said. "Look at my hair!" She swiped at the drooping, flattened curls around her ears, dripping with moisture and Jean Naté.

"It's not that bad," Blanche said, dabbing at Sophia's hairline with a fluffy hand towel.

"My next appointment with Eduardo isn't for two weeks," Sophia moaned. Then she looked at Blanche. "I don't suppose your old boyfriend had a set of hot rollers in his mansion?"

"I doubt that." Blanche sighed. "But he sure had a lot of secrets. Speaking of secrets, did you find anything out on your recon mission?"

Sophia nodded. "We checked out the studio, the body, and the painting our host was working on. You won't believe what we found!"

FINDERS CREEPERS

15

Blanche sat on the edge of the tub and leaned toward Sophia. "Well, spit it out! What did you find?"

"First off, there were spilled paint cans and jars lying all around," Sophia said.

Blanche nodded, vaguely recalling seeing a few when she'd first discovered Declan. But she'd been in such a shock that she didn't remember much besides her old flame lying there motionless. A lump of sadness rose in her throat, and she did her best to swallow it down.

"It was very cluttered in there," Blanche remembered. "Messy. Like a frat house on Sunday morning."

"Well, you would know," Sophia said, standing up in the tub. Water streamed down her slip, making it cling to her skinny legs. "But that wasn't the weird thing. There were more jars on the lanai."

"On the lanai?" Blanche said, puzzled. "Why would he work on something out in the elements?"

"Perhaps he liked to paint en plein air?" Dorothy asked as she grabbed at the pile of folded towels on the bathroom shelf.

Blanche rolled her eyes. Dorothy was always showing off her extensive vocabulary. "It seems unlikely, but I suppose it's possible."

"But there were also some pieces of twine out there," Sophia said as Dorothy wrapped her in a large fluffy towel. "We thought you might have some insight. Was he into . . . you know, into that kind of thing . . . ?"

"He wasn't like that," Blanche snapped, picking up on Sophia's innuendo. "It doesn't make sense to me."

Blanche looked down at her feet, steadying herself against a sudden rush of grief. Declan was a living, breathing person, not long ago. It still seemed so wrong that he wasn't anymore, she thought as she absent-mindedly wrapped a second towel around Sophia's shoulders.

"We saw a mark on the floor," Dorothy said. "Which made it look like his foot slipped in that puddle. That could have caused a fatality. The question is, was it an accident, or set up intentionally to make him fall?"

"Well, how do we find out?" Rose said, handing another towel to Dorothy.

"We need to look for clues, and keep an eye out for anyone saying or doing anything suspicious," Blanche said as Sophia's face disappeared under a third towel.

"But just doing something odd isn't enough," Dorothy said, draping yet another towel over Sophia's still-damp hair. "According to Sherlock Holmes, we need to figure out if they had the means, the motive, and the opportunity to cause El Toro's death."

"Mmmmmf," Sophia said from under a mound of terry cloth. "Mmmmf *mff*."

"What was that?" Blanche said, peeling back a layer to reveal Sophia's face.

"I said, 'Get these towels off me!'"

"Sorry!" Rose said. She quickly pulled away the towels, leaving Sophia in only one wrapped around her, toga-style. "Let's get back to our room, before Mr. Nosypants returns to check on us."

They hurried down the hall and up the stairs, with Sophia leaving dripping footprints on the hardwood floors.

Back in their guest room, Blanche handed her overnight bag to Sophia, who pulled out a set of black satin panties, connected to a pair of thigh-high sheer hose by a lacy garter belt. "Are you kidding me?" she said, peeking through the openings in the skimpy fabric.

"You don't have to wear *those*," Blanche said. "I wasn't exactly packing with you in mind."

Sophia dug around in the bag and pulled out a white silk camisole with a plunging neckline and matching tap pants. "What is this, my wedding night?" Sophia griped. "I wasn't aware we'd booked the bridal suite."

Rose giggled, and even Blanche felt a whisper of a smile trying to form on her lips. No matter what happened, at least they had one another and were able to find the humor in a terribly sad situation. It reminded her of what had happened to the Texas sheet cake Blanche had baked to bring to the reception after Big Daddy's funeral. It was wrapped in tinfoil on the passenger seat of her car, and her brother Clayton had sat right on it. As they gamely tried to smooth out the imprint of Clayton's bottom from the chocolate icing, the siblings laughed until they cried—and cried until they laughed again. They'd managed to salvage the cake that day, and at least a part of their relationship.

"Now give me my dress back," Sophia said to Dorothy.

"Oh no, Ma," Dorothy said, pulling a bundle of coral fabric from Blanche's overnight bag. "The story is that your outfit got dirty, which is why we had to bathe you, remember?"

"But you made that up!" Sophia said. "It's not dirty."

Dorothy shoved Blanche's second cocktail dress at Sophia. "We have to keep our story straight."

Sophia slowly stepped into the bright chiffon dress with bell sleeves and reluctantly allowed Blanche to zip up the back.

"Are you happy now?" Sophia said. She made a tottering attempt to twirl in the too-large dress and matching capelet as it billowed out from her tiny frame. "I feel like Cinderella *and* the pumpkin."

Blanche tried to keep a straight face. To her, Sophia looked exactly like an elderly version of the Peaches 'n Cream Barbie that she had recently purchased for her granddaughter. The doll had been a bribe, of course, since she'd taken Melissa with her to a beauty shop appointment and then a stroll along the docks to observe the local scenery, instead of to the girl's piano lesson as she'd promised her mother. The doll was money well spent; that afternoon she'd gotten the phone number of a stevedore with muscular shoulders and sensuous green eyes.

"You look adorable," Dorothy said. "Just wear it for a little while, then you can change back. In the meantime, we need to come up with a game plan. Right, Blanche? Blanche?"

Dorothy clapped in front of Blanche's face, jolting her out of her reverie.

Blanche blinked, trying to focus on the here and now. Dorothy was always so practical, and Blanche was willing to bet that her mind never wandered from the task at hand. But Blanche had found that life was much easier when she let her mind drift away from harsh realities, such as dead ex-boyfriends or one's slowing metabolism.

"Right, yes," Blanche said. "We're going to find out everything we can, about everyone, is that right?"

"I think we focus on motive before we can determine the means," Dorothy said. "And so far, it seems that almost anyone in this villa had some opportunity, since everyone had access to El Toro in the studio before we found him."

"So we've gotta snoop around, and try to get people talking?" Sophia said.

"That's right," Dorothy said. "Rose, I suggest you keep an eye on Herman, since he's probably going to try to get close to you."

Rose nodded. "All right. I might even have to keep both eyes on him. But if he gets annoying, I'm going to signal for one of you to come save me."

"Sure, honey," Blanche said, remembering how she and her friend Maxine would tug on their earlobes if they wanted to be rescued from an unappealing suitor on a night out at the Roseland or Palladium. "What's the signal?"

"I was going to yell 'Help!'" Rose said.

"Real subtle," Sophia quipped. "Maybe come up with a code word instead, something innocuous."

Rose bit her lip and furrowed her brow. Blanche recognized the confused look on her face—it was the same one Rose wore when attempting the connect-the-dots puzzle in the Sunday paper, or when she had to double a recipe that included fractions.

"She doesn't know what that word means, Sophia," Blanche whispered.

"I mean pick something not so obvious," Sophia said. "Something bland."

Rose nodded, then said, "Dorothy."

"Perfect!" exclaimed Sophia with a chuckle.

"What? No," Rose said, looking at Dorothy for reassurance. "I was just going to ask, Dorothy, how did you get into the studio to begin with?"

Dorothy made eye contact with Blanche and smiled. "After our very own Faye Dunaway here used her feminine wiles and snuck the keys off Ralph, we unlocked the door and wiggled our way in. Speaking of which, we've got to figure out a way to get them back without him knowing. . . ."

"Where are they now?" Rose said.

"In my underwear," Dorothy confessed.

Blanche opened her mouth to make a quip about the key ring boldly going where no one had gone before, but thought the better of it.

"They're in the *waistband*," Dorothy said, moving toward the bathroom. "Jeez. I'll go rinse the cooties off and put the keys in my sleeve, okay? Once we're all together, we can pass them around until whoever is closest to Ralph is able to sneak them back to him. In the meantime, I have more questions. Look here."

She unfolded the salsa flyer with her notes and laid it out

on one of the bureaus. She pointed out the rough drawing she'd made of the crime scene, noting the scattered containers and the ropes, and the location of the body and the smear that indicated Declan's fall.

"If this was someone else's doing, and not an accident, how did the perpetrator get into the studio to set all this up, if only El Toro and Ralph had keys to the space? Didn't Misia say he always kept the studio locked?"

"She did," Sophia said. "And that only she was allowed inside, when El Toro summoned her."

"Then how did someone get in there to kill him?" Rose said. "Does that mean that Ralph is our main suspect?"

"Not necessarily. Perhaps the killer didn't have to get in through the studio door," Dorothy mused. "This stuff could have been set up on the lanai, right over the door. I didn't want to step over the body, and I couldn't get a good look at the entire lanai when I was up there. Or maybe, the killer entered the studio through the lanai—maybe they scaled the wall to the second floor."

Everyone sat in momentary silence, trying to picture the various possibilities. Blanche envisioned an evil, masked intruder in an all-black tactical outfit, rappelling down the side of the building to Declan's lanai. Her mind stuttered to a stop, refusing to go any further and imagine Declan's death. It was too painful.

"How can we know?" Rose said. "We have no security camera footage to see exactly what happened."

"No, but there might be clues that help us," Dorothy said. "For example, if someone climbed to the second floor to get in through the lanai, there might be a ladder nearby. Or footprints in the garden underneath the window. We should keep an eye out for both of those things."

"Will do," said Sophia. "And we'll pump everyone for information as best we can. Maybe we can also figure out some way to contact the mainland."

"Right. We'll do so carefully and try not to reveal that we're running our own investigation," Dorothy said. She folded her notes back up and tucked them into her other sleeve.

Blanche checked the slim watch on her wrist. *We should probably get back downstairs soon*, she thought. The day wasn't getting any younger—and neither were they. They had a collection of clues that didn't really connect, and a bevy of unanswered questions—but she didn't feel ready to interrogate the rest of the household yet. Even though it was still light out, she wanted to burrow into their king-size bed with the covers pulled over her head and revisit the memories of her time with Declan . . . and cry her little heart out. She wished Dorothy and the others could investigate without her, or better yet, they could just leave the detective work to Herman. But if they did that, there was a chance he'd wrongfully accuse them—or just her—of the murder. And she couldn't have that.

What would Big Daddy do in this situation? Blanche wondered. Whenever she'd struggled at home in Atlanta—like the times she had to start over at a brand-new school, or in the disastrous aftermath of her regrettable tap-dancing recital—Big Daddy always told her to dust herself off and grab life by the tail feathers. And that's exactly what she'd do.

"Come on, girls," Blanche said. "We've got a murder to solve!"

THE GAME'S AFOOT

16

The colorless afternoon sky transformed into a vibrant sunset like a woman slipping off her blazer and adding red lipstick for a date after work. The inhabitants of Villa Velado gathered on the terra-cotta patio at the rear of the house. Jasmine bloomed in cloudlike bunches and cascaded over a nearby stone wall, perfuming the air with its musky sweetness. From the patio, Dorothy had an excellent view of the first tier of the elaborate gardens, an ornate expanse of green lawn framed by flat-petaled, waxy anthurium and strands of dramatic lobster claw that hung like holiday garland from heavy green leaves. Under different circumstances, Dorothy would have loved to have spent more time enjoying the villa. Something about not being able to leave made her itchy.

Or perhaps that was the mosquitoes.

Ralph emerged from the house and unloaded a tray bearing wine, a crystal decanter of gin, some tonic water, and sliced lemon and lime along with a tiny bowl of olives and some sad-looking celery stalks onto the weathered patio table.

"Let me help you with that," Misia called as she approached the patio from the far end of the garden. The rest of the group stood up from wrought iron patio chairs and gathered around the table, eager for something to eat and drink. Nobody had eaten lunch—or wanted to—after they'd made the upsetting discovery in El Toro's studio.

Herman began mixing a gin and tonic and scrutinized Misia, who was sweating slightly. "And where have you been?" he said.

"Picking these," Misia said, holding out a basket with an assortment of heirloom tomatoes in a rainbow of colors. "We're running low on food, in case you haven't noticed. We'd only planned on a few guests being here for the party. Not everyone staying for the whole weekend."

"Thoughtful girl," said Vee, eyeing the meager cocktail hour offerings.

"How am I going to do an Albertsons run without the

boat? I'd ask Declan what to do—but I can't," Ralph said sadly.

"What happens if we eat all the food before we can get back to the mainland?" Rose asked.

"I can fish," Ralph said. "We have our little vegetable patch, and some berry bushes at the back of the garden."

"That's a relief," Sophia said. "I made do with less in the Great Depression. One summer, all Sal and I could afford were onions. You could smell us coming from three blocks away."

"Is there anything I could milk?" Rose said hopefully.

"Sorry, we don't keep livestock," Misia said. "Though we do have some bee hives in the garden."

"Maybe you can find a turtle, Rose," said Blanche.

"What?" Sophia said, her wrinkled features contorting with confusion.

"Don't worry. It's a need-to-know thing," Blanche said, patting Sophia's arm.

"There's nothing funny about this," said Akiko as she approached the other side of the table. "I've got clients to attend to, and my Italian greyhound is probably sick of the dogsitter by now. We've got to get out of here soon. Any news on the generator?"

Ralph let out a sound that was part grunt, part sigh, and part belch. "I tried to get it working, but that fallen tree did a number on it."

"Aren't there any flares or other emergency signals we can send?" Dorothy said, reaching for one of the celery stalks.

Hurricanes and other big storms were a fact of life in coastal Florida. She found it hard to believe that a place this remote wouldn't be more prepared.

"When we have storms, we fill the bathtub and ride them out," Ralph said with a shrug.

"Declan was never in a hurry to go back to the mainland," Misia chimed in. "He sent us to town for weekly grocery runs and supplies. Posting mail, picking up the newspaper, that sort of thing. I've worked here just about a year, and he hasn't left the island in that time."

"I didn't realize he'd become such a recluse," Luis said as he placed a few olives onto his plate. "What made him retreat from the world?"

"He was creatively blocked for a long time," Akiko said. "He told me he didn't want to show new work unless he could be certain it would be well received. And I don't blame him. After his last big show, the *New York Times* called him 'overblown' and 'past his prime.' And then there were the mysterious messages he'd been getting."

Dorothy's ears pricked up. This was the second time they'd heard about these messages, and she wanted to know more.

"Those may have been a factor," Herman said. "He telephoned me a few weeks ago with a request for me to reassess his past work and to determine what certain pieces would be worth posthumously. At first, I resisted. I pleaded with him not to speak of such terrible things. But he was adamant that since he was getting older, it was important to do. Then, when he started receiving the messages"—he stabbed a plump olive with a toothpick—"he insisted that I complete my evaluation."

"Well, did you run the numbers?" said Vee coldly. "How much will his work be worth now that he's gone?"

Misia gasped. "How can you talk like that?" she said, her eyes so wide that Dorothy could see how pink the corners had become.

She's been crying, Dorothy noted.

"I'm asking because it appears to me that certain people here stand to make a lot of money." Vee turned to Akiko and crossed her arms. "You could have a nice auction at Christie's and make out like a bandit."

"That's ridiculous," Akiko huffed, setting her drink down with a thunk. "Why would I kill the biggest artist in my roster?"

"So you admit he was your golden goose?" Vee smirked.

Dorothy caught Blanche's gaze and bugged out her eyes as if to say *Are you hearing this?*

"El Toro was my *friend*," Akiko said. She scrunched her features into an expression of pain, and Dorothy couldn't tell if that expression reflected sadness, anger, or both.

"A friend who made you rich," Vee said.

Akiko threw back her shoulders and circled the wooden table until she was face-to-face with Vee. Though over a foot shorter than the model-esque artist, she carried herself as if they were eye to eye. "You know as well as I do that business and personal relationships are entangled in the art world. And you could look at it the other way around. Maybe I made El Toro a lot of money, by selling his work, by bringing him to international acclaim, by taking him from a little art-school nobody to a household name. He was selling watercolors on the subway before I found him, for Pete's sake!"

"Fair enough," Vee said. "But Herman here could also stand to benefit. I know you've been acquiring quite a few pieces over the years."

"That's preposterous!" Herman sputtered, sending teeny bits of olive into the humid evening air. "My whole profession is about safeguarding an artist's work, not killing them!"

Just then, a gray-and-orange bird flew over Rose's shoulder and landed at the edge of the patio, right next to a hibiscus bush. It let out a series of croaking sounds that lasted a few seconds.

"Oh, what a gorgeous bird!" Rose cried, trying to break the tension in the air. "I think it's some kind of cuckoo. Maybe he wants to be friends!"

"Birds of a feather . . ." Sophia quipped.

Rose furrowed her brow. "Well, this bird's a lot friendlier than you . . . and look at its pretty tangerine belly." She watched the bird dip its head and sip from a small puddle of rainwater. Then she tilted her head and quietly pulled Dorothy to the edge of the patio while the others argued about who was closer to El Toro while he was alive.

"Does that puddle look funny to you?" Rose said.

Dorothy looked down at the tiny puddle, noting it had a

rounded, oblong shape topped by a row of smaller impressions.

"Are you thinking what I'm thinking?" Dorothy said.

Rose nodded eagerly. "Bigfoot!"

"I was going to say it's a foot*print*, Rose," Dorothy intoned. "I highly doubt it belongs to Bigfoot . . . even if he were real."

"But look how large the print is! It stands to reason that it might be him."

Dorothy waved Blanche and Sophia over before taking another look. "It's not so big," Dorothy said, holding her own foot just above the print, careful not to step into the watery mud. "It's a similar size to mine."

Sophia and Blanche stared at Dorothy, until she sheepishly lowered her foot. "Not a word."

Blanche covered her mouth with her hand, stifling her laughter.

"I knew I heard something roaring last night—remember?" Rose said, pointing to the wet grass. "And look—there are more prints! Weren't we supposed to keep our eyes peeled for mysterious footprints?"

"It does seem a little suspicious," Blanche said.

"It could be a clue!" Sophia said, a little too loudly.

Dorothy glared at her to keep quiet. They'd agreed to investigate Declan's death secretly, just among themselves.

"A clue, you say?" Herman trotted over, his bushy eyebrows aloft with curiosity.

"It's probably nothing," Dorothy said, stepping in front of the footprint, trying to block it from Herman's view.

"I quite distinctly heard the word *clue*," Herman said. "As we all have the same goal in finding out what happened to El Toro, we must follow each and every lead. Unless you have something to hide, madame?"

"No, she doesn't," Rose sputtered. "And *I* found the clue. See? It looks like a footprint."

Herman leaned down. He pulled out his miniature magnifying glass, polished it on his cuff, and peered through it. "Most definitively, the foot of a *Homo sapiens*."

"Look, I don't care who Bigfoot is dating, only that there's a whole set of prints leading off that way," Rose said, pointing toward the lawn. "And we did hear strange noises last night. . . . Maybe this was the cause!"

Herman's eyebrows floated even higher on his wrinkled forehead. "Well then, we must follow this trail."

The little man led the four women onto the wet grass alongside the line of footprints. Dorothy felt her heels sink into the squishy ground and briefly considered taking off her shoes before she realized that meant her feet would be covered in muck. Instead, the women grasped each other's arms for support as Herman charged on ahead.

"Wait!" bellowed Ralph from behind them. "You shouldn't be wandering the grounds. There might be fallen branches from the storm, loose masonry . . ."

Herman didn't break his stride. "We'll be careful," he called over his shoulder.

Ralph shook his head in exasperation as he caught up to their group. "I'm coming with you."

Herman spun to meet the groundskeeper's eye. "You certainly seem eager to prevent us from pursuing this lead. . . ." He paused to scrutinize Ralph over the rim of his glasses. "How peculiar."

"There could be snakes, crocs, flooded from their lairs," Ralph explained, then swept his arm forward with a flourish. "But, please, don't let that stop you."

"Snakes?" Blanche cried, making the word last at least three syllables. She clung to Ralph's arm. "You can scare them away for us, right?"

Dorothy noted movement in her peripheral vision and turned to see the rest of the group following their commotion—clearly, their conversation had drawn everyone's interest. Luis was the first, his notebook clutched in his palm.

There are either snakes in the grass, or snakes in the villa, she thought, realizing she felt a little safer with everyone together.

The group followed the twisting path across the lawn to a flower bed, then past a few stone urns to a hedge wall. Occasionally the footprints disappeared, only to reappear a few feet later. Finally, the prints stopped at an alcove, which had been carved into the hedge, housing a low stone bench and decorated with flowerpots overflowing with hot pink petunias and bleeding hearts.

"The prints just end," Rose said. "I guess this wasn't much of a clue after all."

Rose sat on the bench while Herman inspected the ground around the alcove, as did Dorothy. She noticed that Luis had put away his notebook, clearly not expecting anything of interest to come from this evening's little detour.

But something about the footprints tickled the back of Dorothy's brain. The indentations were fresh enough to not have been completely washed away by the weather. And since toes were clearly visible, the marks must have been from bare feet, not someone in shoes.

"Why would someone creep around here in bare feet?" Dorothy wondered as she sat next to Rose on the hard stone bench.

"So they'd make less noise?" Sophia suggested as she joined them.

Blanche leaned one hand on the bench and bent to inspect her shoes. "I hope I didn't ruin these!" She lifted one dripping leather slingback, with blades of grass and globs of dirt stuck to the sole.

Of course. For stealth, or to protect expensive shoes, Dorothy thought.

But why did the prints just stop? They led away from the main house, not anywhere near the lanai where El Toro had been found. There was nothing here but a bench, a hedge, and some flowerpots.

Dorothy stood up and took a closer look at those flowerpots. One had a smudge of dirt spilling over the scalloped edge, and a few of the petunias were crushed, their stems snapped like necks. *Odd.* She parted the broken petunias and saw something glinting in the soil. She reached for it and grasped cold metal. She pulled it free from the pot, revealing a palm-size golden object. Though the glow of its jewels were dulled by a layer of wet dirt, it was unmistakably the missing butterfly brooch.

Everyone gasped.

Dorothy shook the dirt from the brooch and turned to give it to Blanche.

"Most peculiar, indeed," Herman said, intercepting the gesture and plucking the brooch from Dorothy's hand.

Dorothy fought the urge to grab it back from the bossy little man. But she didn't want to do anything that would make her look guilty, and so she let him take it

"How did that get all the way out here?" Blanche said, sidling next to Herman. Dorothy thought Blanche looked like she wanted to snatch the brooch from him and pin it to her dress, mud and all.

Herman scowled. "My preliminary hypothesis is that the disreputable individual who made these footprints carried it here to conceal it from the rest of us. Who knows what illicit plans they had for it?"

Rose scoffed. "Why would Bigfoot want any jewelry?"

"Rose, it was *clearly* a person's foot," Dorothy grumbled. Sometimes her dear friend's airheaded behavior could wear thinner than a pair of L'Eggs pantyhose.

"And if it were actually Bigfoot, the prints would be much larger, and have claws," Ralph added.

"Finally, someone talking sense!" Rose said, smiling up at him.

"An adorable theory, if misguided, my dear," Herman said, patting Rose on the arm. "Reason states that these mysterious prints must belong to someone in this villa. There's no one else on this island, correct?"

"That's right," Misia said. "Just us."

"I will prove, by scientific deduction, who they belong to," Herman said. "Everyone, please remove your shoes."

Everyone groaned, except for Vee, who had smartly already done so before following the others across the lawn. The girls added their now-damp heels to a pile with Akiko's leather boots, Misia's new-looking high-tops, Luis's polished loafers, Herman's scuffed wingtips, and Ralph's muddy Red Wings.

One by one, each guest held their bare foot next to the clearest footprint they'd found, conveniently next to the flowerpot.

Sophia, Rose, and Blanche's feet were much too small to be a match. Misia's were about an inch too short. Luis's and Herman's feet were too wide, and Akiko's feet were as tiny as Sophia's. Then Ralph dangled his foot by the print. It was obvious to everyone that the length seemed pretty close. He put his foot back down with a grunt.

When it was Dorothy's turn, she felt like Cinderella's stepsister, curling her toes to make her foot look as small as she could.

"Yours is a good match, too," Akiko pointed out.

Dorothy snatched her foot back quickly and slipped it into her shoe. "I promise you all, it wasn't me," she said firmly. "Why would I lead us to the brooch if it were?"

"A very good point . . ." Herman agreed. "Or a *ruse* to confuse us!"

Dorothy wanted to shake the self-appointed detective for being so annoyingly contentious. Instead, she attempted to wrench her features into an innocent-looking expression, which she feared would only make her look more suspicious—or constipated.

The last person in line was Vee. Her feet, with a perfect cherry red pedicure, were a similar length to Dorothy's, Dorothy realized with a sigh of relief. They both were tall women, so it made sense they'd both wear around a size nine, maybe nine and a half. That meant that she, Ralph, and Vee would be seen as the most likely brooch thieves. And since she knew it wasn't her, that meant either Vee or Ralph were the culprits. She couldn't wait to get her friends alone and ask them if they remembered where Ralph and Vee were when the lights went out and the brooch had been snatched from her mother's neck.

"The brooch thief must be one of you," Herman said, pointing to the three of them. Dorothy's stomach clenched as the other guests eyed her, Vee, and Ralph. "If I had more equipment, and if it weren't so wet, I would dust for fingerprints."

"Don't look at me—I was in my bed all night. And the rest of the time I've been with everyone else. When would I have stolen away?" Vee said with a dismissive wave of her hand.

"It's not me," Dorothy insisted. "Why would I rob my own mother? We already had the brooch."

They've got to understand logic, she hoped.

"I'd never walk around here barefoot," Ralph said simply.

Every member of the group scrutinized the rest, and by their crossed arms, narrowed eyes, and lack of smiles, Dorothy could tell that distrust had taken firm root in people's minds. She wondered who each of them suspected the most. Dorothy wasn't 100 percent certain that the culprit had to be Ralph or Vee—their foot-measuring method seemed highly unscientific. Did mud shrink or grow over time? Was the size even accurate? Furthermore, who knew if it was really true that no one else was lurking on the island? Could someone have snuck into the dining room fast enough to steal the brooch, right after the lights went out? Her head swirled with questions, churning harder than the margarita machine behind the bar at the Rusty Anchor.

BROOCH-ING THE SUBJECT

17

After the discovery in thc flowerpot, Vee strode back toward the house in a huff. Misia and Akiko trotted behind her, followed by Luis and Herman, with Ralph sullenly bringing up the rear.

"Wait here a minute, girls," Blanche whispered. "What did you all think of that?"

"There's definitely a thief in this house," Sophia said. "And since we know it's not Dorothy, it's gotta be Vee or Ralph."

"So which one do you think did it?" Rose asked the group.

"Ralph has had the most opportunities to go off on his own, and he has keys to the studio," Dorothy mused. "And I must admit, I haven't been paying much attention to Vee's whereabouts."

Something clicked in Blanche's mind. Clumps of soil had tumbled from Dorothy's fingers as she lifted the dirt-covered pin from under the petunias.

"Girls, I just realized something!" she gasped. "When I was expertly creating a diversion . . ." Blanche put a hand to her chest and lowered her voice to a husky whisper. "When Vee dumped water on me, I saw that one of her rings had some dirt on it. Just as if she'd been *digging around in a flowerpot*!"

Rose's eyes went wide. "Why didn't you say anything?"

"At the time I didn't know what it meant," Blanche said. "Maybe she washed her hands, but there was enough stuck on the setting of the ring for me to notice."

"Well done, Blanche," Dorothy said. "Even if we don't know for sure, that's pretty convincing circumstantial evidence."

"So what are you waiting for? Let's confront her!" Sophia said, assuming a boxer's stance. "Shame on her, attacking her elder, and stealing from me, to boot!"

"Calm down, Ma," Dorothy said. "We can't let on yet that we think it was her."

"Why not?" Sophia asked. "I have a few choice words I'd like to share with her."

"We need to keep information close to our vests until we

have outside help," Dorothy said. "We don't know who we can trust here. We don't know how she'd react if confronted, or if it truly was her. And we don't know enough yet about everyone else."

"That's right," Rose added sagely. "One time, back in St. Olaf, the bank downtown was robbed. Everyone was shocked when the culprit turned out to be the only person with the key to the vault: the president of the bank! He apparently wasn't very good with money, and needed the funds to pay for his collection of designer toupees. He was the nicest man, always giving out free toasters. But it's a good reminder that anyone can be a suspect."

"Except the four of us," Blanche said, recalling the unpleasant tension between Rose and Dorothy the last time they solved a mystery. "We're not doubting or turning against one another this time, no matter how hard things get. And we have to get to the bottom of this, for Declan—deal?"

"Deal!" the others said in unison.

The girls stood there in silence for a moment, sure of one another, but unsure of their next move. Then a light rain began to fall.

"We'd better join everyone else, before we start to look suspicious," Dorothy said.

"True," said Rose. "But I'm in no hurry to rejoin a group that likely includes a killer!" Blanche nodded and placed one arm around Rose's shoulders. The gesture was meant to comfort Rose, but Blanche drew strength from it as well.

"I know exactly what you mean," Blanche said. "That's why we have to stick together."

The four women shielded their faces from the drops and hurried across the wet grass back toward the patio, whispering among themselves.

"I had a feeling that Vee was up to something," Blanche said.

"You're just saying that because you both went out with El Toro," Dorothy said. "Anyone can see there's a rivalry between you two."

"It may be a foreign concept to you, but other women feeling threatened by me is a daily occurrence," Blanche scoffed. "I pay them no mind. But I just know she wanted that brooch for herself. She was watching Sophia like a hawk . . . and you should have seen the dirty look she gave when Declan said it was meant for me!"

"That's true," said Rose, trying not to slip on the wet grass. "But we can't rule out Ralph. His feet fit the prints, too."

"Now what would a rough-hewn guy like Ralph do with some delicate jewelry?" Blanche asked, wondering if her friend might, in fact, be just as empty-headed as she looked. "We need to keep an eye on *Vee* for many reasons."

The beautiful installation artist was hiding something, she was sure of it. Her mysterious, carefully composed demeanor, the way she'd splashed water in Blanche's face—and the fact that she looked so darn perfect, even in hand-me-down pajamas—it all just didn't sit right with Blanche.

"Are you saying she's responsible for El Toro's death?" Dorothy asked. "All just because she took a brooch?"

"I'm not saying that *exactly*." Blanche kept her voice down, now that they had almost reached the patio and the other guests. "But I'm not *not* saying that."

"What's the motive?" Dorothy asked.

Blanche thought about it. Vee clearly wanted the golden butterfly, and probably felt entitled to other things from Declan. But she also seemed to want Declan himself, so murdering him wouldn't make any sense.

"I don't know . . . yet," she said at last. "But if she's guilty of one crime, she could be guilty of another."

"There you are," Misia said sourly as the girls finally joined the others on the patio. The sky had faded to a mellow gold, and the sound of crickets filled the air. "Since it's raining, Ralph and I will serve dinner in the music conservatory. We'll have a bit more ambient light through the windows until the sun sets, so we can conserve our candles."

She led the group into the house and through the halls until they reached a glass-walled room filled with musical instruments of all types and a variety of sculptures. Scattered throughout were wicker armchairs and side tables. An entire wall was papered in sheet music, and an ebony baby grand piano dominated one corner of the room.

"Oh, a flügelhorn!" Rose said, pointing to a shiny trumpet-like instrument mounted on the wall. "Did I ever tell you that my cousin Gustave was a prodigy?"

"My dear, this is actually a flumpet," Herman corrected her, pointing to the double brass loops. "Observe the unique central design." Then he surveyed the room, lifting his finger as he spoke to those assembled. "As you can see, no minute detail escapes Herman Price. So if there is a murderer in our midst, heed this warning: what you do not confess to Herman, he will find out."

At that, everyone gave Herman a wide berth as they chose their seats. Whether to avoid suspicion—or to avoid being unnecessarily corrected, Blanche couldn't say.

Misia brought in the wine and gin from the patio, placing them on a marble table in the center of the room as the girls located a cluster of armchairs around a low table and sat down.

Then Ralph appeared, placing a tray with serving bowls of spaghetti, sauce, and a vegetarian antipasto on a marble side table. "Help yourselves," he grunted, then made himself a plate and took a seat.

"Ralph's a culinary genius, but he's working with what's left in the pantry. I'm sure none of you will complain about the offerings, or the portions," Misia said.

"Of course not," Vee said, pouring herself a glass of wine. "Thank you, Misia."

"I suppose we can't call out for pizza," Luis joked weakly.

Akiko tsked as she approached the marble table. "I'm supposed to be on a flight to Amsterdam today, can you believe it? There's this new graffiti artist I'm trying to sign—"

"I'm sure you'll make up the funds selling Declan's final work," Vee said. "What perfect timing for you."

"I don't appreciate your insinuations, Vee," Akiko said. "And you know what? I think it was you who took that brooch!"

Vee whirled to face Akiko, nearly spilling her wine. "Excuse me?"

"You were on that trip to London when Declan got the brooch, back in '66," Akiko said, calmly pouring herself a fresh drink. "I recall you two being pretty cozy, shacked up at the Savoy, partying with George Harrison—"

"I recall," Vee cut in, "that Declan was networking hard—at your behest. Didn't George and Pattie buy a painting after that trip? How much did you make from that sale?"

"You were jealous that Declan was doing so well," Akiko said. She squeezed a lime wedge into the clear liquid so hard that her knuckles turned white. "You just couldn't get over the fact that it was El Toro's work that got honored by the queen. That he was the one who got the brooch, instead of you."

Blanche's jaw dropped, watching these two powerful forces in the art world go at each other like alley cats. And she couldn't believe Declan had partied with one of the Beatles! Blanche had only hung out with the Monkees, when her husband George took her to see them at the Miami Beach Convention Hall. When they were invited backstage, Davy Jones scribbled his phone number on the back of a ticket stub and slipped it in Blanche's purse when George wasn't looking.

Of course, she'd never called it, being a married woman at the time. She'd completely forgotten about that interaction until today. *I wonder where that ticket stub is now*, Blanche thought. She'd have to ransack her pocketbook collection when they got home.

"Of course it was Declan who got honored," Vee spat. "How many female artists got even a fraction of the opportunities that he got?"

"Oh please, it was all about his talent," Akiko said. She took a long swig of her drink without breaking eye contact with Vee.

Vee scoffed. "You know just as well as I do that there are dozens of equally talented artists out there. Just because he happened to be handsome, and charming, and . . . *male* meant you paid more attention to him."

"I paid plenty of attention to you!" Akiko roared. "After the success of your *Valise* installation, you insisted on doing *Venereal*. You should have taken my advice." She gestured to Luis and then the girls to prove the point. "*No one* wanted to see something like that."

Vee looked up at the glass-paned ceiling, then took an angry sip of her wine.

Rose mouthed *Yikes* to Blanche, who raised her eyebrows in agreement. The claws had come out, and as far as Blanche was concerned, this was even more ammunition for her theory that Vee had likely stolen the brooch and had years of professional jealousy as fuel for other potential crimes.

And Blanche knew that the significance of the butterfly meant much more than the monetary value of its precious metals and stones. Big Daddy had given her jewelry for each of her birthdays, and each piece had a story and a meaning behind it: A strand of seed pearls for her tenth birthday, a tiny version of the Mikimoto choker her mother wore on special occasions. Twenty-four-karat studs when she was finally allowed to get her ears pierced at age twelve, to show she wasn't a little girl anymore. And finally, an emerald cocktail ring on her eighteenth birthday, which Big Daddy told her to wear on her left hand so that boys would think she was engaged and wouldn't make moves on her. Blanche chuckled to herself now—even a diamond on that finger rarely stopped men from chatting her up.

"What would I need that old dusty brooch for? Clearly I can afford my own jewelry. I've been very successful since then." She wiggled her fingers, showing off her elaborate rings.

"That's right!" Rose cried from the sidelines. "Her ring. Remember, Blanche?"

"Hush," Blanche said, remembering that they were trying to keep a low profile until they had more information. She kicked Rose's foot under the table. "I was just remarking how pretty those rings are, wasn't I, Rose?"

"No, we were saying that— Oh, right," Rose said awkwardly.

"Please continue, my dear," Herman said, his eyes traveling

back and forth from Vee's glittering rings to Rose's face. "Don't be shy. One wouldn't want to suspect even an innocent Rose to be hiding a thorn."

Rose glanced at her friends, then hung her head. "We thought we saw some dirt on one of Vee's rings. That's all. It could have come from anywhere."

Herman's eyes lit up and he stood so quickly that he almost knocked his wicker chair over. He grasped Vee's hands, inspecting every finger. "My initial analysis—and professional opinion—is that traces of North American potting soil *are* present, most likely from a flowerpot. Ergo, this woman is who has hidden the brooch!"

The room fell silent, except for the sound of Luis's pen scratching in his notebook. *He's getting a juicy story*, Blanche thought. She wondered how he'd describe her if he wrote up this whole evening. She hoped he'd use words like *shapely*, *alluring*, and, perhaps, *captivating*. Maybe she could ask him to include the fact that she was single in the article.

Vee did a slow, sarcastic clap. "Bravo," she said. "You figured it out. Fine! I took the brooch. Only because it was rightfully mine!"

Blanche's cheeks flushed with heat and sudden anger. *She* was the one who had inspired Declan. He'd intended the brooch to be hers and had said so in front of everyone.

"Now wait a minute here—Declan gave it to me," Blanche said, her voice shaking with emotion. "For being his muse."

"He gave it to *Bianca*," Vee hissed. "And Bianca doesn't

exist—at least not anymore. Bianca was young and carefree, a fleeting feminine ideal for a young man at a very particular time in his life. I was his true muse. We were together for *years*, working side by side, inspiring and challenging each other. Not an illusion who disappeared on him. Not some temporary *libertine belle*."

Blanche's jaw dropped. Vee's words made her feel small and empty, and she didn't want them to be true. She hadn't intentionally disappeared on Declan. Big Daddy and Charmaine had eventually tracked her to New York—after a moment of weakness in which she'd used his purloined credit card at Gimbels—and brought her home. She hadn't even had time to leave a forwarding address. Soon enough she'd met George, and she hadn't really thought much of other men during her decades of marriage.

And she had to have been more than a fleeting illusion, even if she'd used a fake name. After all, Declan had tracked down her real identity and been so happy to see her, even all these years later. Why, there was an entire gallery dedicated to her!

"Bless your heart," Blanche said coldly. "If you're so desperate to feel important to Declan, you can keep it."

"No, she will not," Herman said, patting the pocket in which he'd secreted the brooch. "It's evidence, and part of Declan's estate. I'll have to evaluate it along with everything else. Though I may not be a member of the Miami Police Department, investigation is integral to my profession, and one might say that being a detective is my vocation."

The more he talked, the more Blanche's heart rate calmed. If he could just find the right piece of evidence to figure out what really happened to Declan, they could all relax and stop worrying about who the killer was. And, she realized, if he did his job well, then she and her friends wouldn't have to worry about getting falsely accused. She took a long breath, crossed her legs, and massaged the back of her calf. All this running around the villa and stress about Declan's death had strained her bountiful energy reserves. She longed for a hot bath—or better yet, some time in a Jacuzzi—to soothe her tired legs. She didn't dare develop spider veins at her tender age.

Herman prattled on about the time he'd saved a Pomeranian from a wayward crocodile as a child. Whisking the puppy out of danger from its sharp, snapping jaws had given him a taste for helping the helpless, which developed into a strong sense of justice. As he detailed the various forgery scandals and insurance scams he'd uncovered in the art world over the years, Blanche allowed herself to sink back into the plush cushions of the armchair. Usually she kept her spine ramrod straight and her shoulders pushed back, as she had been trained to do by her mama. Good posture was a requirement in the Hollingsworth household, and Blanche had always liked to give her chest a little boost—especially when she was sitting next to Rose, who had more of a "front porch" than she did.

But then Blanche sat bolt upright again. Even if Herman found out who the killer was, that meant they were still trapped on this island *with* that killer. Since Declan's death, there had been no hint of violence. But if the killer were publicly identified, would they lash out? Blanche's moment of calm had lasted just about as long as it took Mel Bushman to get from first to second base, and worry reared its ugly head. There could be dangerous consequences for them all.

"I have single-handedly determined that Vee is our brooch thief," Herman crowed, pacing around the music room with his hands clasped behind his back.

Blanche saw Dorothy roll her eyes and she stifled the urge to do so herself. It was Rose who'd found the footprints, and Blanche who'd noticed the dirt on Vee's rings. *Typical*, Blanche thought. It reminded her of the time that her mama invited the bank president's wife over for tea, serving Viola's most delicious cakes and pouring on so much Southern charm that the women were practically best friends by the time they'd run out of Earl Grey. When Big Daddy got his loan approved for the new barn the following week, he'd boasted that it was his killer pitch that had carried the day. Blanche thought Big Daddy hung the moon, but she knew it was her mama who often cleared away the clouds so that moon could shine.

"But does that mean she's also, in fact, a *killer*?" Herman said, sending a piercing look to Vee, who shot an equally piercing one right back.

"Oh please. There are much more likely suspects. Like Akiko," Vee said, jerking her head toward the petite gallery owner.

"I told you, I had no reason to want him dead! Shouldn't we look to see who would benefit from El Toro's death? It's probably in his will," Akiko said.

"Why didn't we think of that?" Dorothy leaned over and muttered to Blanche. "Maybe we can find it before anyone else does."

Blanche briefly wondered if she'd be mentioned in Declan's will, if they could even find it. "Even if I were Meryl Streep, I'm not sure I could create a similarly convincing distraction for y'all to go snooping around again," she said.

Though the girls had tried to keep their voices down, their whispered conversation drew Herman's attention. "Do you have something to share with the group, madame?"

Blanche suddenly felt like a schoolgirl getting called out for gossiping during class. She'd chitchatted all the way through high school, passing notes to—or about—boys. She'd only paid attention in biology, when they learned about the birds and the bees, and in English, because she loved *Romeo and Juliet* and *Pride and Prejudice*. She hadn't been such a fan of *The Scarlet Letter*, though.

"I was just agreeing with Akiko," Blanche fibbed. "I think it just might clear things up for all of us if we read Declan's will. Does anyone know if he even had one?"

"I'm not sure," Misia said. "He was pretty private about that kind of thing, I never heard him mention a will."

"Me neither," said Ralph, as the rain outdoors increased to an insistent patter against the room's tall windows.

"Hmmm," Herman said, striding over to Blanche. The smell of mothballs and Aqua Velva trailed in his wake. She frowned. She'd have thought that a European man would have worn a more sophisticated scent.

"I wonder: Would you be named in such a document, Madame Devereaux? Or should I say, Miss Holloway?" he said.

Blanche wasn't so sure she wanted to be named in Declan's will, especially if it made her look guilty. Blanche quickly widened her eyes and dropped her jaw in surprise, hoping her expression was more Betty Boop than Bette Davis. Looking innocent was a skill she'd practiced many a time, such as after climbing back through her window at the Alpha Gamma Delta house at three a.m., or when she'd accidentally given Rose's childhood teddy bear to a mercenary young girl named Daisy.

"I'm sure I don't know what you mean," she said, her tone as smooth and sweet as buttermilk pie.

"Perhaps El Toro left everything to you, his long-lost muse! If that were the case, you'd benefit greatly from his unfortunate demise," Herman said. Every person in the room stared at Blanche, and not in the way that she preferred. The accusation in their eyes felt like a slap in the face.

"That's ridiculous!" Blanche exclaimed, placing a hand on her chest. "I cared for that man! Deeply!"

"Then a crime of passion, perhaps?" Herman continued, pacing around the room. "Perhaps you were angry at him for some current slight—or a romantic betrayal from years ago! A hot-blooded woman like you could easily have a strong temper. One so inflamed, you might even kill your lover!"

Blanche stood, suddenly feeling spicier than a Scotch bonnet and ready to give Herman the dressing down of his life. But Rose tugged at her hem.

"Don't play right into what he's accusing you of," Rose whispered. "You've got to stay cool as kjøttpålegg."

At Blanche's confused expression, she added, "That's Norwegian for cold cuts."

Blanche nodded. She hated to admit it, but this was one of the rare cases where her scatterbrained friend was right. She sat down primly, smoothing her dress over her knees. She imagined dipping her toes in the Mississippi River to calm her anger. "I don't need to kill a man to make him suffer," she said, giving Herman an icy look. "For such an esteemed investigator, it's a shame to see you barking up the wrong tree."

Blanche knew that poking at a man's insecurity wouldn't win her his affection, but in this case, she didn't want it. She just wanted to point his suspicion somewhere else.

But Herman arched one eyebrow and turned his attention in the wrong direction—right to Dorothy, Sophia, and Rose. "Perhaps not as individuals . . . but as a group, you and your friends could overpower a man as strong as El Toro."

"You think we're *killers?*" Sophia said. She slapped one hand against her forearm, making a rude gesture with the other, which Dorothy tried to stop by grasping her elbow.

"Glad you got that mosquito, Ma," Dorothy said, fooling nobody.

"We're as innocent as the Virgin Mary! Well, if she'd had a dozen children," Sophia continued.

"That's right! We'd never do something like that!" Rose cried.

"Perhaps *you* would not, my innocent Rose," Herman said, drawing a finger under her chin in an overly intimate gesture.

Rose tensed, clearly uncomfortable with the physical contact. She glanced at her girlfriends with a bewildered expression, then dubiously back down to Herman's hand. Blanche worried for a second that she would bite the man. Rose was sweet and mild-mannered 99 percent of the time . . . but Blanche had seen Rose shatter a mug to smithereens in her bare hands when she'd thought Dorothy had taken her boyfriend, and of course there was that infamous field hockey incident in high school. She hoped Rose would control herself. They needed to play off Herman's little crush on her to get back on his good side. Rose bared her teeth in an awkward smile, drawing her chin slowly out of Herman's reach.

"I'm sick and tired of being belittled, infantilized, and underestimated," Rose ranted indignantly. "All because I'm friendly, and kind, and—and—*blond*."

"Oh, honey, that's not the reason—" Dorothy began, but Rose wasn't done.

"You know what? Maybe I *could* commit murder! I think I could do it, if I was mad enough!"

Sophia jumped out of her seat to clap a wrinkled hand over Rose's mouth.

Blanche cleared her throat and flashed a nervous smile around the room. "What my friend means to say is that we shouldn't judge people superficially. Not that she would *actually* commit murder." A scared little laugh escaped her throat. "Trust me, she's incapable of hurting anyone. As are the rest of my friends."

"And how come Mr. Price is only accusing women?" Dorothy pointed out suddenly. "If El Toro was killed—and that's a big *if*—isn't it much more likely that El Toro was taken out by a man? Not just because of his strength, but don't statistics show that men commit far more murders?"

Herman froze, stepping away from Rose and turning to Dorothy. "An interesting theory, though perhaps one born out of deflection, rather than deduction." He continued his circuit of the music room and stopped next to Ralph, who shuffled behind an antique harp as if he were trying to disappear. The shimmering strings did nothing to conceal Ralph's hefty form and sweaty face as Herman pointed a finger at his chest.

"This gentleman certainly has the strength and the opportunity to commit such a dastardly deed," Herman said. "Perhaps it was the act of a disgruntled employee, trying to get what he felt he had earned! Or, more simply, revenge on a tyrannical boss, who ordered Ralph about, day and night. Although it would be a cliché—perhaps the butler did, in fact, do it!"

Ralph knit his heavy brows, deepening the weatherworn creases of his face. "We didn't always get along. But we respected each other. We'd walk the grounds and watch the birds. . . ." His voice broke, and as he looked down at his calloused hands a high-pitched whimper escaped from his lips. Misia left her perch on the piano bench and put a gentle arm around the groundskeeper.

The poor man's crying, Blanche thought. Her heart twinged witnessing Ralph's grief, but she fought the instinct to go comfort him herself. A man in distress never failed to activate her nurturing instincts. But . . . what if those were crocodile tears? Until they knew more, she couldn't write anyone off as the killer. And one of the girls would need to get close to Ralph to replace his keys, but with everyone's attention on him now, they'd have to wait for a better moment.

"Clearly, he didn't do it," Misia said. "Ralph wouldn't hurt a fly! Just last week he rehabilitated a pelican with a broken wing. And Declan told me that years ago when Ralph found an abandoned baby crocodile, he fed it kitchen scraps until it could fend for itself."

Ralph smiled sadly at Misia. "It's true. Elizabeth's thriving."

"Elizabeth?" said Vee.

"Elizabeth Taylor, the crocodile. She's a teenager now," Ralph said, wiping his eyes.

"So he's more Doctor Doolittle than Nurse Ratched," Sophia whispered. "But that's just us taking Misia's word for it."

Herman listened with his head tilted to one side. "How touching! This gentle giant, incapable of violence . . . Although people are more difficult than animals, I think, no? Still, he's not the only employee who could have turned disgruntled, yes? Young Misia doesn't have quite the same reputation for tenderness. Why, just yesterday, I saw her screaming at a *peacock* no less."

Misia faced Herman with her arms crossed. "For your information, that peacock deserved it! It got inside the house and pooped on the carpet, and guess who had to clean it up?"

"That doesn't prove anything," Vee cut in, stretching out an arm like she was shielding Misia from afar. "You seem to be grasping at straws, Mr. Price. Why don't we stop this charade of yours? We can all stay out of one another's way and wait for the authorities."

"Great idea," Akiko chimed in, as murmurs of agreement rumbled around the room.

Herman scowled as if Vee's suggestion pained him. "I wish I could allow that," he said. "But since one of us is a murderer, I don't think we should split up."

"But why not?" Dorothy said. "It's not like the murderer can get away."

"Because," Herman said ominously just as a crack of thunder rocked the house and Rose shrieked. "What if the murderer kills again?"

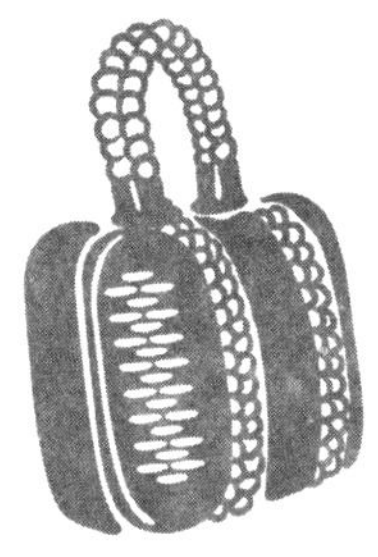

J'ACCUSE ALL OF YOUS

18

Dorothy paced from the harpsichord to the flumpet and subtly passed the set of keys to Rose as she stepped past her. She was surrounded by suspects, each offering a very good reason why they wouldn't—or couldn't—have killed El Toro. Many of them could have a strong enough motive and, some of them, opportunity. Yet that insufferable little man kept focusing on Dorothy and her friends. After being accused of a previous crime she hadn't committed, Dorothy had had it right up to her chunky earrings.

"You know what rubs me the wrong the way?" Dorothy said, pausing just a few steps away from Herman. She enjoyed towering over him—except for the fact that it gave her a better view of the liver spots on his bald head.

"Other than Stan?" Sophia said.

"The feeling of corduroy pants between your thighs?" Rose asked.

"No, Rose," Dorothy said.

"Oh—riding a cow without a saddle?" Rose said. "That never feels good. Or when you're on the Exercycle and . . ."

Blanche tittered, then silenced herself as if remembering the gravity of the situation.

Dorothy shot a long-suffering glare to her friends and mother, then turned back to Herman. "What bothers me is that you're pointing fingers at everyone but yourself."

Herman chuckled and turned to Dorothy with a condescending smile. "I'm just asking questions," the little man said. "The backbone of any investigation."

"But you're as likely as any of us to be the killer, just by virtue of being here," Dorothy said, slightly raising her voice. "Right, everyone?" Dorothy expected the rest of the room to make sounds of agreement, or at least nod their heads, but instead they studiously examined their laps or picked at their cuticles.

No one else wants to get in his crosshairs, she realized.

Sophia pushed herself up from her chair and tottered over to Dorothy. "Excuse me, everyone. I need a word with my daughter." She yanked Dorothy by the arm to a corner of the room, where an unusual guitar with three different-size necks hung on the wall.

"Simmer down, pussycat. I know you want to figure out what happened, but you have to stop drawing attention to yourself!"

"I'm not trying to, Ma," Dorothy said.

"You're a five-foot-ten woman with an attitude problem," Sophia said. "You're going to draw attention no matter what. The deck is stacked against you."

"I don't have an attitude problem!" Dorothy growled, crossing her arms. She quickly uncrossed them, recognizing with annoyance that she just might be proving her mother's point.

"You need to be more subtle with this appraiser guy," Sophia urged. "We can't have any more false accusations against us. After the fire at Shady Pines, and the dead guy in that freezer . . . my heart can't take it." She placed her hands over Dorothy's and squeezed. When her mother blinked up at her like an elderly Kewpie doll, it was easy to forget all the times Dorothy disagreed with her.

"Fine. I'll try to keep a lower profile," Dorothy whispered. "But I don't agree with this wannabe Columbo interrogating everyone but himself."

Sophia widened her eyes and let out a fake-sounding cough.

"He's right behind me, isn't he?" Dorothy said.

Herman chuckled as he tapped Dorothy on the shoulder. "And why would I interrogate myself? It would be as silly as accusing the police of committing a crime, or a firefighter of arson!"

"Of course you're right," Sophia said in a placating tone. Dorothy recognized it as fake, since her mother had never placated anyone in her life. "Though stranger things have happened. Not with you, of course, but just ask my cousin Gino, who was railroaded all the way to the clink. They planted that evidence in his Camaro like they were stuffing a cannoli."

Herman's eyebrows danced upward and he smiled smugly at Sophia. "Thank you for sharing the fact that your family is intimately familiar with the criminal justice system," he said. "That's most illuminating."

"See, Ma? You're not helping!" Dorothy said. Then she addressed the room. "I simply believe Mr. Price should answer the same questions that everyone else did."

"Perhaps you are right. Fair is fair," Herman mused. "Please go ahead. I have nothing to hide."

For a moment, Dorothy doubted herself. She didn't really think Herman was the killer; she simply disagreed with how he'd been excluding himself from suspicion simply because of his profession. Maybe it was the way he acted, as if he was a little smarter, a little more knowledgeable than everyone else. He bugged her the same way Stan did when he was trying to explain his latest "risk-free" investment to her.

"All right," she began. She searched her mind for the right question as the other guests watched her expectantly. Dorothy really didn't have any concrete reason to suspect him over anyone else, so she channeled her inner Perry Mason and decided to ask Herman the question he'd been using to hound the rest of them. "What did you have to gain from El Toro's death?"

Herman pulled his hands out of his pockets, lifting his palms in a gesture of innocence. "As long as the great El Toro produced more work to circulate through the art market, that meant job security for me. I would never wish him harm, especially because I believe—ahem, *believed*—him to be the world's most bold and breathtaking living artist. Over the years we became more friends than colleagues with each painting I authenticated and insured for buyers. I apologize for how crass this may sound—but I could never be the killer, because El Toro was worth more to me alive than dead, do you not see?"

Despite her annoyance with the man, Dorothy saw sincerity in the eyes growing moist behind smudged lenses. Hearing his clear affection and respect for El Toro nudged Dorothy toward believing him. Even though he was irritatingly self-important, that didn't mean he was a cold-blooded killer. She looked over to her mother to get her reaction. Sophia's eyes were half closed—meaning she was still suspicious, or had fallen asleep, either being equally possible. They'd have to compare notes on what everyone had said later, away from prying eyes. So far, to Dorothy, nobody seemed guiltier than anybody else.

Just then, Rose suddenly sneezed, causing the keys to slide from where they were hidden in her lap onto the floor with a soft *clank*.

Dorothy let out a loud, fake cough to cover the sound and tensed, waiting to see if anyone else had noticed.

But Herman blathered on, paying attention only to the sound of his own voice. "I looked up to him, and I most certainly didn't want him dead," he continued. "Our friendship was one of the most important things in my life."

Blanche elbowed Rose. *The keys*, she mouthed, then pointed with her chin to Rose's feet, where they were just out of Blanche's reach.

"Huh?" said Rose, her brow furrowed in confusion.

Oh no, Dorothy thought. *There goes our attempt to return the keys without anyone knowing.*

"The *keys*," Blanche hissed, making her eyes wide.

"Oh! The keys!" Rose said, much too loudly. Herman turned his head toward her with an inquisitive look on his face.

Dorothy groaned inwardly, barely preventing herself from smacking her forehead in frustration. Dorothy caught Rose's eye just as the realization dawned on her friend.

"The *keys* . . ." Rose said more loudly, grasping about for a way to recover. "The keys to a wonderful life surely include strong friendships like yours and El Toro's."

Herman sniffed and nodded. All eyes remained on Rose, so she continued. "Some of my most important friendships began in St. Olaf, of course," she said. "When I was four, my best friend was a chicken named Gordon. Oh, how we'd laugh and laugh."

"Oh? Was that the one who saved your life?" Dorothy asked, trying to keep the room distracted from the shiny key ring on the floor.

"Oh no," Rose said. "Gordon often led me *into* danger. I can't tell you how many times I got in trouble for following him across the two-lane highway at the edge of our farm. I always asked him why he crossed the road, and he had a different answer every time!"

Herman chuckled. "What a wonderful imagination you have, my dear."

"I'm being quite serious," Rose said, surreptitiously placing her foot over the keys as she spoke. "We were very close until we started growing apart. He became more interested in chasing the hens than in playing chase the grasshopper with me." Rose shook her head sadly and drew her foot back, pulling the keys underneath her seat. She gave them another little nudge to push them closer to Blanche's side.

Then Blanche "accidentally" dropped her purse, right between her chair and Rose's, blocking the keys from anyone else's view.

Dorothy realized that they needed to maintain the group's attention on Rose so that Blanche could bend down and pick up the keys unnoticed. Dorothy never thought she'd ask for more detail during one of Rose's St. Olaf stories, but desperate times called for desperate measures.

"And then what happened, Rose? Did you ever reconnect with Gordon?" she asked.

"I sure did, Dorothy," Rose said as she stood up, stalking across the room to pluck a pickle from the antipasto plate. She popped it in her mouth with a flourish, then continued. "We teamed up for the St. Olaf talent show and sang 'People Will Say We're in Love' from *Oklahoma!*" Rose stopped by the grand piano and played a few rousing chords from the song, banging loudly on the instrument to give Blanche cover to snatch the keys from behind her purse. "Unfortunately we only got second place, losing to Hans the Plate Spinner."

"It's a real mystery what his talent was," Sophia said sarcastically.

"Do tell," Dorothy said, mustering all the strength she could to continue the ruse. "Did he stick to dinner plates, or did he branch out into saucers?"

"What? No," said Rose with a chuckle. "He did a killer Humphrey Bogart impression. Not domestic circusry."

As Herman watched Rose with a bemused smile, Blanche stood up to pour herself a gin and tonic from the sideboard. While returning to her seat, Blanche tripped on the corner of the large, walnut base of the harp—spilling a little bit of her drink on Akiko along the way—and clutched at Ralph to get her footing. Only Dorothy noticed that Blanche masterfully slid the keys back into the pocket of his work shirt as Akiko complained about the spill and brushed a few droplets of gin from her leather sleeve. Dorothy unclenched her jaw slightly, now that the keys had been successfully returned.

"Speaking of killers," Herman said. "We shall wake the sleeping dogs, and throw needles into the haystack until we find him or her, despite these captivating stories from our delightful Rose."

He resumed his pacing around the music room, staring keenly at each person. So deeply, Dorothy felt like he was cataloging the contents of her pores.

Herman stopped at the baby grand piano and inhaled dramatically. "El Toro wasn't just receiving mysterious messages before he died—he was getting death threats! And one of you was behind them."

DEAD LETTER DAY

19

Herman pulled out a sheaf of papers from his blazer's inner pocket and waved them in the air.

"Death threats?" Blanche said. She clasped her hands together to try to stop them from trembling.

"Here is the menacing correspondence so you can all see for yourselves!" Herman pushed aside a collection of kazoos displayed on the piano lid and spread the letters across it.

Everyone clustered around to peer at the overlapping

pages composed of letters cut out from magazines in the style favored by anonymous ransom-note writers in TV and film.

"'Stop painting or else,'" Vee read aloud, pointing at one on black construction paper.

"'I'm watching you. Your days are numbered,'" Rose read slowly.

"'You've painted your last portrait,'" Blanche read, a shiver going up her spine as she realized the note had come true. Her Declan would never create another masterpiece. She scanned the faces around the piano, looking for anyone who seemed particularly guilt-ridden—or anyone trying to hide their happiness that their dastardly plan had come to fruition. Though Blanche knew she was an excellent judge of character—she could tell when a man was fibbing about where he'd been on a Friday night, or when her sister Virginia was making up stories—this group was hard to read. Ralph and Misia both had pinched expressions that looked like pain or sadness to Blanche. Akiko's face had turned as pale as a blank canvas, and Vee, normally coolly composed, looked queasy. Luis's eyes were wide as he made hurried notes, his tongue poking out of the corner of his mouth in concentration. Even Herman seemed fully disturbed by the threats. He'd flung the letters on the table as if they'd burned him.

Blanche skimmed the rest of the notes. They were short, blunt, and terrifying. *How awful*, she thought. If Declan and she had reconnected sooner, she would have made him take these straight to the FBI. The jaunty collection of fonts from various magazine and newspaper cutouts made the chilling messages seem even more sinister.

"While these messages of ill intent are shocking news to most of you, I know of at least one person here who already knew about them," Herman said, rapping his knuckles next to one made with red construction paper. "Akiko, it's quite curious that you didn't do anything when you first learned of these dastardly notes."

Akiko looked up, looking even paler than before. "Yes, it's true, I didn't take action right away. But when El Toro first told me about them I figured they were from some crazed fan, trying to get a rise out of him. It was a hectic time—Art Basel was coming up, and I'd been opening a new gallery in Singapore. Now that he's . . ." She trailed off. She patted her pockets for her gum. Finding the colorful package empty, she crumpled it in one hand.

"Dead as a doornail?" Sophia added.

Blanche elbowed her. In the South, they were never that blunt. Her family would say things like "gone to his eternal rest" or "gone to glory" if someone had died. As a little girl she'd found it confusing that there was a woman named Glory who had kindly taken in all of their elderly pets yet would not accept human visitors.

"Shady Pines, Ma," Dorothy hissed under her breath.

Akiko shoved the crumpled pack back into her pocket and sighed. "I realize I should have taken them seriously sooner."

"I'll say," Vee grumbled. "These are *death* threats! What were you thinking?"

"I'm sorry." Akiko's voice cracked. "I thought they were harmless. Some crank having a little fun. And since El Toro lived out here, so secluded from the world, I never imagined that anyone could actually hurt him."

"You should have told *us* about this!" Misia hissed. "Ralph and I had no idea."

"We could have protected him better," Ralph said, his face darkened by growing shadows as the ambient light outside the windows faded. "And by not telling us, you put all of us in danger."

Akiko shifted uncomfortably in her spot between the piano and a set of bongos. "After I got this one I asked Herman to investigate," she said as she pulled out a wrinkled piece of paper from her pocket. She unfolded it and placed it next to the others. It read: *I'M WATCHING EL TORO. HIS NEXT PAINTING WILL BE HIS LAST!*

"When Akiko alerted me to these threats, I told El Toro that we needed to involve the police—or hire a bodyguard," Herman said softly. "He refused. So I decided, if he would not take them seriously, the least I could do was a full investigation myself. And I've been quietly looking into them ever since. . . . I only wish I had been able to stop this terrible tragedy from happening."

Blanche could see the real pain in Herman's eyes and the strain the investigation must be causing him.

Luis then spoke up. "I also received notes about El Toro at the paper. Warning me not to write about him or his latest painting."

Akiko and Herman looked at each other with raised eyebrows, clearly surprised.

Herman whirled on him. "Why did you not tell me this sooner?"

Luis flipped through his notebook, looking for an earlier page. "Here it is. I made a note of that conversation. When I called El Toro to tell him about the threats, he laughed them off. Said it was all fodder for my story on him, but it was nothing to worry about. Of course, now it'll be more of an exposé on his suspicious death, a *preeminent artist struck down in his prime* type of thing, rather than the career-renaissance piece I had planned."

"Let me get this straight," Vee began. "All three of you knew about the danger Declan was in and are only deigning to tell the rest of us now? You downplayed them as 'mysterious messages' before—but these are *death threats*." She pressed her hands into the ebony piano lid as if to steady herself. "To echo your words, Mr. Price, I find that very odd indeed."

Herman sniffed. "I don't appreciate what you are insinuating. I've been working very hard to find out which one of you—supposedly, those closest to El Toro—was sending them!"

Poor Declan, Blanche thought. She remembered his big-hearted laugh, his keen intensity with a paintbrush, and felt a fresh sense of mourning for herself, but also for the world to have lost such a talent. She knew he could be brusque—even harsh at times—such as when he barked at Misia about the milk for his coffee or yelled at Ralph about the generator. She knew he'd been ruthlessly competitive with the other students at art school, often complaining that their work was boring and uninspired. But he was hardest on himself, she remembered, like the time he'd spent an entire week trying to capture the way the light hit the Hudson River at sunset. He'd even missed one of their dates to do so, and she'd given him the cold shoulder in the stairwell of their building the next day. So the following evening, he'd invited Blanche to eat hot pretzels and sip lemonade with him on the pier while he worked. As the sun had set over Hoboken, they'd shared a kiss that was sweeter than any bite of the Big Apple. It was also the cheapest date she'd ever agreed to, but it had been one of her favorites.

Not only had Declan's beautiful life been threatened, but if Herman was right, it meant that it had been by someone he was close to. The deception reminded her of the time Big Daddy had hired a man from Decatur to help run their farm. Rufus had been friendly and smart, with a voice as melodious as a preacher's and enough wit to charm a ballroom full of debutantes. When Big Daddy found out that he'd been skimming off the profits from the pecan harvest, he'd been heartbroken to have to fire the man he'd trusted.

Thank goodness I have my girls, Blanche thought, looking at the steadfast, loving friends with whom she shared a home. Though they might disagree at times, they'd never betray each other like someone in Declan's inner circle had. "I wasn't as close with him as all of you," Luis said. "I only knew El Toro because he wrote to me at the *Herald*, telling me how much he enjoyed my writing, and to suggest that I cover his upcoming return to the art scene. I began visiting him here from time to time, to interview him for my story."

"And yet you were getting notes, too," Herman said. "Most unusual. Do you have any idea who sent them?"

"They were dropped off—anonymously—in a manila envelope in the *Herald*'s mail slot after hours."

"You know, I did something similar when I sent an anonymous note to the St. Olaf *Courier-Dispatch* about Mean Old Lady Hickenlooper," Rose said. "But they found out it was me. Maybe we can use a similar tactic!"

"Pray tell, what happened?" Herman said, his eyebrows aloft with interest.

"That woman drove her tractor over my petunia patch, and never even apologized! I hoped they'd print how awful she was on the front page, or at least in the gossip column, but instead they returned my letter and told me that they didn't publish personal gripes, can you believe that?" Rose said. "I was extremely careful not to sign my name or put a return address on the envelope. But that didn't stop one of the reporters there from discovering that I was the letter-writer."

"How did they know it was you?" Sophia asked.

"Perhaps you had used some type of rare ink in your pen? Did they perform a handwriting analysis?" Herman pressed.

"No. No, I think they examined the paper fibers and used them to track down the supplier for my personalized stationery," Rose said.

Dorothy grimaced as everyone else realized what had happened.

"Your innocence is a marvelous thing," Herman said.

"Yes, well, we weren't that lucky," Luis said. "And since there was no return address on the envelopes, we couldn't trace them."

"Did you develop any theories as to who sent them?" Herman asked eagerly.

"We get a lot of crank letters at the paper. It's hard to tell what's legitimate. For example, just last week we got a letter from a concerned citizen complaining that Miami was too beautiful and was attracting too many tourists. They suggested the city should produce more smog to keep the tourists away!"

"What did the ones about Declan say?" Blanche said, trying to get the investigation back to her departed suitor.

"See for yourself," Luis said, producing some papers from his inner breast pocket. He added them to the others on the piano lid. One said: *KILL YOUR PIECE ON EL TORO IF YOU KNOW WHAT'S GOOD FOR YOU.*

Blanche traced the cutout letters with her finger. "These are meaner than a hornet in a hairnet!"

"They're poison-pen letters, sweet cheeks, what did you

expect?" Sophia said as Luis stuffed the note back into his blazer pocket. "No one's gonna write 'You're a great artist with a fabulous personality, so I have to kill you.'"

Blanche dug her fingernails into her palms, trying not to display the temper that Herman had accused her of having. This wasn't a time for joking around, and she very much wanted to give the petite Sicilian a piece of her mind. But more than that, she wanted to find out what had happened to Declan.

"Someone was very angry with El Toro," Herman agreed. He began to pace slowly around the piano.

"Well, obviously, if they killed him," Sophia said.

"But we're missing a piece here," Dorothy said, waving her hand over the notes. "Except for the one to Luis, these messages aren't asking for anything—there's no mention of blackmail, for example."

"That's right," Rose said. "They're just threats. It's like when you take a warning shot."

"You mean *send* a warning shot," Dorothy corrected.

"No, I mean when you take one," Rose explained. "Or you drink one, to be more precise. For example, when you're at the Rusty Anchor and you want to let everyone know you're going to get a little wild and belt some Irving Berlin? You take a shot first, to warn everyone."

Blanche rolled her eyes.

"So?" Vee said. "What does that mean?"

"My guess is that these threats were meant only to scare El

Toro, not to get him to do—or not do—anything," Dorothy said. "But why?"

The malicious letters circled around Blanche's mind, making her feel like she was walking through a swamp of sadness in stilettoes—and sinking deeper with every step. She realized she'd been clinging to the hypothesis somewhere deep in her subconscious that Declan had died from a sudden malady or an accidental slip, because in her heart, she couldn't imagine anyone really wanting to extinguish her old flame. She felt sorry for Declan, for herself, and she also felt for his friends and staff—but only to a point. Any one of them could be his killer, even though they all seemed to have some love—or at least respect—for their erstwhile host.

"I suppose that puts a big strike against the natural causes theory," Blanche sighed.

"The final doornail in the coffin . . ." Sophia muttered.

"Shady *Pines*, Ma," Dorothy muttered back.

"Maybe to be sure we should go take another look," Luis suggested. "When we first checked out the scene, we were all in shock. I wouldn't mind getting a few more details."

"Me too," Misia said. "And I know we're supposed to wait for the cops, but I want to cover him, out of respect."

"I don't believe we should tamper with the evidence," said Herman. "But another look may be a necessary step to further my investigation. If you please, follow me." Herman gathered up the notes from the piano lid and led the group out of the music room through the foyer.

"This again?" Sophia said, looking up at the curving staircase with trepidation. "I'm too tired for all this up and down, up and down!"

Despite her melancholy, Blanche let out a little laugh. The idea of Sophia getting frisky at her age was just too comical for her to keep a straight face.

"Get your mind out of the gutter, Blanche," Sophia said. "I meant my knees can't take it anymore."

Blanche covered her mouth, trying to stifle another giggle. Dorothy shook her head.

"Is sex all you can think about at a time like this? I thought you were in mourning," Sophia said.

"Of course I am," Blanche said. "But I can't help it if you're making innuendos."

"Oh, I *love* innuendos!" Rose squealed. "Can I have mine with grated cheese on top?"

Dorothy strategically placed herself between Rose and her mother, and Blanche could tell she was hoping to interrupt the silliness. But sometimes, when stress and grief clung to her limbs like Spanish moss, Blanche found that laughter was the only thing that helped.

"Ma," Dorothy said. "You don't have to come up. You can wait here."

"And be left alone in an unfamiliar house with a killer at large? No, thank you." Sophia shook her head vehemently.

"Then take your time," Dorothy said.

"I'm staring down ninety, pussycat. Time isn't exactly an unlimited resource."

"Don't talk like that!" Dorothy said.

Sophia hooked her arm around Dorothy's elbow and followed the rest of the group up the steps and down the hall.

The girls took a deep breath together to steady themselves before entering the studio. As Blanche stepped through the door, she was grateful for the scent of paint and other materials that filled her nose instead of that of a dead body. Thank goodness the cool, fresh air from the lanai had kept the room from filling with the unpleasant odor of death.

Both Herman and Luis made a show of jotting down notes as the group traversed the studio and approached the motionless body at the threshold of the lanai, taking care to avoid stepping in the drying puddle of liquid. Misia shook out the white sheet she'd carried and handed one end to Ralph.

The sheet billowed like a cloud as they lifted it to place the makeshift shroud over Declan's body.

"Wait!" cried Herman. "Look!" He pointed a shaking finger at something near Declan's left side.

CAUGHT RED-FOOTED

20

Dorothy lifted herself on the balls of her feet to peer over everyone else's heads. Herman pointed to a partial shoe print, pressed halfway into the drying puddle of goo at El Toro's left side, right next to the smear that indicated he'd slipped.

"Oops, was that me?" Ralph asked. He lifted one foot to check the bottom, then the other. His soles were clean.

"You're good," Misia said.

"Then that must be another clue!" Rose clapped.

"That's correct, my little Rose," Herman said. "Clearly, this must have been left by the killer!"

Dorothy heard a few gasps as everyone craned their necks for a better look at the print.

"I don't remember seeing this before," Vee said.

"Me neither," Akiko said. "How about you, Luis?"

"I'm not sure," Luis said, frowning. He squatted down near the puddle to take a closer look. "We were all in a state of shock when we first saw him. It's no wonder we missed this."

"That was definitely not here before," Sophia whispered as she tugged at Dorothy's arm.

"I agree," whispered Dorothy, stepping back from the group so as not to be overheard. "I would have included it in my drawings."

"Are you sure?" Sophia said.

Dorothy nodded firmly and put a finger to her lips. Neither of them could let on that they'd already been back here an additional time. A sense of unease settled over Dorothy like a cloud of hairspray. Someone must have entered the studio after she and her mother had snuck in.

"Another suspicious footprint," Herman said. "Perhaps our killer should have been more careful!" He knelt next to the body, careful not to let his pant leg touch the border of liquid, and pulled out a magnifying glass from his pocket.

"I'm afraid to ask . . . but what is that liquid? Shouldn't

you try to figure that out as well?" Blanche said. "It might be relevant to the case."

"It could be an oil or varnish he was using to create a sheen over his layers of paint," Misia said. "He was always experimenting with different materials."

"You know what?" Dorothy said, just realizing something. "It looks like a similar shade to the ink used on the invitation we got to El Toro's so-called gala."

Akiko looked up sharply. "Invitation?"

"Yes, that beautiful wood-cut style print, with the flowers and the butterflies," Blanche said. "Oh, it was just gorgeous! Of course, ours also came with a beautiful wooden box for the brooch."

"I didn't get any invitation," Akiko said. "I got a telegram from El Toro, begging me to fly down here for a very important conversation about his career."

"I got an invitation," Vee said. "But mine had a watercolor on the front, and it wasn't for a gala, it was for an artistic salon. And mine had a much more . . . *ahem*, personal message written inside."

"That's odd," Dorothy said. "How about you, Luis?"

"He phoned me at the paper and said he was throwing a dinner party I wouldn't want to miss. That it would provide some good intel for our—I mean *my*—story."

"What did your invitation look like?" Rose asked Herman.

Herman shifted from one foot to the other. "I didn't exactly get an invitation," he mumbled.

"Then how did you know to show up?" Rose said.

"Akiko told me she was coming in to meet with El Toro," he said. "I joined her, thinking the two of us could talk some sense into him regarding these threats."

Dorothy drummed her fingers against her thigh. Why would each guest have gotten a different type of invitation from El Toro—for a different type of event?

"I still think that stuff looks like blood," Akiko said bluntly, bringing everyone's attention back to the body on the floor. "We should check."

"Wait one moment while I set up my portable forensics kit," Sophia said. "I never leave home without it."

"I'm willing to do a rudimentary analysis," Herman said. "But that would necessitate me coming into contact with the substance. And we'd agreed as a group not to disturb evidence."

"But we don't have that luxury," Vee said. "We've decided to cover the body with a sheet, and we're going to pull him inside to close the door. It's the respectful—and practical—thing to do. We can't leave him half-exposed to the elements any longer."

"Very true," Herman allowed. "But if I touch it as part of my investigation, it is with all of you agreeing that it should not incriminate me."

"I don't care, I'll do it," Sophia said. "Then can we move on? I've given birth three times and survived a stint at Shady Pines. Mysterious puddles don't faze me anymore."

"No, Ma, let him do it," Dorothy said, placing a cautioning hand on Sophia's shoulder. "He's the experienced investigator."

Herman nodded approvingly at Dorothy, then gingerly squatted down and dipped one finger into the tacky substance. He brought his finger close to his face, peering at the congealing liquid over the rim of his glasses, and gave an inquisitive sniff.

"This is definitely not blood," he said. The room let out a sigh of relief. "It smells like paint mixed with castor oil, or something like it."

"That's basically what I said," Misia grumbled. "No one listens to me, and I was the one working by his side, day and night."

"Did you ever pose for him?" Blanche asked. "I did, many a time."

"Ew, no," Misia said. "Never."

Blanche's face softened into the faraway look that Dorothy had seen many a time when Blanche was lost in a romantic reverie. "He told me I was an excellent sitter. Why, I could hold any position for as long as it took."

"We should put that on the flyers you hand out at Fleet Week," Sophia cracked.

Blanche's eyes glowed with a private memory as she ignored the older woman's remark.

Vee cleared her throat. "Right. So if you all are quite finished, I'd like to find out what happened to Declan."

"Quite right," Herman said. "Now we must examine the shoe print."

Dorothy craned her neck for a better view. Only the top part of the shoe had landed in the puddle, leaving a softly rounded outline with a honeycombed pattern of tiny circles. She quickly glanced around the room, wondering whose shoes matched the imprint.

She breathed a quiet sigh of relief knowing that the shape didn't look anything like the pointy-toed dress shoes she and her friends were wearing, similar to the silver slingbacks Vee had on, which also ruled her out. Luis's loafers had more of a square toe, she noticed . . . but Akiko's boots had a rounded one. Dorothy elbowed Blanche and pointed with her chin at the gallery owner. Blanche peeked at Akiko's feet and raised her eyebrows. Dorothy had no idea what type of tread was on Akiko's soles, but they were one possibility so far.

"I guess we'll have to check everyone's shoes," Dorothy said, trying not to look directly at Akiko.

"Did someone step in dog poop?" Rose asked, bewildered. "I don't smell anything!"

Dorothy was about to correct her when Herman stepped in and clasped Rose's hands in his. "Your charming naivete is as refreshing as the ocean breezes of my childhood home. But finally we have some cold hard evidence! For whoever's shoe bears this stain is our killer. I must ask everyone to form a line, if you please."

Everyone shuffled uneasily into a rough line along the studio wall while Herman tapped his foot with impatience.

"To prove that I have nothing to hide, I will go first," he announced. He lifted one foot and then the other, rotating his ankle to show the bottoms of his shoes. His wingtips had smooth worn soles, without a trace of the red stain anywhere to be seen. "Obviously, it cannot be me. Next!"

Dorothy and her friends obediently revealed the bottoms of their shoes to Herman and the others. Their soles were clear, except for a blotch of dried pink bubblegum on Rose's heel.

"I was wondering where that went," said Akiko.

"All clear." Herman smiled. "I knew it could never have been you."

"Of course it wasn't me! But I don't think you should have suspected my friends either," Rose insisted.

"An investigator must be impartial, my dear! Just because they are your friends does not mean I could assume their innocence," Herman said, tapping his temple as if he'd imparted a precious morsel of investigative brilliance.

Then it was Vee's turn, followed by Ralph, who insisted on showing his soles again. Both of their shoes seemed too large for the partial print, and the wrong shape. Neither had the red stain on the bottom, though Ralph's were crusted in dirt. Dorothy held her breath as Akiko stepped forward. The gallery owner leaned on Ralph as she presented her leather boots for inspection. The black rubber sole bore a pattern of perpendicular wavy lines, not a match for the little circles.

There goes that theory, Dorothy thought.

That left Misia and Luis. Luis's loafer soles were smooth and unstained, and Misia's Doc Martens had a chunky sole, flecked with paint and a little bit of dirt in between the ridges of the straight, horizonal tread pattern. Herman bent to examine the multicolor specks of paint with his magnifying glass.

"I'm an artist's assistant," Misia said. "Of course I'm going to have some paint on my shoes."

"And as you can see, the pattern doesn't match," Dorothy pointed out.

Misia smiled up gratefully at Dorothy while Herman knit his brows.

"So no one here is caught red-footed, so to speak," he said, tucking his magnifying glass back into his pocket. "But perhaps the culprit changed their shoes!"

"No one has extra clothes or shoes," Blanche said. "I brought an itty-bitty overnight bag, but none of us were planning to get stuck here."

"Alas, you have forgotten about the staff," Herman said, shaking his finger in the air. "Certainly they would have more than one pair of shoes on hand! Or on foot, one might say." He allowed himself a satisfied little chuckle as Ralph and Misia stared at each other in horror.

"We would never have hurt Declan!" Misia cried.

Dorothy noticed that Ralph's hands were clenched into fists and he looked like he just might punch the self-appointed investigator. Next to him, Blanche pulled at the neckline of her dress, trying to get a little airflow as the two men faced off, the tension (and testosterone) in the room rising to dangerous heights. Misia wordlessly shook her head at Ralph and he stepped back from the shorter man. His broad chest rose and fell as he forced a deep breath.

"My detective's instincts require that we search the house for any and all shoes to compare to this pattern. The one that matches *must* belong to the killer," Herman announced.

Dorothy found herself nodding along with Herman's plan, though she found it hard to believe that Ralph or Misia had murdered El Toro. They seemed devoted to their employer even if they'd had their gripes, which to Dorothy's mind were completely legitimate. She didn't love the way that Declan had bossed Misia around, but was that enough motive to commit murder? And even though Ralph had the brute strength, he seemed far too gentle and attached to his friendship with the artist.

Still, she remembered what Rose had told her after they'd solved their last mystery: Anyone could be a criminal, anyone at all.

"All agreed?" Herman didn't wait for a reply and turned on his heel. "To the servants' quarters!"

"Wait," said Ralph. "Now that we've all taken a good look, it's time to cover him."

Dorothy winced inwardly as he and Misia carefully draped the sheet over El Toro, then gently pulled him fully inside the studio by his feet, leaving a smear of the red liquid across the floor. The sheet and the movement would interfere with evidence-gathering from real detectives, Dorothy thought as Ralph muttered a quiet prayer. But after considering the realities of keeping a corpse on the premises, and being respectful of everyone's feelings, Dorothy knew that this was the best, if imperfect, course of action.

Then Ralph closed the lanai doors firmly and locked them. "We can't risk any critters getting in here."

Dorothy nodded. She wondered just how long it would be until they'd be able to get help, and El Toro's body would be taken to a morgue—and desperately hoped it would be before any decomposition set in.

"Now that our sad duty is concluded, we must follow the trail where it leads," Herman said. He charged out of the studio and led the way down the hall.

Ralph hustled to catch up with him. "Just how do you know where our rooms are?" he called. "Maybe they're on the third floor, or on the first floor."

"El Toro gave me the blueprints to his home at my request," Herman said while the group followed behind him. "Once I learned of the threats against him, I campaigned to institute some safety measures. This weekend, I thought I would be able to convince him to set up a security system—an alarm, and maybe some video cameras." Then he added sadly, "Of course, now it is too late."

"Maybe if you'd done your job sooner, he'd still be alive," Akiko snapped.

"It's my greatest regret that I couldn't convince him earlier," Herman said. "But you know what a stubborn bull El Toro could be!"

Vee and Akiko both nodded. Herman paused before the third door in the hallway.

"My room is not prepared for visitors!" Ralph said, leaning his meaty frame across the doorway. "It's my private space. At least let me neaten up first."

"So you can possibly destroy evidence? No, monsieur," Herman said, pushing past Ralph to open the door. It was unlocked and swung open, releasing a pungent, earthy scent and an otherworldly glow.

LIGHTS, CAMERA, LIZARDS!

21

Blanche staggered backward a few steps as she took in Ralph's room. Two walls held a collection of glass terrariums, each with their own set of lights, vegetation, and rocks, with various scaly creatures housed inside. Another wall was covered in glossy black-and-white headshots from the golden age of cinema up to modern day and an almost life-size poster of David Hasselhoff wearing a leather jacket—and not much else.

"A bearded dragon!" Rose cried, pointing to one of the

terrariums. "How adorable. Hey, how come their heat lamps are working? I thought the electricity was out."

Blanche blinked, surprised that Rose knew the difference between one critter and another, and that she was keen enough to notice the heat lamps. Rose trotted over to the bearded dragon and cooed at it.

"I have battery-powered ones for backup," Ralph said. "I don't take any chances when it comes to my ladies." He strode over to the creature Rose was pointing to. "This one's Madeline Khan," he said. "And the chameleon is Angela Lansbury."

Blanche thought the lizard looked more like Ham Lushbough—a man worth less than five minutes of her time—than some of the most beautiful and talented performers of stage and screen. But thanks to her Southern manners, she kept her mouth shut. A true lady never criticized another person's pets.

"Your closet?" Herman said, stepping into the center of the room.

Ralph pointed to a door on the left next to a movie poster for *Attack of the 50 Foot Woman*. Inside hung neat rows of casual shirts, pants, and more rugged workwear, including a pair of denim overalls. Herman rummaged around the floor, holding up a pair of barely used men's dress shoes, which had nothing suspicious on their smooth soles. He next picked up and discarded a pair of fuzzy Garfield slippers and flipped over a set of worn men's tennis shoes. Those were grimy, but without any reddish stains, and featured a triangular tread pattern very different from the one in the shoe print.

Blanche let out a breath she'd been holding since Herman opened Ralph's closet, relieved that the seemingly kind boatsman/groundskeeper/chef wasn't the culprit. She had a soft spot for strong, burly men, even if they had dirt under their fingernails and an assembly of exotic pets.

"I told you, he's innocent," Misia said, as the group backed out of Ralph's bedroom/reptile habitat.

"Well then, we have just one more closet to check," Herman said, barreling his way down the hall to the next door. He rattled the handle, but it was locked. He turned to Ralph.

"Key," he demanded.

"I'd rather not," Ralph said.

"This is an unlawful search," Misia said. "You don't have a warrant."

Herman adjusted his tweed suit jacket. "Spoken like someone with something to hide!" He sneered.

"Just because she knows her rights doesn't mean she's guilty," Dorothy interjected.

Blanche shot Dorothy a questioning glance, curious why she was suddenly sticking her neck out for the young woman. Especially when, by the process of elimination, Misia was the most likely of them all to have left the print—and therefore, to be guilty of the crime. She had motive, as did several others, but she also had the most access. In general, Blanche maintained a general wariness around all young, pretty women, since she never knew if a man's attention would wander from herself to them. But something about the idea of Misia being the killer didn't feel quite right, like wearing seersucker after Labor Day.

Herman glared at Ralph, then at Misia. Blanche bit her lip, wondering who would win the standoff. Something about Ralph's steadfast refusal reminded Blanche of a broad-shouldered cowboy in an old western. She patted her cheeks with a handkerchief from her purse. *If only the power hadn't gone out*, she thought. *I could use an icy blast of air-conditioning right about now.*

"As you wish," he said. "I will simply pick the lock." Herman pulled out a tiny eyeglass repair kit from his breast pocket and knelt in front of the door.

"You're not even a real cop," Misia pointed out.

"Maybe so, but I am the closest thing we have on this island," Herman said, poking at the lock with a miniature screwdriver.

"Do you think you'll be able to get it in?" Rose whispered as she peeked over Herman's shoulder.

"Bah!" Herman grunted. "If I can just find the right angle for my little tool."

Blanche let out a little snort. When everyone stopped to look at her, she tried to revert to a serious expression. But she couldn't and laughed again. "I'm sorry, I'm sorry," she said, trying to blur her mental image of Herman getting it on. "I just can't help it!"

At last, the lock finally clicked. Herman barged into a room wallpapered with framed prints, loose sketches, and photographs ripped out of magazines. Against the back wall, a mirrored vanity held a mug full of charcoal and colored pencils, a pile of makeup brushes and a bottle of Paloma Picasso perfume, a tangle of jelly bracelets, and a tub of Dippity-Do. Next to an unmade bed stood a nightstand with a small tape deck and a stack of cassettes. Blanche read the labels: Madonna, Whitney Houston, Cyndi Lauper, and some she wasn't as familiar with, like New Edition and Inner Circle. The room reminded Blanche of a cross between Declan's studio and the joyful chaos of her own daughter's bedrooms when they were teenagers. Though she'd struggled to get along with Janet and Rebecca (especially during those turbulent years), she realized in that moment how much she missed them. If they ever got out of this predicament and off of this island—when, Blanche told herself, *when*—she vowed to telephone both of them.

Above the vanity hung a vision board with bold phrases.

MAKE RAD ART

"ALL ART REQUIRES COURAGE"—ANNE WILKES TUCKER

"PAINT THE WAY A BIRD SINGS"—CLAUDE MONET

Each of these phrases contained words carefully cut from magazine headlines, layered over hand-drawn designs and pictures of female artists such as Frida Kahlo, Yayoi Kusama, and Ann Norton.

They immediately brought to Blanche's mind the collage-style notes Declan had received. *Interesting*, Blanche thought, and mentally filed that detail away.

"Misia, before we check your shoes, is there anything you'd like to confess?" Herman said as he stepped over piles of books and clothing to the closet.

Blanche watched Misia's face carefully and noticed that Dorothy was doing the same.

"No, there is not," she said, her voice weary with annoyance. "Go for it."

Herman searched the closet floor and tossed out a pair of white Keds, stylish teal pumps with a conical heel, and some wooden Dr. Scholl's sandals, turning each one upside down to examine the soles. None of them matched the circular pattern from the studio, and none of them bore a reddish stain.

"See?" Misia smirked. "I told you that you wouldn't find anything."

"But wait—there is one more pair." Herman groaned as he crawled on all fours halfway into the closet, returning with two Reebok high-tops.

Blanche leaned forward as he turned the first shoe over, only to find a blue paint splotch in the center. When he turned over the second shoe, the room collectively gasped as he revealed a reddish-brown stain across the top half of the sole.

"That's impossible!" Misia shrieked.

"Oh, but it's *possible*!" Herman said triumphantly and then passed the shoe around so everyone could examine the tread: a series of small circles in a honeycomb pattern. Even the rounded toe of the high-tops matched the shape of the shoe print in the puddle around Declan, Blanche thought.

"The smoking gun—er, shoes," Herman said, standing a little taller. "What have you to say for yourself, *petite fille*?"

Blanche stared at Misia in stunned silence along with the rest of the room. She hadn't wanted to suspect Misia, but the shoe was damning evidence, plain as day.

Misia looked at Herman with a strange expression, then exploded. "This is unbelievable! *I didn't kill him!* I'm not saying anything more until I have a lawyer."

"I believe you," said Ralph.

"Thanks," Misia sniffled. Suddenly, tears poured over the young woman's cheeks, soaking into the collar of her jumpsuit. Blanche couldn't tell if the tears were from the guilt of murdering Declan or from frustration at getting caught. Or was she, as she insisted, somehow totally innocent?

The rest of the room remained silent, trading uneasy glances as Misia sat on her bed and sobbed. Had they finally solved the mystery? Had they caught the killer? At the end of most murder mysteries, the suspects all ended up in a room with the detective, who outed the killer just as Herman had done. Was this what that felt like? Blanche thought she'd feel something closer to relief than the mixture of confusion and uneasiness that pervaded the air.

"So what do we do now?" she asked.

"Beats me," Sophia said.

Herman frowned and patted his pockets. "Is there a room in the villa that locks only from the outside? We could contain her, so as not to endanger ourselves."

Ralph crossed his arms. "Not while I'm here and in charge of this property, there isn't. And I don't think she did it."

"But the *shoe*—" Herman spluttered.

"It's damning," Dorothy chimed in. "But it's not perfect. It's just one piece of evidence, and it could be circumstantial. As civilians, I don't think we can—or should—detain someone without due process."

Blanche wrung her hands, wishing Big Daddy would magically appear and tell them what to do. On one hand, Dorothy was correct. Her well-educated friend knew the law and knew her rights. On the other, how could they safely let Misia roam around the island, if she was, in fact, the killer? Maybe Dorothy was trying to appease Misia so she wouldn't murder them, too. With Dorothy's Mensa-level smarts, she could be playing three-dimensional Scrabble for all Blanche knew.

"Perhaps we can talk this out," Blanche suggested, remembering how Big Daddy always took control of tense situations at Twin Oaks. Calming the catfights between Blanche and her sisters had taken legendary levels of diplomacy.

"Good idea," said Vee. "We don't know what's what."

"Would you like to make a statement?" Luis said to Misia, holding his mini tape recorder up to her face. His thumb hovered over the Record button.

"What? No! I didn't do anything," she said, batting the tape recorder away.

"I can tell your side sympathetically if you share your story. Was El Toro an abusive boss? Was it self-defense?" Luis pressed. His eyes were alight with the possibility of getting an exclusive, Blanche noticed.

Akiko shook her head in disbelief, and Vee watched Misia with an unreadable look on her face.

"How about I stay in my room and promise not to come out," Misia said through her tears. "You can post someone outside to watch the door. I'd *love* to get a break from you all."

Blanche and Rose locked eyes, and shrugged. Then Blanche tugged Dorothy's arm and moved to exit Misia's crowded bedroom. If they could just get away by themselves, they could figure out what to do next.

"That will have to do—for now," Herman said ominously. He stepped carefully across Misia's cluttered floor toward the door, then his toe caught on something sticking out from under the bed. Herman stumbled to the floor, then used his prone position to look under the bohemian quilted bedspread. He yanked at the corner of something, and pulled out a painted canvas.

Then he pulled out another, and another. As he turned the last one right-side up, he revealed an interpretation of *Girl with a Pearl Earring*, except the face was different: more catlike and suntanned than the original, in a three-quarter profile. Blanche recognized herself, remembering when she'd sat for that painting on a late Sunday afternoon after a particularly grueling Rockettes matinee. Light had streamed into Declan's flat through the windows, which had been flung open and let in the sound of traffic and occasional wafts of roasting nuts from the city street below. After he'd finished the undercoat, he'd massaged her tired legs and sore feet, then helped her out of her undergarments. They'd found wonderful ways to pass the time as they waited for the layer of paint to dry.

"What have we here?" Herman gloated. "An early El Toro!"

Blanche's mouth went dry. If the shoe was a major piece of evidence, this painting was another. Herman pawed through the rest of the canvases, checking each one against something written in his notebooks. "Each of these paintings match a recent sale that I have recorded. All bought up by mysterious buyers, previously unknown in the global art scene."

He flashed his open notebook to the group, too quickly for them to see anything except for columns of words and prices. "My hypothesis has been proven correct!" he crowed. "I suspected that the person who was threatening El Toro was also buying up some of his lesser-known paintings. See this one?" He tapped the first canvas. "This was purchased by Rosie Spoonbill. This one, by Ann Hinga. And Sandy Ling bought the last three. I work with most of the important collectors, and these names were unfamiliar to me. I looked into all of them and found that every single one gave the same P.O. box in Miami at the point of sale. And when I looked deeper, to try to trace these women, I found that not one of them actually exists!"

Misia swallowed, looking nervously from Herman to the paintings. Sophia frowned, and Blanche noticed that the older woman had the same look in her eyes that she wore when she was trying to remember if she'd taken her medication.

"You were buying up El Toro's early work. Then, when news of his death hit the press, you were going to sell these pieces and make a fortune! Quite a way for Misia to get out of the shadow—and from under the foot—of her boss, eh?"

"That's not true," Misia said. "You don't understand!"

"Silence!" Herman said. "You can tell it to the police, when they finally arrive. As the great Hercule Poirot once said, it is one thing to know that a woman is guilty, and it was an easy matter to prove it so. You are guilty, guilty, guilty!" He jabbed a finger toward Misia with each repetition of the damning word.

Misia's face crumpled as more tears streamed down her cheeks. She crouched down into a little ball and hugged her knees.

"You better be sure about this," Akiko said to Herman. "Those are serious accusations."

Misia sobbed so loudly that Blanche could hardly think

and she looked to her friends for guidance. Dorothy jerked her head to one side, indicating that they should make a quick exit.

"Let's leave Misia to compose herself," Blanche said. "I think we all need some time to process the twists and turns of this eventful evening."

"She's not a threat to us," Vee pointed out. "She's tiny, and she's not going to hurt anyone."

"That young woman is a *killer*!" Herman said.

"Even if that's true," Dorothy interjected, "she can't kill all of us."

"That's right," Sophia said. "There's more of us than her. Safety in numbers."

"One, two, three, four . . ." Rose whispered to herself.

Blanche turned to Rose with an incredulous expression on her face. "What in heaven's name are you doing?" Blanche said.

"Sophia just said there's safety in numbers!" Rose said. "Twenty-seven, forty-two, nineteen, six . . ."

"I think we should lock her up," said Herman.

"Where's she going to go? We're stuck on this island!" Sophia said.

"Why are you defending her?" Herman said, pounding the heel of one hand into the palm of the other. "Misia had unique permission to enter El Toro's studio as his assistant. She could have at any time had a chance to kill him! And she had ample time to commit the murder, as she wasn't with us every moment on the day El Toro died."

"Because I was running around waiting on you all!" Misia said. "You know, serving food, drinks, bringing everyone coffee, setting up, cleaning up, finding more candles. I wouldn't have had time to kill him, even if I wanted to!"

The younger woman had a point, Blanche had to admit. Misia was constantly on the move, taking orders from Declan like the Cinderella of Villa Velado.

Misia shook her head, her face pinched and angry.

"You also had motive," Herman said, pointing to the vision board. "You wanted to be a great artist and you were jealous of El Toro's success!"

Blanche glanced at the vision board quotations, which, on second thought, *did* look similar in nature to the death threats. She was about to share this thought aloud, but then stopped herself. Those notes had the individual letters cut out, not whole words like this. Rather than potentially make things worse—and raise the temperature of the room even higher—she figured she'd wait until she had a chance to discuss it with her friends.

She also wondered why Dorothy was going so easy on Misia. Blanche couldn't exactly ask her in front of everyone. Did she suspect someone else? Or did she feel for the poor girl? And even after being confronted by all the evidence against her, Misia hadn't admitted anything, which made Blanche even more confused. At the end of most of the murder mysteries on TV, the killer usually confessed, the pieces all fell into place, and everyone breathed a sigh of relief.

But that's not what this feels like, she thought.

"Let's take a vote on it," Dorothy said. "All in favor of everyone going back to their rooms and locking their doors until tomorrow morning, raise your hand."

Blanche, Rose, Sophia, and Dorothy raised their hands, as did Vee and Ralph. Akiko hesitantly raised hers, and Herman's remained rigidly at his sides.

"Luis, what about you?" Dorothy asked.

"I want to get to the bottom of this," he said. "I have more questions for Misia and all of you. No way am I just going to go to bed!"

"I suppose Misia is abstaining," Blanche said, as Misia dropped her head onto her knees and continued crying into her crossed arms.

"Listen to me," Sophia said. "I'm the oldest one here, so I have seniority. It's late, tensions are running high, and I need to lie down in bed before my ankles swell up like grapefruits. If you think things look rough now, imagine me without my beauty sleep!"

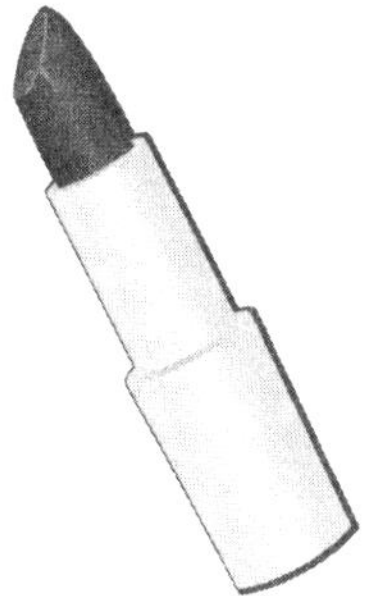

MIRROR, MIRROR, ON THE WALL, WHO'S THE GUILTIEST OF THEM ALL?

22

After hustling her companions into their room, Dorothy locked the door. Blanche dragged over the chair they'd used to wedge against the doorknob the previous night.

"We can't be too careful," Blanche said. "We're still trapped here with a killer."

"Good idea—let's not take any chances," Sophia said. "I'm desperate for a good night's sleep, and I don't want it disturbed by someone trying to attack you idiots."

"Aren't you scared for yourself?" Rose asked.

"Eh, I sleep like the dead—meaning I look dead when I'm asleep, meaning the murderer will think they got a freebie."

"Not funny, Ma," Dorothy said. She kicked off her shoes and sat at the edge of the bed. She'd gotten blisters on the backs of her heels, and her legs ached from all of the flights of stairs they'd climbed. "I'm just as tired as you, but after the day we've had, I have more questions than answers."

"Do you really think Misia did it?" Rose asked.

"All signs point to yes," Blanche said. "But I'm not sure. Perhaps my judgment is clouded because I felt sorry for her, getting ordered around all the time."

"I'm also not convinced that she's the killer," Dorothy said. "But like you I'm not sure why. We've got to figure out who killed El Toro, in a rational way, not just because we have some vague funny feelings."

"We could sing Ring Around the Rooster," Rose suggested.

"This isn't the schoolyard, Rose," said Blanche. "This is serious."

"Of course it's not a schoolyard game!" Rose chided. "Do you think that's how we would elect the St. Olaf mayor if it were? It's quite solemn when all the candidates line up in the town square so we can sing the song in unison and land on the last 'cock-a-doodle-doo' for the winner."

Dorothy couldn't help herself. "Wouldn't you just stand in the spot you know would end with 'cock-a-doodle-doo'?"

Rose's jaw dropped. "Now, Dorothy, I'm surprised at you! Politics is *serious*—and that would be *cheating*!"

"Can we please get back to the matter at hand?" Blanche said. "A man is dead, and we've got a very guilty-looking young woman just one floor down from us!"

"Right," Dorothy said. "Where can we write things down?" Her salsa flyer was already filled with notes, and she hadn't thought to grab any paper from the rest of the house. She wished she had the large blackboard from her classroom to write on. Dorothy glanced around the room, her eye catching on the antique bureau with a huge ornate mirror hung above it.

"Everyone, give me some lipstick," Dorothy said.

"Oh, honey," Blanche said. "We're not going back downstairs. And I don't think any of the men here are interested in you at all."

"We're not going to wear it; we're going to write with it," Dorothy said, gesturing to the mirror. "We're going to map out everything we know and see if it truly leads to Misia. And thank you for pointing out yet again that you think I'm some sort of man-repeller!"

"I'm not saying you're a man-repeller," Blanche said, rummaging in her purse. She pulled out three different lipsticks. "It's just that . . . well, you could soften your tone a little bit when dealing with members of the masculine persuasion."

"My *tone?*" Dorothy growled.

"Yes, that's the one," Blanche said in a singsong voice.

Dorothy scoffed. "We're not here to make friends," she said. "We're trying to catch a killer!"

"And I'm trying not to get killed!" Blanche said. "Declan

was a strong, robust man—and he was struck down! So what chance does a dainty little flower like me have? We have to tread lightly. And you know the saying, you catch more flies—"

"In a jar!" Rose said. "And you should cut holes in the top so they don't suffocate."

Dorothy grimaced. "You catch more flies with *honey*, Rose." She hated to admit it, but in these particular circumstances, Blanche just might be right about a gentle approach.

"We have a saying like that in St. Olaf," Rose said. "You catch more fish with a net."

"As opposed to what, dear?" Dorothy said, trying to quash the annoyance in her voice. She didn't want another citation from the tone police.

"As opposed to your bare hands! It's just so much easier," Rose explained.

Sophia knocked on the mirror, making everyone jump. "Ahem! I'm not getting any younger here. We have a bunch of clues, a likely suspect, and I have a date with Paul Newman in my dreams."

"Thanks, Ma. Here's how I see it," Dorothy said, grabbing one of Blanche's lipsticks. She uncapped it and started writing on the mirror.

"Wait, not that one! It's Chanel," Blanche said, handing Dorothy two different tubes. "These are CoverGirl."

"Thank you. Anything written in—" Dorothy checked the bottom of the lipstick tube. Since she didn't have her reading glasses, she had to hold it a foot and a half away from her to see the fine print. "Sienna Sunset . . . is everything we know."

She listed the names of each suspect along the top of the mirror in a brownish-red shade. "Everything else, in Rose Rapture, is what we still don't know."

The four women took turns, writing out details and questions under each name with boxes labeled *Motive*, *Opportunity*, and *Means*. By the time they were done, the mirror was a riot of red and pink lines, with a few stick figures drawn by Rose to illustrate each suspect. Only a few of the boxes remained empty.

"It looks like everyone had nearly similar amounts of opportunity," Dorothy mused. "We've all been cooped up together, with very few chances for someone to sneak off by themselves to commit a murder."

"But you and Sophia were able to sneak away," Rose pointed out.

"True," said Sophia. "And there was not much time between when we last saw El Toro and when he bought the farm."

Blanche visibly stiffened.

"I'm sorry, Blanche," Sophia said. "I mean, when he went to the great museum in the sky. Is that better?"

"I don't expect you to understand my grief," Blanche said.

"You barely knew him!" Sophia said. "Sorry if I'm being insensitive."

"He was a wonderful man." Blanche sniffed. "Talented, passionate, with an eye for true beauty."

"But you'd only just remembered he existed yesterday," Sophia said.

Blanche nodded. "That's true," she said. "But he was a part of my youth. Now that he's gone, I feel like that part of me—young, carefree, with all of Manhattan wrapped around my little finger—is gone, too."

"Oh, Blanche, your youth is not gone," said Rose. "It's just in the distant past."

Blanche scowled.

"Ahem," Dorothy said, tapping at the bureau mirror. "We still don't have much information about Luis, other than his professional interest in El Toro and the theory that he could make his career by engineering a huge scoop about a famous artist's murder. We have Misia, who has two substantial pieces of evidence against her, but something feels a bit off. I can't put my finger on it."

"Why don't you think it's her?" Blanche said. "I thought she might have confessed once we found that shoe, but she didn't."

"And the paintings," Rose said. "Don't forget about those. Herman seemed very excited since he'd been trying to track them down for a while."

"She clammed up tighter than a witness to a mob hit," Sophia said.

"She's smart," Dorothy said. "She's not wrong to wait for a lawyer, whether she's guilty or innocent."

"How could a young woman afford those paintings on an assistant's salary, even before they went up in value?" Blanche said.

"Good question," Dorothy said, adding it to the list.

"And why were those buyers' names familiar?" Sophia said. "I know they're made up, but something about them rings a bell."

"Something else is bothering me," Rose said. "If you did get some of that mixture on your shoe, wouldn't you clean if off? If she's so smart, she wouldn't want to be tracking it everywhere, like the time my cousin Gustave stepped in a cow patty on the way to school. He stunk up the whole classroom! Needless to say, we didn't learn very much that day."

"Or any other day," Blanche murmured. "But, still, it's a good point. I'm surprised we didn't notice any other footprints in the studio."

"You're both on to something," Dorothy said. "Even if only part of Misia's high top landed in the varnish, it would have left at least some marks on the floor itself." Dorothy picked up the salsa flyer, checking her notes and drawings. "I didn't see anything like that, did you, Ma?"

"Nope," Sophia said. "Not when we snuck in on our own the first time, and not when we all went in together the last time. Then again, we could have missed them. We didn't exactly know what to look for."

"Maybe it doesn't matter about the tracks," Blanche said. "They would have led to Misia's room anyway, because that's where the shoe was. Right in her closet."

"She must not have realized that she stepped in that gunk," Sophia said.

"But wouldn't there still be tracks?" Dorothy said. She remembered how Stan would leave trails of mud and dirt all over their house in the winter, completely oblivious to the fact that he'd stepped in anything at all. It had taken Dorothy years to realize that Stan was allergic to using a doormat, cleaning the sink after he shaved, and the concept of monogamy. "If there weren't, what does that mean?"

"Maybe she cleaned them up, but forgot to clean her shoes. Or maybe she didn't make that footprint after all," Sophia said.

"What if somebody else did?" Dorothy asked.

"You're saying someone took her shoe and dipped it into the goo without her knowing?" Blanche said, raising her eyebrows sky-high.

"Maybe El Toro's paintings aren't the only thing being framed in this villa," Sophia said.

"An interesting theory," Dorothy said, stroking her chin.

"You sound like Herman," Rose joked.

"But how would someone get into Misia's room, which I presume was locked, and into Declan's studio, which was also locked, and protected by the webbing of tape?" Dorothy asked.

The girls sat in silence for a few minutes, stumped.

"I really don't know," Sophia said. "But if you think the shoe was planted, do you think the paintings were, too?"

"It's possible," Dorothy said. "What do you all think?"

"I think she knew about the paintings," Blanche said. "I was watching her. She didn't act shocked that they were in her room."

Dorothy nodded thoughtfully. It was helpful to have all four of them to brainstorm about this case. In fact, she thought, working together made everything easier. . . .

"What if the killer didn't do it alone?" Dorothy said. "What if they had help?"

"You mean more than one person here might be involved?" Rose said.

"Maybe. Are there any people who seem closer than others?" Dorothy said.

"Ralph and Misia are both in similar roles as Declan's employees and have worked with each other for a while," Blanche pointed out.

"And Ralph keeps sticking up for Misia," Rose added. "Of course, it could just mean that they're friends."

"Or that they're in cahoots!" Sophia said.

"And Vee and Akiko know each other from the art scene," Dorothy mused. "Same with Herman."

"Luis is the biggest mystery," Blanche said. "He doesn't seem to have previous ties to anyone else here. Maybe I should get close to him tomorrow and see what's going on behind those sexy aviators."

"You just want to get close to him because he's young and handsome," Sophia said.

"So what if he is?" Blanche said. "I wouldn't let that cloud my judgment. I've barely noticed his chiseled cheekbones or his broad shoulders."

"Maybe you can find out what else he was going to put in his article," Dorothy said. "He kept that death threat detail from all of us for a while, so he may be sitting on some other helpful information we can use."

"Aye, aye," Blanche said. "And maybe Rose can do the same with Herman. Just use your feminine wiles."

"I'll try," Rose said. "But I'm *not* sleeping with him! I'm okay with some hanky-panky to get to the truth, but I have to draw the line somewhere."

"No one is saying you should sleep with him, Rose," Dorothy said. "Just flirt with him a little and find out what's in his notebook."

"I can do that!" Rose said, her shoulders sagging with relief. "Besides, I don't have the number of handkerchiefs *or* the pancakes I'd really need for hanky-panky."

"Okay . . ." Dorothy said. "That leaves Vee and Akiko."

"I'll take Akiko, because she's short, and you take Vee, because she's tall," Sophia said. "That way we're more likely to see eye to eye."

"Don't forget Ralph and Misia," Rose said.

"There are more of them than us," Blanche said, falling backward on the bed with an exhausted sigh.

"We'll just have to do our best—at least until we can get back to the mainland. And, Ma, I'm a little nervous about you going off to talk to anyone on your own after what happened with the brooch, so let's you and me stick together."

For the next two hours, Dorothy scrutinized the notes on the mirror while Blanche, Rose, and Sophia took very short, very cold showers and got ready for bed. She knew there were connections she was missing, questions they hadn't yet even thought to ask. All the evidence so far pointed to Misia. On top of the fishy footprint, the hidden paintings were very suspicious.

"Come to bed, pussycat," Sophia called. "You can have the cot tonight. I'll share with Tweedledum and Fiddledeedee."

Dorothy smiled gratefully and lay down on the cot, scrunching up her long legs so that she'd fit. Just as she was about to drift off to the sound of her mother's whistling snores, an inhuman, primal scream jolted her fully awake.

"It's probably that crocodile Ralph raised," Rose said as she hopped out of the bed and opened the window. "Good night, Elizabeth Taylor!" she shouted.

PEEPING TOM, DICK, OR HARRY

23

After a tumultuous night of tossing and turning between Rose and Sophia, Blanche awoke glistening with sweat. Probably because they'd slept with the window closed, and definitely not for any biological reason, she told herself. She'd had only fitful sleep, her dreams more like commercial breaks instead of the cinematic episodes she was used to. In one dream, she was helping Big Daddy file important papers in his office after church as he took discreet nips of whiskey. *You've got to look beneath the surface*, he said, stretching his long legs onto his roll-top desk. In another, she was dressed in a chicken costume, ballroom dancing with Fidel Santiago. And her final dream before waking was of a young Declan, painting in his Greenwich Village studio. *Help me*, he said, then smeared a hand across his face, the streaks of paint shining like blood.

When she sat up in bed, she found that Rose was sucking her thumb and that Sophia had stolen Blanche's pillow.

"I had the oddest dreams last night," Blanche said, nudging her friends awake. They'd certainly enjoy hearing about the one with the chicken costume, and she loved sharing her more colorful dreams with her friends and hearing their interpretations.

"Me too," Rose said, rubbing the sleep from her eyes. "I dreamed that Herman Price was right here in this room, watching us as we slept!"

"That's rather creepy," Dorothy said, rousing herself from the cot.

"It sure was," said Rose. "I almost called out, but then I realized it was only a dream. But it was so realistic! He was standing right here." Rose stood up and walked to the far corner of the room. She gestured to the decorative wall panel, then placed her hand upon it. "And—"

Suddenly the panel swung open with a low creak, emitting a gust of dusty air into the room. Rose gaped at her friends, and they gaped right back.

"What in heaven's name?" Blanche said, jumping out of bed and scurrying over to the opening.

"Has that been here the whole time?" Rose asked, her eyes as round as Frisbees.

"I suppose so," said Dorothy, eyeballing the hidden door. "Another secret passage, just like the one leading from the library to El Toro's hidden gallery."

"Oh my!" Rose said. "If there's a secret entrance here—does that mean that my dream was real?"

Blanche thought a moment. Usually the idea of a strange man creeping into her bedroom gave her a hot, tingly feeling all over. Sometimes she even fantasized about a robber coming to steal her jewelry, who, when faced with her beauty, forgets his criminal intentions, reforms into a true Southern gentleman, and falls passionately in love with her. Another favorite of Blanche's featured a fireman wrapping his soot-stained arms around her lithe form to carry her out her bedroom window as she swooned against his pectoral muscles. But now she only felt chills up her spine, and not the good kind.

"It's possible," Dorothy said. "Didn't Herman say he had the blueprints to the house?"

"Then he'd know about the passageways, and how to get to our room. It's no secret he has the hots for Rose," Blanche said.

"Yuck," Rose said. "I feel so exposed! This is worse than the time my underwear slid down my pantleg during St. Olaf's annual Cod-Calling Tournament."

"How in the world did that happen?" Dorothy asked.

"Do you really wanna know?" Sophia said. "The point is, that guy's a creep."

"You may be right," Blanche agreed. "I thought his interest in Rose was sweet, if a bit misguided. If that was really him, then I think we should steer clear."

"But last night you told me to get close to him so I could pump him for information!" Rose said.

"You'll have to be careful," Blanche said, stepping past Rose to push the secret door open wider. "And if he gets fresh with you, just tell him no means no."

"A swift kick in the arancini works, too," said Sophia.

Blanche peered into the dark space with a mix of curiosity and familiarity. There had been a few hidden passages at her childhood home of Twin Oaks, born out of the prohibition days when her ancestors would hide crates of bootleg liquor away from prying eyes.

"I wonder where it leads. And how many of these does this house have?" Blanche said, her nose twitching from the dust.

"There's only one way to find out," Dorothy said.

"Are you sure that's a good idea?" Sophia said. "Maybe we should focus on getting off this island, rather than, I don't know, farther inside its dark, mysterious corridors?"

"It's so dusty—and covered in cobwebs!" Rose said, peeking through the door.

"It's a rarely used passageway," Dorothy said. "A few cobwebs never hurt anyone."

"Is that what you tell the men you bring home?" Blanche joked.

"Put a sock in it," Sophia said to Blanche. "You've made enough cracks at my daughter's expense this weekend."

"Thanks for sticking up for me, Ma," Dorothy said.

Sophia winked. "It's *my* God-given right as a mother to tease you, not hers."

Blanche was about to make another dig just to spite Sophia when she noticed Dorothy's face. Her friend's shoulders drooped, and her face had taken on an exhausted pallor. *Maybe I've gone a little too far and it's taking a toll on her*, Blanche thought. Or maybe it was the lack of sleep, horrible lighting, and strain of a murder investigation.

"I think we should see where it goes," Blanche said. "In my dreams last night, Big Daddy told me to 'look beneath the surface.' I think this counts."

The girls quickly changed out of their makeshift pajamas and slipped on their shoes. They each grabbed a candlestick, plus two glass hurricane holders, and Blanche lit them with a matchbook from El Cid that she'd found in her purse.

Blanche stepped carefully into the murky passage. The light from the candles barely illuminated two feet ahead of her. She dragged her fingers against the wood-paneled inner wall to help orient and steady herself as she led the way, hoping that she wouldn't dislodge any spiders—or any vermin. Who knew what lurked in the walls of this estate, cut off from the mainland and covered in vines? A few yards ahead, a faint patch of light cut across the darkness.

As she approached it, she realized the light was actually from an interior window with a view of an empty bedroom.

"This must be one-way glass," Blanche whispered. "The other side's probably a mirror."

"Your old boyfriend must have been quite the voyeur," Sophia quipped.

"I'm sure he was *not*," Blanche said indignantly. Declan hadn't needed to resort to spying on women to get an eyeful. All he had to do back then was unfurl one of his sultry smiles or a sly wink—or ask them to pose for him. "He might not even have known about all this."

"I'm sure he was aware of these passages," Dorothy said. "Remember, Herman said he got the villa's blueprints from him."

Something about the hidden passageways gnawed at Blanche as they walked. It wasn't that shocking that an old mansion would have them. Plenty of old homes in the South still had hideaways from the bootlegging days. Big Daddy's entreaty continued to echo in her head, and she felt in her bones that they were on the right track, but they were still a few side dishes short of a barbecue.

"Who else could have known about this?" Blanche said.

"Herman, apparently," said Rose. "And El Toro. I don't think Ralph and Misia do."

"What about Luis?" Sophia said. "He might have had access to historical documents like blueprints at the newspaper. Or at least he'd know where to find them."

"Good point," Blanche said. "When I cozy up to him, I'll try to find out."

"How about Vee or Akiko?" Dorothy said. "Could they have known about these passageways?"

Blanche thought a moment. "I don't know, but I got the impression that it was their first time at the villa. It was the way they were gawking at everything, same as us."

Then the four women rounded a corner and found themselves at an intersection illuminated by a grimy skylight above, facing two corridors branching off and a set of steps going down. All three passageways were forebodingly dark beyond their candlelight.

"Let's go down the stairs," Blanche said. "The only other rooms up here are empty."

"Let me go first," Sophia said. "That way, if I slip, I won't take the rest of you out like a set of human bowling pins."

"Someone else should go first," Dorothy said. "Like Blanche."

Blanche stiffened.

"Why should I go first?" She wasn't scared exactly, but skulking around in the dark wasn't her forte, not unless there was a man waiting with champagne in an ice bucket and Johnny Mathis on the stereo.

"Because you're the reason we're even here, stuck in the middle of all of this," said Rose. "Instead of coming to this party, we could've gone to the movies, or rearranged our sock drawers, or cleaned the lint trap in the dryer."

"She's got a point." Dorothy laughed.

Blanche huffed. Sure, they were in the middle of a murder investigation, but didn't they have a nice time before that?

"You all wanted to get dressed up and see the inside of this mysterious mansion, don't you forget it," she said, shaking a finger at Rose.

"I suppose that's true," Rose said. "Before it ran out, the food was pretty good."

"That's the spirit," said Blanche. "Let's look on the bright side."

"And the room we're staying in *is* rather elegant," Dorothy said. "Even if it only has one bed and a hidden door for perverts."

"Dorothy, I think you should go first," Blanche said. "Sophia's far too senior, I'm too dainty, and Rose is . . . well, would you want Rose leading anyone in a life-or-death situation? You're the tallest and have the most brute strength."

Dorothy glowered at Blanche. "Being tall doesn't mean I'm some sort of beast. I'll have you know that I've been compared to a young Lauren Bacall!"

"It was your own *mother* who said that about you," Blanche said. "It doesn't count."

"Girls!" Rose cried. "What does anyone's physical appearance have to do with any of this? We're trying to solve a murder!"

"And get off this godforsaken island," Sophia said. "Blanche, you need to apologize to Dorothy so we can move on."

Blanche bristled. They were in a stressful situation and she didn't have time to think about everyone else's feelings. Not to mention that on plenty of occasions, she'd heard Dorothy dish it out as well.

But they couldn't spend all day bickering, and she truly hadn't meant to hurt her friend.

"Fine! I'll go first," she said. "It's not like there's anything— Ahhh!" Blanche shrieked as a small, furry creature whirled around her legs and brushed against her ankles. "Was that a—a rat?"

Blanche quavered. She scratched her legs, which had instantly started itching. *What if it had fleas?*

"That was a big one, if it was," Sophia said as the sound of nails scrabbling on the wooden floor receded in the distance. "Haven't seen ones that size since my tenement days in Brooklyn. . . . Wait . . . *Pssst*, King Whiskers, is that you?"

"I didn't smell a rat," Rose said. "And that's a talent I've honed since my first Little Miss St. Olaf Pageant. Of course, in later years I placed higher in cooking a goose and in opening a can of worms."

Blanche recovered her footing—and her composure. She

remembered Declan's face in her dream, imploring her for help. And Big Daddy—well, he never let anything stop him. If there was a fox in their henhouse, he'd say, "Baby girl, sometimes you gotta do the tough stuff," and then he'd roll up his elegant sleeves and chase it away with a broom.

Blanche swallowed, trying to clear the lump in her throat. Big Daddy wasn't around anymore to encourage her. And Declan was gone now, too. Blanche didn't like doing the tough stuff even on her best day, but she certainly couldn't do it all alone.

"Are you okay?" Rose said, putting a soft hand on Blanche's shoulder. Blanche grasped it, and then fumbled around for Dorothy's. She wasn't alone, she realized. She was with her friends. And with their help, they could get through this together.

"Why are you three standing around in the dark holding hands? It's too early in the day to summon a demon," Sophia said.

Blanche smiled. "I just realized how lucky I am to have my good friends around at a time like this."

"Friends?" Dorothy intoned, yanking her hand out of Blanche's. "I've downgraded you to 'streetwalker I happen to pay rent to,' after the comments you've made all weekend."

"Oh, Dorothy, I'm so sorry," Blanche said, hearing the hurt in Dorothy's voice. "I've been jumpier than a cat on a hot tin roof since losing Declan. And I guess I've been taking it out on you especially." She reached for Dorothy's hand again and squeezed it, hoping her friend would know that her apology was sincere.

Blanche took a deep breath. She could follow Big Daddy's example and be brave—for Declan's sake, and for her friends.

"Come on, girls. I'll lead the way. Let's see what we can find out!"

JEEPERS PEEPERS

24

As Dorothy followed Blanche, Rose, and Sophia down the dark steps, she hoped they wouldn't trip and fall—especially her mother. Mostly because she knew that whenever Sophia was laid up, it tickled her too much to ring a little silver bell and call Dorothy to wait on her hand and foot. Dorothy gripped the back of Sophia's elbow. She would not give her the satisfaction of ringing that little bell.

Soon they reached the second floor and followed a musty hall toward the next patch of light. The girls clustered around another pane of one-way glass, this time revealing a view of Ralph's bedroom, which was empty except for his collection of reptiles. Angela Lansbury turned to the mirror as if she could sense the girls watching through the glass. She blinked slowly at them.

"Nothing to see here," Blanche said, hurrying on to the next room.

This one-way glass was clearly part of a built-in vanity mirror, and Dorothy peered past makeup and art paraphernalia to see Misia slumped on her bed. As she wiped her eyes with a tissue, Ralph gently patted her back.

"What do you think they're saying?" Dorothy whispered.

"Maybe they're having an affair," Blanche said. "They could be in on the crime together."

"I'm pretty sure he's a friend of Dorothy's," Sophia said.

"But Dorothy never met him before this weekend," Rose said, confused.

"Different Dorothy," Dorothy said. "She thinks he's like Blanche's brother."

"But what do Dorothy's friend and Blanche's brother have to do with it?" Rose said.

"Sophia's saying Ralph here might not swing our way, sweetie," Blanche said. "Do I need to spell it out for you?"

"Aha," said Rose, with a knowing smile. "Like our old friend Coco! Gosh, I wonder how he's doing."

Misia and Ralph suddenly stopped speaking and peered around as if they'd heard something. Rose covered her mouth with her hand and the girls immediately quieted. When they resumed their conversation, they were more cautious.

"Can you hear anything?" Dorothy whispered.

"He's comforting her," Rose said. "And he's just so sweet with his pets, I find it hard to believe he's up to no good."

Dorothy wasn't sure what to believe as they continued down the passage. Was Misia upset because she'd been falsely accused of a crime? Or was she crying because she'd been caught? Was Ralph simply a kind friend and coworker, or were they in cahoots?

They scurried to the window into the next room, which revealed Luis fast asleep in his bed with one bare shoulder visible above the covers. Dorothy peered over the heads of her friends, noticing a narrow glimmer of gray coming in at Blanche's roots. *Father Time comes for us all*, Dorothy thought to herself and chuckled inwardly. She wondered if she should tell Blanche that it was time for a touch-up, or let her find out for herself.

"I'm curious if he sleeps in the nude," said Blanche, licking her lips. "Or maybe he's got on boxer briefs?"

"You're just as bad as Herman," Dorothy chided.

"That's right, you don't want to come off like a Peeping Agnes," Rose said.

"The phrase is Peeping *Tom*, Rose," Dorothy said gently. Correcting Rose was a Sisyphean task, but the teacher in her couldn't help but try.

"Says who? In St. Olaf, a Peeping Agnes is a baby chick

who watches you sleep," Rose explained. "Then she goes *peep peep peep* when it's time to wake up."

"Let's keep moving. If I stand still any longer, my knees will end up stiffer than the stiff down the hall." Sophia clapped a hand over her own mouth. "Sorry, Blanche."

Dorothy prodded Blanche, then prodded her again until she finally tore her gaze away from Luis's sleeping form. He was even more handsome without his glasses, Dorothy noticed, though she refrained from saying so out loud.

The view into the next room was partially obstructed by a vase, a lamp, and a fedora.

"This one's Herman's," Blanche whispered. "Come look!"

"It's empty," Rose said. "He must be an early riser, like us."

Dorothy ran her finger along a crack in the wall and was surprised to discover that a section of the wall moved ever so slightly. She stepped back, holding her candle higher to get a better view.

"Ladies, I think we have something here," she whispered. "Another secret door!"

"Where do you think it goes?" Rose asked.

"Presumably right into the room we're looking at," Dorothy said. Perhaps they should take Rose to see a specialist, she thought.

"To paraphrase our little Swiss friend," Blanche said, "most interesting."

"I'll say," said Sophia. "This house holds more secrets than the confessional at St. Mary's."

"Let's take advantage of this opportunity and see what we can find out," Dorothy said. She pulled the hidden door until it swung open. The acrid scent of woodsmoke filled her nose as they crept inside.

"Look!" Rose pointed to a leather briefcase on a tufted armchair.

The girls clustered together and crept quietly over to the chair, fearful of being discovered snooping. Rose opened the briefcase as the others peered over her shoulders. Pulling out a small black sketchbook, she flipped through it to reveal a series of pencil sketches, many of which looked familiar to Dorothy. Each one was heavily annotated with descriptions of brushwork, technique, and dimensions, with swatches of paint colors along the edges of the pages.

"Do you recognize these?" Dorothy asked the group.

"They all look like paintings Declan has done," Blanche said. "It's almost like Herman was making a study of each one."

"Is that typical for an insurance appraiser?" Dorothy asked.

Blanche frowned. "I'm not sure. I suppose it could be part of his process of authentication. Or maybe he has aspirations of being an artist himself?"

"Why does it stink in here?" Sophia asked, holding a section of Blanche's coral dress up over her nose. "I can hardly breathe!"

"You're right," Blanche said. "It's worse than a smokehouse in here!"

Dorothy stepped over to the fireplace and rummaged

through the pile of cinders with a small iron poker. Chunks of ash fell away to reveal a few half-melted white shapes.

"These look like shirt buttons," Dorothy said. "Don't they?"

The others nodded.

"Why would he have put a shirt in the fireplace?" Rose said. "Do you think he was trying to dry it after handwashing?"

Before Dorothy could answer, the sound of footsteps over a hardwood floor emanated from the hall. She drew a finger to her lips as the footsteps stopped right by the door. The girls quickly turned and tiptoed through the secret door and back into the hidden passageway. Dorothy pulled it shut behind them, just as the guest room door began to swing open.

The four women stared at one another and tried to control their breathing as they recovered from the close call. Dorothy was too scared to look through the window and verify who had come in, but she assumed it was Herman. After her heart rate finally slowed, she realized she was still holding Herman's sketchbook. Not knowing what else to do, she shoved it inside one of her loose-fitting sleeves and pinned her arm to her chest to hold it in place. Then she nudged her friends down the passageway. The girls tried to muffle the sounds of their shoes so as not to attract attention. After all, Herman knew about the secret corridors, so he was much more likely to pinpoint the source of any unusual noises, and Dorothy sure didn't want to explain what they were up to.

Shortly, they came to another window and stopped to peer through it. They had a clear view of an empty canopied bed and Vee's silver dress flung over the back of a striped armchair. The bedsheets were twisted and tossed to one side, as if she'd had a fitful sleep. Dorothy scanned as much of the room as she could see but found nothing out of the ordinary among the antique furnishings.

They reached the end of the hall and the final window. Inside, Akiko slept, surrounded by crumpled tissues as if she'd cried herself to sleep. *Were they tears of sadness, or of guilt?* Dorothy wondered. Either way, El Toro had touched so many lives through his life and his work, and Dorothy felt a little small in comparison. Well, not small exactly, since everyone had been making jokes about her height and shoe size all weekend. Even though Blanche had apologized for her comments, and Dorothy knew that she was a good-looking woman, she was beginning to feel like the Ugly Duckling once again.

Dorothy tried to brush the negative thoughts from her mind as quickly as she'd sweep wilted flower petals from their lanai back on Richmond Street. She wasn't one for self-pity, but she had to remind herself that there was more to life than one's physical appearance. And what was so bad about her height? *Ingrid Bergman was tall, and so was Charlotte Greenwood*, she told herself. Yet Dorothy couldn't help but wonder: What if she had been born more petite, like her mother? Would she have been happier?

She imagined herself shrinking like Alice in Wonderland, getting smaller and smaller until she was shorter than Blanche and Rose, until she was the same height as Sophia. She saw herself disconcertingly shrunk down to size, with diminutive hands and feet—and a voice as tinny as Steamboat Willie's.

She shook the disturbing image from her head. Playing small was *not* for her. Dorothy made a vow to herself right then and there: Once they got home, she would take in a performance at the Philharmonic or the Coconut Grove Playhouse. Maybe she could find a good lecture to attend at the University of Miami—anything to feed her mind and prevent it from dwelling on superficial insecurities.

"What do you say, shall we go down to the first floor, or head back to our room and regroup?" Dorothy asked.

"I say head back," Sophia said. "My bunions are killing me and my throat is dustier than the plastic ferns at Shady Pines."

"Me too," said Rose. "We don't know why there were buttons in Herman's fireplace, or if that has any connection with the contents of his sketchbook. And we need to come up with a new game plan, based on everything we've seen."

"Very astute, Rose," Sophia said. "I'm surprised."

"You all think just because I'm a wide-eyed tenderfoot with a childlike sense of wonder, often confused about how the world works, who doesn't really understand why nine dimes are worth less than four quarters that I'm dumb, is that it?" Rose demanded.

"Pretty much," Blanche quipped.

"Well, I know a thing or two! Maybe even three," Rose said, shaking a finger at her friends. "And I know there's a lot more going on here than we've bargained for."

"You're right, Rose," Dorothy said. She thought back to some of her favorite crime novels and their fictional sleuths: Spade, Wimsey, even Marple. What would they focus on in this situation? Dorothy and her friends still had a lot of suspects, a variety of motives, but not a lot of clear answers. She peered through the gloom at the notes on her salsa dancing flyer. So many questions, and they had answers, or partial answers to some of them. But one word jumped out at her, underlined twice: *WILL*.

"Remember last night when Herman was asking us all how we'd benefit from El Toro's death?" Dorothy said, raising her eyebrows.

"Why yes," Blanche said. "It was very ungentlemanly of him to accuse me—I mean, any of us."

"Akiko mentioned something about a will," Dorothy said. "Then we got sidetracked."

"A will would certainly tell us who'd directly benefit from his death," Blanche said, tapping her chin as she thought. "But it would only really make sense if that person knew they were in it, and what they were getting."

"That's why I change mine once a month. Gotta keep my offspring on their toes," Sophia said.

"We've got to find that will," Dorothy said. "Blanche, any ideas where your old flame would keep something like that?"

"I sure do," Blanche said suddenly, pushing in front of Dorothy. "I think he'd keep personal things somewhere . . . personal. Follow me!"

WHERE THERE'S A WILL, THERE'S A SUSPECT

25

Blanche led the girls back through the secret passageways to the opposite end of the villa.

"There's one place we haven't looked at all," she said. "Declan's bedroom. I would assume that the main bedroom would be connected to these corridors, or else why have them? They're perfect for midnight trysts."

"Are we almost there?" Sophia grumbled. "If I don't get something to eat soon, I might start gnawing on Rose here."

After a few moments, they spotted an offshoot hallway they hadn't noticed before. "Come on, it must be this way."

"Blanche, how on earth do you know your way around this mansion so well?" Dorothy asked.

"What," Sophia said, "you think it's the first time she's roamed through a strange man's house?"

Blanche gave her friends a sly smile. "I guess I just have an uncanny knack for knowing where a man's bedroom is."

They followed a twisting path and reached a solid wall at the end, with no one-way glass window in sight.

"He probably covered up any way to peek into his own room," Blanche said. She ran her fingers along the dusty wall. "But I feel something here!"

She gave the wooden panel a hard shove and practically tumbled into a dark bedroom. She clicked on a battery-powered lamp made of glass blocks, illuminating a room covered in hand-painted wallpaper that looked almost like graffiti. An artistic mobile made of recycled bicycle parts hung from the ceiling. When Blanche saw the king-size mattress on the floor in one corner of the room, she pressed a hand to her mouth and stifled a sob. Even though he'd become world famous and could certainly have afforded a real bed, in some ways Declan hadn't changed.

Then she smiled again when she noticed a painting hung above the bed, a portrait of herself, turned to the side, wearing a blue turban and a lustrous pearl earring. *Wait a minute*, she thought.

"Didn't we already see this painting in Misia's room?" Blanche asked.

Rose, Sophia, and Dorothy crowded around.

"Could he have painted two of them?" Dorothy asked.

"That wasn't really his style," Blanche said. "At least back then."

"I'll make a note of it," Dorothy said. "Everyone, look around for clues." Rose hurried to the bed and shook out the sheets and flipped over the pillows.

"What exactly are you doing?" Blanche said. "That's an odd place to look for clues."

"Well, if I knew *where they were*, I'd start there!" Rose said as Sophia skirted the room.

Sophia stopped by a wooden dresser, on top of which sat a cardboard Bankers Box. "This looks promising," she said.

Dorothy lowered the box to the floor and the four women set their candles aside and pawed through it, discovering bundles of folded-up papers, crumpled receipts, and a pile of business-size envelopes, all mixed up together.

"There must be something useful in here," Dorothy said as she dumped the box out onto the carpeted floor.

Blanche's head swam as she considered the piles of paper. She wasn't sure exactly what they'd found, or what it meant. The papery mess reminded Blanche of the time a famous author had bequeathed crates of documents to the museum when their archivist was on vacation. The head of the museum had tasked Blanche with making sense of it, cataloging it, and preparing it for an exhibition, with only a handful of interns to help her. She'd been chagrined when her boss took credit for Blanche's hard work, but she realized now that the experience was coming in handy.

"Everyone, take a manageable stack and sort it," she said. "Once you've finished a section, report back to me with a summary." As her friends worked, Blanche organized the papers by type, arranging any dated materials in chronological order.

After spending several minutes reading materials and listening to her friends' summaries, Blanche realized that the box held quite a few secrets. Secrets that several people in this villa would prefer to keep hidden. *But would they kill to keep these secrets?*

As she and her friends discussed what they'd found and compared it to what they'd written down in lipstick the night before, threads connected like lovers finding each other across a crowded ballroom.

"We know a lot more than we did yesterday," Blanche said, folding up some of the papers into a neat bundle.

"But we still don't know everything," Rose said.

"Like who the killer is," said Dorothy. "Or what's in El Toro's will."

"Or when we're getting something to eat," grumbled Sophia. "We've got to beat everyone to breakfast or we'll be fighting over the last crust of bread."

"And we'd better get back," Rose said. "Before they all wake up and come looking for us!"

"We need to hang on to these papers," Blanche said. "Here."

She handed a few to Sophia, but her purse was too full to hold anything else. So Blanche handed some to Rose, who shimmied them under her dress until the waistband held them in place, and Dorothy stuck a few in her billowing sleeves.

"Perhaps we should check the library," Blanche said. "I remember it being on the first floor. If we hurry, maybe we can find it!" She folded up the rest of the papers as small as she could and stuffed them into her bra, enjoying the extra cup size that this batch of clues had given her. Then she waved the girls back through Declan's secret door into the passageway. After several moments of wandering, a few dead ends, bruised toes, and muttered insults, they found the hidden staircase again and followed the twisting steps down.

At the bottom of the stairs, their candles finally petered out. Blanche felt around at the wall and gave the bottom of it a hard shove. A wooden panel juddered open into a storage pantry lined with shelves.

"Come on, girls," Blanche whispered as she dipped through the low doorway. Once they all emerged on the other side, she led them tiptoeing past rows of crockery and glassware. Peering through the slats of the outer door into the kitchen, she said softly, "The coast is clear."

The four friends crept through the kitchen, a narrow room with white cabinets and appliances dating back to the Roosevelt administration. Dirty dishes sat piled in the sink and on the counters.

Somebody ought to clean this up, Blanche thought.

The four women hurried through the elegant rooms of the first floor, trying not to wake the rest of the house. When they reached the library, Blanche felt something like butterflies in her stomach, but not the good kind. More like big fat June bugs zipping around under her ribcage as she wondered if they'd able to find Declan's will.

And if they did, what would it say? she wondered. Would she be in it?

"This is the only other place I'd expect Declan to keep his important papers," Blanche said. "Everybody pick a section of the room and start looking!"

Buttery sunlight poured through two tall windows at one end of the library, framing an antique wooden desk in pillars of light. Dorothy and Sophia checked a series of drawers beneath some bookshelves on the other side of the room, and Rose ran her hands over a wooden file cabinet, trying to figure out how to open it. Blanche hurried over and pulled out one of its drawers. The first held pens, pencils, rubber bands, and paper clips. The next held a batch of envelopes, tied together with a red ribbon.

This is promising, Blanche thought.

She undid the ribbon and opened the first envelope. The handwriting was expansive, a few lines filling each page with lots of flourishes, as if written in an artistic hand.

My dearest Declan— the first one began.

Blanche read, her eyes widening with each line as the June

bugs in her stomach whizzed faster and faster. These were love letters, she realized. She flipped over the first letter to jump to the signature: a dramatic *V* inside a heart.

Blanche went through the rest of the letters—all from Vee, though sometimes the heart surrounding her initial was drawn with broken, jagged edges, or dripping drops of blood. Blanche read fragments of each, noticing how the tone changed from exuberant when talking about a new artistic installation, to sensuous when recapping romantic getaways they'd had together, to accusatory and vengeful when she felt he'd wronged her.

Blanche paused for a moment and pinched the bridge of her nose. Of course she knew that Declan would have been with other women throughout his life—just as she'd had a number of romantic adventures with other men. But reading these letters felt like getting a front-row seat to their relationship—even the R-rated parts. Clearly, these letters had meant something to Declan; otherwise, why would he keep them? She turned to the last letter, dated at the tail end of the 1960s. The postmark was from California this time, unlike the New York addresses on the others.

I haven't heard from you in weeks. I can't go on like this, especially with what I'm going through right now. Come to California. If not . . . goodbye—forever.

"What did you find?" Dorothy said over Blanche's shoulder, making her jump.

"These are love letters from Vee to Declan," Blanche said. "I just got a crash course in their whole relationship. Looks like things abruptly ended in the late sixties, when he didn't follow her to California."

Dorothy looked down at the flowing script and frowned. "Is there anything in there that could be a hint about his murder?"

"I'm not sure," Blanche said. "It cements the fact that they had a steamy love affair for many years. But I didn't know it had ended so suddenly, and this last one makes me think that maybe they hadn't spoken again until this weekend."

"So when Vee said she hadn't spoken to Declan in a while, she meant the last twenty years?" Dorothy said.

"Based on these, it's possible," said Blanche. "It sounds like he wasn't there for her when she needed him, or wasn't as invested in the relationship as she was. But still—he kept these letters. All tied up in a bow and everything. That has to mean something, right?"

"He could be sentimental," Dorothy said.

"Or an egomaniac," Rose quipped. "Though I suppose every man imagines he's the greatest thing since sliced Vanskapkaka."

Blanche shook her head, momentarily derailed by Rose's remark, then added, "Lots of important artists have historically been seen as egotistical. There's nothing wrong with having high self-esteem if you're doing something extraordinary."

"Are you talking about yourself again, Blanche?" Dorothy joked.

"It's just a fact," Blanche said, patting her honey-colored waves into place. "Some people are just more special than others."

"It's interesting that they stopped talking about twenty years ago," Rose said. "Since this weekend it seemed like they got along like peanut butter and herring."

"It's true. You all saw the way Vee flung herself at him the other night," Blanche said. "As much as it pains me to admit Declan had other relationships."

"The question is, was this one dangerous?" Dorothy said.

"I don't think so. From what I gathered from Vee's letters, it sounds like they had a tumultuous relationship, more Diego and Frida than anything . . . murderous." Blanche placed the letters back in the drawer and closed it. "I don't feel like we're any closer to finding out what happened to Declan—or what's in his will."

"There's another file cabinet over here!" Rose called from behind a decorative screen. Blanche and Dorothy jogged over, followed by a slower Sophia. Behind the screen, next to a large ficus and under some art nouveau vases, sat an ugly metal file cabinet. Blanche smiled. It was very much like Declan to conceal something so mundane with beautiful objects.

Blanche pulled out each drawer, skimming over file names such as *awards*, *colors to source*, *festivals*, *photographs*, and *publicity*.

"See if there's anything interesting in here," she said, pulling out the one marked *publicity* and handing it to Dorothy.

Blanche yanked open another drawer, this one with various household receipts and papers related to the villa and its utilities. She traced her finger down a line of files and paused on one named *legal documents*.

Jackpot! she thought.

She pulled it out and spread it open on the top of the file cabinet, revealing subfolders for deeds, titles, and one marked *last will and testament*. She pulled it from the file, her heart racing as if she'd swallowed a gallon of Tab.

But the folder was empty.

"It's gone!" Blanche wailed.

"Somebody must have taken it," Sophia said.

Blanche's heart sank. They'd come so far, only to be thwarted by an empty folder.

Dorothy put a reassuring hand on Blanche's shoulder. "I know it was years ago, but can you remember anything at all from your time with Declan that would help us figure out what he would have put in his will?"

"We were so young then! He never mentioned a will. But he always kept a diary," Blanche said, as forgotten memories slowly came back to her. "I remember him scribbling in it late at night when I'd get back from high-kicking with the Rockettes. He never let me read it, though I tried to peek over his shoulder a few times."

"Maybe he kept up that practice," Dorothy said. "He was

a very thoughtful man, it seems. Did any of you see anything that looked like a diary since we've been here?"

"Think, everybody, think!" Blanche cried.

"I got nothin'," Sophia said, lifting her hands in surrender.

"Well, think harder!" Blanche snapped.

Rose frowned in concentration.

"I can practically see the smoke coming out of your ears, Rose," Dorothy said. "Try to use a lower gear."

"Maybe the fluffy little bunnies that live up there are electing a new pope," Sophia cracked as Rose narrowed her eyes.

"I don't think I've seen anything like a diary since we've been here, other than Herman's and Luis's notebooks," Blanche said.

"Think back to New York," Dorothy said. "Do you remember where El Toro kept his diary in that apartment? Maybe he's a creature of habit."

Blanche closed her eyes and her mind's eye wavered as she pictured Declan's tiny studio apartment. Paintings in various stages leaned against the walls, and a mattress made up in fresh linens sagged in one corner. The room smelled like paint and turpentine and Declan's rugged, intoxicating scent. There was hardly any room for furniture, but Declan did have a small bookshelf with works by Jack Kerouac and Gertrude Stein next to biographies of da Vinci and Dalí. In this mental vision she was young again, lounging on Declan's mattress as he pulled a small leather-bound book from that bookshelf and scribbled some notes about his day. Blanche knew that he'd been writing about her, because he'd asked her how to spell *evanescent*. When he finished, he slipped the diary back on the bookshelf.

"The bookshelf!" Blanche said. "Of course!"

"That sure narrows it down," Sophia said, looking around at the dozens of bookshelves holding hundreds of books.

The four women quickly split up, each taking a different corner of the room and moving inward. Blanche ran her fingers over the spines of Declan's collection, looking for a leather-bound book, or anything that looked like a diary, since he might not have kept using the same style so many years later. But after scanning dozens of spines of published works in fiction and nonfiction, she realized with a sinking feeling that none of them were a diary or journal.

"Any luck?" she asked her girlfriends.

"No dice," said Sophia. "Maybe it's in another room, like his studio."

Blanche rubbed her temples, as if that would help her think better. Based on the amount of sunlight streaming through the windows, it wouldn't be morning for much longer. The rest of the house would be waking up soon, and they were running out of time to investigate without interference. And even if they could sneak back into the studio, she didn't think she could face seeing Declan's shrouded, motionless form again. It was just too painful.

If only she could ask Big Daddy what to do. He always—*Wait a minute*, Blanche thought. When she was going through all Big Daddy's things after he'd gone to glory, she'd found a whiskey bottle hidden inside his Bible. Since Declan had grown more secretive over the years, perhaps he'd done something similar.

"What if it's hidden *inside* another book?" Blanche said.

"Wonderful," Sophia said sarcastically. "We've got our work cut out for us."

Blanche circled the library slowly, looking for books big enough to hide another one within. There were many books large enough, as much of the collection consisted of oversize art monographs and volumes of prints. What book would Declan have chosen, based on what Blanche knew about him and his personality? He was a talented artist, and like Blanche had been blessed with stunning good looks, a sparkling personality, and a healthy dose of self-confidence.

"I think I have it," she said, reaching for a thick coffee-table book. Blanche pulled *The Greatest Artists of All Time* from the shelf and opened it. Inside a section of carved-out pages sat a small Borlino notebook with a paint-flecked leather cover. She eagerly flipped to the end, ready to learn everything about Declan and his last days.

But there was one problem. The tiny letters looked odd and were almost illegible.

"It's in some kind of foreign language or secret code!" Blanche cried. "I can't read it."

"Is it a Romance language?" Dorothy asked, taking the diary from Blanche's hands. "I know a little French and Spanish."

"I thought Blanche of all people would be fluent in romance," Rose said.

Blanche tried again, but the nonsense words swam before her eyes as they filled with tears.

"Oh, sweetie, we know you miss him," Sophia said. "It's tough, losing someone."

"This is too damn hard!" Blanche said. "I wish Big Daddy were here. He'd know just what to do!"

"Well, what would Big Daddy say if he were here right now?" Rose said.

"Blanche, my little clementine," Sophia said in a deep, manly voice and fake Southern accent. "Why don't you give the bigger bedroom in your house to the nice Italian lady?"

"Ma, stop!" Dorothy said. "We know you're not channeling Blanche's father from the Great Beyond."

"Don't interrupt her—she's an excellent medium for someone so small," Rose said.

Blanche thought for a minute and fiddled with one of her earrings. They weren't a pair a man had given her. They were a pair she'd bought for herself with her first paycheck from the museum. "He'd probably still be mad at me for running off to New York." Blanche chuckled through her tears. "I suppose Big Daddy would say, 'Blanche, there's nothin' in the world you can't do if you set your mind to it, and if you need help, don't be a ninny, and ask for it.'"

"That sounds like good advice," Dorothy said kindly.

"Can you make sense of this?" Blanche said.

"Let me see," Dorothy said. She peeked at a few pages, then laughed. "Try it this way," she said, holding the pages about a foot from Blanche's face.

From farther away Declan's tiny handwriting became readable, and Blanche realized that the diary wasn't written in another language. She just needed to get her eyes checked.

"I won't be caught dead in those little half-glasses!" Blanche said with a shudder.

Though if anyone could make them look chic, she thought, it would be her.

Just then the library door slammed open. Misia, Ralph, and Herman fumbled against one another, each one trying to get in first.

"Just what on earth are you four doing?" Herman thundered. "Most suspicious indeed!"

HUNGRY FOR THE TRUTH

26

Blanche whipped the diary behind her back and passed it to Dorothy, who quickly shoved it inside her voluminous suit jacket sleeve next to Herman's sketchbook. She hoped that the bulging items wouldn't poke out and attract Herman's notice.

"What are you all doing in here?" he demanded.

"We—ha, we—uh," Rose stuttered, whirling around with a panicked look on her face, unable to think of an excuse quickly enough.

"We were looking for the bathroom," Sophia said.

"We were doing some light reading," Blanche said at the same time.

"We were looking for El Toro's will," Dorothy said.

She figured the truth was the simplest way to go, and if for some reason Herman had been the one to take it from its file, then this might be a good way to gauge his reaction to the subject.

Herman's eyebrows shot up. "And you took this most serious task upon yourselves? Without notifying the rest of us, particularly myself, the elected leader of the investigation?"

"I don't remember a vote," Dorothy muttered.

Herman squinted at her, then surveyed the library. Misia and Ralph followed, stealing nervous glances at each other.

"Did you find it?" Misia asked. She chewed on her fingernail, looking from Dorothy to her friends.

"We almost did," Dorothy said, waving the empty file folder in the air. "But it looks like someone got to it before we did."

Ralph blinked in surprise as Misia snatched the empty file. "Who gave you permission to poke around Declan's private papers?" she said.

"Well, somebody beat us to it," Blanche said brightly. "Do any of you know who it could be?"

Dorothy wondered if perhaps they could get closer to the truth with a mix of Blanche's Southern charm and her own blunt honesty.

Herman glanced angrily around the library. "I do not, but I would very much like to know!"

"Because you think whoever is named in the will is the most likely suspect, is that it?" Dorothy said.

"Yes," Herman said. "I would consider it most damning as far as motive."

"Then maybe we can put our heads together and find out who took it," Dorothy said.

Just then, Sophia's stomach grumbled. "Can't we have breakfast first? I think better when I'm not distracted by hunger pangs."

"Me too," Rose said. She turned to Ralph and Misia. "What's for breakfast?"

Ralph shifted his weight and looked at Misia.

"Do you all still consider me a suspect?" she asked.

Dorothy kept her mouth shut. Even though there was evidence against Misia, she didn't feel like they had the whole story. And if she was the killer, Dorothy certainly didn't want to get on her bad side.

"Of course," Herman said. "The evidence, it does not lie."

"Then you can get your own stupid breakfast!" Misia said.

"I'm not cooking anything out of solidarity with Misia," Ralph added as Misia stormed out of the library. "Also, we're practically out of food anyway," he called over his shoulder on his way after her.

"That was interesting," Dorothy said. She crossed her

arms, trying to stop El Toro's journal from sliding around inside her sleeve without attracting attention. She searched her mind for a way to get Herman out of their hair so they could examine the diary in private.

"I don't blame them," Sophia said.

"Why don't we find the kitchen and see if we can't rustle up something to eat?" Blanche purred, pasting a sunny smile on her face. "We'll make something for you, too, Mr. Price. Do you have any dietary restrictions?"

"Thank you, but that won't be necessary," Herman said. "Bringing Misia to justice is all the sustenance I need."

Dorothy shot a glance to Blanche; Blanche then nudged Rose.

"But—but surely you need to eat sometime, to fuel that *massive* investigative brain of yours," Rose said, attempting a flirtatious tone. "If we were at our house, I'd make you my famous herring pancakes à la mode. Why don't you take a seat in the dining room, and I'll whip up something yummy."

Blanche nodded encouragingly, and Rose put her hand on the small of Herman's back to gently lead him out of the library.

"I suppose I could eat," Herman said as Rose deftly reached into his pocket and pulled out his wallet, then hid it behind her back. "This investigation has been most taxing."

"I can't even imagine the strain. Why don't you tell me all about it?" Rose said with a sweet smile. As soon as Herman and Rose disappeared down the hall, Dorothy, Blanche, and Sophia headed to the archaic kitchen.

"What now?" Sophia said. She rummaged through a cabinet and selected a box of cereal. "There's nothing here but Apple Jacks, can you believe that?"

"We've got to read this diary," Dorothy said.

"What was that about a diary?" a gravelly woman's voice said.

Akiko entered the room in a men's pajama shirt belted around the waist like a dress, having finally given up on a third day in her leather ensemble.

"Dairy!" Dorothy yelled suddenly. "If only we had dairy! Rose was just telling me that back in St. Olaf they would read the dairy report every morning to check, uhm, the price of milk, and so they knew how much butter to churn for breakfast—"

"Fascinating," Akiko said. "Let me know if you figure that out." She turned and walked out of the kitchen.

"That was a close one," said Blanche.

"I feel like Rose is taking over my brain because I know for a fact that the churning part is true—" Dorothy began, but Blanche was in a hurry and snatched the diary from her hands.

Blanche pushed up her sleeves and held the diary at arm's length. "Okay, this one is recent. 'Today I had a tuna sandwich for lunch. . . .'"

"Skip ahead to the good stuff!" Dorothy urged.

"'I painted for six hours straight today,'" Blanche read. "'This is either going to be my greatest masterpiece or will make me the laughingstock of the art world. I can't tell until I show it to someone. . . .'"

"Does it say anything about the threats?" Dorothy asked as Sophia poured herself an overflowing bowl of Apple Jacks.

"Darn it, there's no milk," Sophia said.

"I'm skimming as fast as I can," Blanche said. "Here's something! This is dated a few months ago. 'I'm tired of my solitude. Perhaps it is time for my reentry to the world. But what if I'm well and truly forgotten? What if my best days are behind me?'"

"There's no two percent either," Sophia grumbled.

"Of course there isn't," Dorothy said. "Just eat it dry. Or put some water in it!"

"Water?" Sophia lifted a hand to her forehead with a horrified expression on her wrinkled face. "Did I raise a monster?"

"So he was nervous," Dorothy said. "Makes sense, after years of being out of the public eye."

Dorothy looked longingly at the coffee maker, useless without electricity. She rummaged through another cabinet, located a glass, and filled it with water from the sink.

"I'm going to see if I can find something edible. Maybe there's a candy drawer somewhere," Sophia called over her shoulder.

"If you find one, get me an Almond Joy," Blanche said, and

leaned against the kitchen island, trying to block the sight of the diary should anyone else push through the swinging doors.

She continued reading. "Hang on . . . he says a few lines down that he's working on a plan. He writes, 'My latest work must be received with much fanfare—positive or negative, it matters not. For the worst thing would be for it to make no ripples at all.' That sounds like Declan, all right. Even in the early days, he wanted to make his mark. I think he'd rather die than have no one recognize his greatness."

Dorothy put down her water glass with a *thunk*. Something Blanche had said set off tiny little bells in her head. "Say that again, Blanche."

"I said he'd rather die. . . ." Blanche paused, then quickly covered her mouth. "You don't think he took his own life, do you? Or . . . or faked his own death?"

Dorothy frowned, then took Blanche's hands in hers. "Oh, honey. I don't think he faked his own death, because we saw the body. Ma and I got an up-close look and he's truly gone. But suicide . . . as terrible as that is to consider, do you think that's a possibility?"

Blanche dabbed at her eyes. "I just had a glimmer of hope there, for a second. But as for . . . taking his own life, I just can't see that happening. From what I knew of him, it wasn't in his nature."

"I tend to agree with you, based on what you've told us, and my impressions of him before he died," Dorothy said.

"But you hadn't seen him for years. He may have changed, or something may have driven him to it."

"I don't think so," Blanche said, shaking her head. "Besides his usual artistic angst, nothing in here suggests he was feeling that way."

"Keep reading," Dorothy said. "And skip to the end. We need to find out what his last days were like."

"Oh, here's something," Blanche said. "'I have concocted a plan to bring my work back into the spotlight where it belongs. First, I must drum up publicity—'"

"Girls!" Rose poked her head through the swinging kitchen door. "Herman is getting hungry and so I thought I'd check and see if you've found anything we can eat? Otherwise I think he might come in here and start looking for himself!" She raised her eyebrows comically in warning.

"Got it. Give him this to start," Dorothy said, handing her Sophia's abandoned bowl of cereal. Her mother could pour another bowl when she returned. "Explain to him that there's no milk so he doesn't come looking for it. And, Blanche, we'd better find another place to read that diary before more people barge in."

Dorothy and Blanche crept out of the kitchen and located a powder room. They squeezed inside, marveling at the all-black marble fixtures, the hand-painted wallpaper, and the inexplicably mirrored ceiling.

Blanche perched on the toilet lid and read from the diary

while Dorothy leaned against the sink, their knees pressing against each other in the tiny space.

As the story of Declan's final months spilled from Blanche's lips, Dorothy's eyes opened wider in shock. Members of the villa had been keeping secrets from Declan—but he'd been keeping others from them. As Blanche flipped through the pages, it was clear that El Toro swung wildly from brimming with confidence and an inflated sense of self to the depths of despair, born from a craving for approval and yearning for the fame that his work had brought him before his yearslong creative block. He'd hatched a plan to ensure that his artistic return would be a triumph even as he struggled to finish his latest work.

"Can you believe this?" Blanche said. "We have to tell everyone!"

Dorothy nodded. "Keep going," she said. "We know a lot more, but we still don't know why he died—or who did it."

Blanche bent her head and ran her finger along the words, reading faster. Dorothy wished they could compare some of the pages with their lipstick notes and cross-reference all of the documents they'd found in El Toro's bedroom, but there wasn't time. She had to rely on her memory, the notes in her pocket and Blanche's brassiere, and the connections she could make as fragments of the full picture came to light.

"Oh!" Blanche said. "He talks about Misia here, and mentions when she first came to the villa about a year ago."

Blanche flipped back toward the beginning of the diary.

"But we really only need to know about his last days," Dorothy said. "Stay on track."

"No," Blanche said. "Look." She pointed to a specific page and handed the diary to Dorothy.

"It seems Misia isn't who we think she is," Dorothy said after reading several entries. Her mind whirred with questions, possibilities, tenuous connections, and memories of the past weekend.

"So what does this mean?" Blanche said. "Does it mean she's guilty?"

"I think it means the opposite," Dorothy said. "Think about everything we know about the threats, the shoe print, and her reactions to Herman's accusations."

"Someone could be protecting her," Blanche said.

"True," Dorothy said. "Especially since the will has disappeared. But what El Toro says here means that she had even less reason to kill him, don't you agree?"

Blanche nodded.

"I'm not exactly sure why—or how," Dorothy said, "but it's becoming clear that someone really wants us to think that she's guilty."

She gave her friend a determined look, then added, "And I think it's time we confront that person."

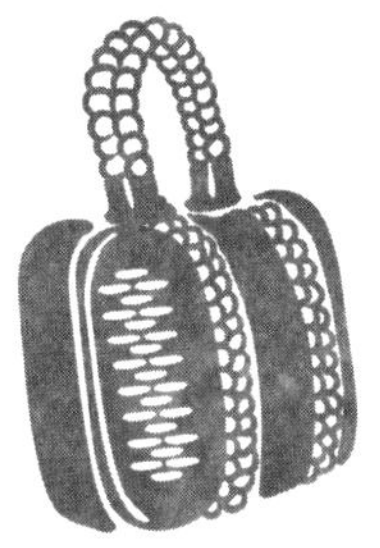

A NOT-SO-PRETTY PICTURE

27

Dorothy and Blanche entered the dining room and pulled Rose to one side, out of earshot of the rest of the guests who had assembled there. As they shared the final pieces of the puzzle with Rose, she gulped.

Dorothy scanned the room to tell her mother, but Sophia was nowhere to be seen. *Probably in the bathroom*, she thought. She decided not to wait for her, in case she lost her nerve.

Taking a deep breath, she surveyed the group of individuals representing so many glittering facets of the art world. On one hand, they were an intimidating sight, with all they had achieved on their own, and in relation to El Toro, whose name would echo through museum halls for many years to come.

On the other hand, they were all sitting around the stately dining table in wrinkled, sweat-stained clothing and borrowed pajamas, eating handfuls of Apple Jacks. She could do this.

She cleared her throat. "My friends and I have done a lot of thinking, and some investigating of our own," she said, trying to keep her voice steady. It wasn't easy to accuse anyone, let alone the person she most suspected. "And we have found several pieces of new evidence that change everything."

Nervous glances whirled around the room as Dorothy's words sank in.

"Excusez-moi!" Herman cried. "What is the meaning of this? I am the chief investigator, and the only one authorized to make such inquiries and accusations."

"Hang on to your butter beans," Blanche said. "We're in for a bumpy ride."

"And why should we listen to them?" Herman asked, wheeling around to address the rest of the group. "Except for Blanche, this coven of women have no connection to El Toro, and therefore don't belong here. They know nothing of our host, nor his sudden demise."

Blanche opened her mouth to give Herman a piece of her mind, but Dorothy stopped her. "It's a fair question. You may think we're just a bunch of grandmothers—well, we are a bunch of grandmothers. But we've solved a murder before. Have any of *you*?"

She paused to let that resonate with the group. Then she added, "And in *this* crime, we've become privy to details that turn the suspicion away from Misia and onto someone else."

"Then spit it out. Who is it?" Akiko said.

The room fell silent and Dorothy looked to her friends for encouragement. Was she crazy to do this? Did she really know what she was talking about?

She mentally reviewed all the notes and connections they'd made over the course of the weekend, the clues they'd discovered in the diary and the Bankers Box, and checked them against her gut. Whether it was feminine intuition, a keen sense of pattern recognition, or the mountain of evidence they'd unearthed, Dorothy knew when things felt right. She was learning to trust that feeling.

She swallowed, trying to get her mouth to form the words.

"We believe that there are *several* guilty parties in this room," Dorothy said. "At least half of you were hiding something from El Toro."

Blanche pulled out a crumpled ball of receipts and paperwork from her brassiere and waved them under Akiko's nose. A few Post-it notes fluttered to the floor. "Declan found out that you'd been cheating him," she said. "He hired someone to investigate sales through your gallery over the last several years. Look here."

Blanche pointed to a column of numbers highlighted in yellow. "This is what he was supposed to have been paid," she said. Then she tapped another column, highlighted in blue. "And here's what you actually paid him. See the difference? Also, it looks like you sold multiple copies of a few works, which seems to me means *forgeries*."

Akiko looked from the numbers to Blanche's scowling face. "You don't know what you're talking about! You're a nobody who cannot possibly understand the workings of the international art scene."

"I understand that this could get you kicked out of the Art Dealers Association of America, as it violates their code of ethics," Blanche said. "But what do I know? I'm just a nobody."

Akiko snatched at the pages, but Blanche jerked them out of her grasp. She began handing them around the room.

"We also discovered that Vee had her own secrets," Rose mumbled. From under her skirt, she pulled out a stack of envelopes held together with a giant alligator clip. "Apparently she tried to sell off her stash of private letters from El Toro to a gallery on the West Coast for quite a tidy sum."

"Give me those!" Vee exclaimed, reaching for the letters. Rose danced out of reach.

"Luckily the gallery owner wrote to El Toro and informed him of the situation," Dorothy said. "And El Toro bought them back himself."

"Tsk-tsk." Blanche sniffed. "I thought you loved that man! Did you know we also found your letters to him? For all these years, he kept yours tied with a red ribbon in his desk."

Vee's face fell. "He did?" she warbled. "I thought he didn't care about me or our history. That's why I finally decided to sell those letters. I needed closure—and I have a mortgage! The business of avant-garde art installation doesn't pay as well as it used to." She placed her head in her hands and wept quietly.

"And we found more. Except for Ralph, all of you were hiding secrets from El Toro. We believe that Declan was going to confront you all this weekend," Blanche said in a wavering voice. "But he was killed before he had the chance. And the person who did this is . . . is . . ." Blanche faltered and looked at Dorothy with pleading, red-rimmed eyes.

Even though they'd agreed that Blanche should be the one to name El Toro's murderer, Dorothy knew that Blanche needed her to do the hard part. It wasn't easy, but Dorothy knew she could be an island of strength for her friend as she struggled in a sea of grief.

Dorothy cleared her throat. "Herman Price is behind all of this," she said.

The room erupted in gasps as everyone stared at Herman. Misia's eyes bulged as they darted between him and Dorothy.

"What?" Herman roared. "No one admired El Toro more than me! When I found out about the threats on his life, it

was as if someone had held a knife to my own throat." He pointed to his neck to drive home the point.

"We don't know exactly why he did it," Dorothy interjected. "But we think he's framing someone else for the murder, and also possibly trying to capitalize on his death."

"Why would I kill El Toro? I was his friend! I coaxed him for years to produce more work. I wanted him to know that he hadn't been forgotten. The public would clamor for more if he came out of hiding and had a new show. His death was the worst possible thing to happen—it's inconceivable that I would benefit from it!"

Dorothy, Rose, and Blanche inched closer to Herman, hanging on every word.

"I was the one who found out people were buying up his early work all of a sudden, and I suspected they weren't legitimate. The fake names proved it. At the same time, the threats were escalating against El Toro. So I came to Miami and implored him to take proper precautions—an alarm system, perhaps some surveillance. El Toro only scoffed at that." Herman sighed loudly and stared down at his shoes. "He laughed at me. It seems I was not one he would take seriously after all."

"Tell us what happened," Dorothy urged. "We know Misia's shoe print wasn't at the scene from the beginning. My mother and I snuck in through the tape after you'd put it up to get a better look at the body, and it wasn't there then, or when we all first viewed the body. Luis suggested that maybe we were all too distracted and upset to notice it, but really it's because you planted it afterward. The only reason to cast false suspicion on someone is if you wanted to turn it away from yourself!"

"Your insinuations are preposterous!" Herman growled.

"I saw you peeking at me in the night!" Rose said. "You'd been creeping around the secret passageways. Only El Toro and maybe his staff would have known about their existence, except you'd gotten the blueprints."

"Passageways?" Misia said, and shared a look with Ralph, who looked equally confused.

"He didn't just use them to get an eyeful," Blanche added. "He used them to access Misia's room in secret, borrow her shoe, then get into Declan's locked studio. He was able to replace the shoe at the back of her closet when no one was paying attention."

"A colorful story, but you have no proof," Herman sneered.

"We have some proof," Rose said. "Though you were careful—and very smart—to try to confuse everyone."

"Like with Misia's shoe," Blanche said. "You were craftier than a fox, passing it around so everyone's fingerprints would get on it—not just yours."

"That is still not proof!" Herman said.

"Then there's the matter of the buttons," Dorothy said. "We poked around your bedroom and saw a few melted buttons among the ashes in your fireplace. On Saturday morning you wore a shirt borrowed from El Toro, isn't that right?"

Herman harrumphed. "El Toro offered us *all* clothes when we had to spend the night," he said. "Nothing is suspicious in this."

"But if you just wanted a fresh shirt, why burn your old one? Why not simply take it home, or wash it?" Rose said. "You were clearly hiding something!"

"We think you had something incriminating on your shirt," Blanche said. "And you didn't want any of us seeing it. My guess is that you spilled some varnish on it, or you tore it in your efforts to kill my dear Declan."

"And there's just one more thing," Dorothy said, relishing the chance to quote Columbo, one of her favorite television sleuths. "How do you explain these?"

At that, Dorothy wrestled with the hidden items in her sleeve as the tension in the room grew. She finally revealed the sketchbook they'd taken from Herman's room. She held it open and flipped through the pages as everyone peered to get a closer look. Dorothy carried it over to Misia and let her examine its contents more carefully.

"What is this?" she said. "These look like instructions."

Blanche held up the gallery paperwork. "Some of these match paintings that Akiko recently sold through her gallery. Isn't that interesting?"

"Those are just notes! I was an ardent student of his work!" Herman cried.

"Then how come there are two copies of *Bianca with a*

Pearl Earring?" Dorothy asked. "One original, hanging in El Toro's bedroom, and one very excellent forgery in the stack of canvases in Misia's room."

Herman sputtered. "Then she must be a forger, as well as a murderer!"

"No," Dorothy said. "She's not. Though she might have the skills and the talent, she wouldn't have the time, with the amount of work El Toro had her doing."

"Your sketchbook is one piece of evidence," Blanche said. "I'm sure that when the police search your home, they'll find more."

"We could go on all day," Rose said, patting his arm gently. "We have lots of evidence against you. It's better if you come clean."

Finally, Herman spoke in a small voice with barely a trace of his European accent. "You don't understand . . . I was *helping* El Toro. As you know, I was dismayed by the threats against him, and I took it upon myself to capture the person or persons targeting him. I thought they'd come for him through the external entrance to his studio, since some of the final notes mentioned watching him while he worked. On Friday night I booby-trapped the lanai, so I could catch them in the act. But I certainly wasn't trying to kill anyone!" He broke off into loud, hiccupping sobs. "It was a horrible accident."

The rest of the room was deathly quiet as everyone absorbed what Herman had said.

"But you set up those cans and jars with twine, ready to fall on someone," Rose said. "Maybe you didn't mean to kill anyone, but it wasn't an accident."

Herman looked up from his tear-splattered shoes. "Misia had mentioned that he never went out on that lanai, as the breeze from opening the door would disturb his materials, so I knew it was a foolproof plan," he said. "But I was clumsy. The apparatus I set up was rickety, and I cracked one of the jars prematurely. It dripped down my sleeve and left a puddle near the threshold. There was no way I could clean it up. It's terribly bad luck that El Toro didn't see it before he stepped out there."

"And yet," Dorothy said. "For some reason he *did* step out onto the lanai. Whether it was the tumbling items from the booby trap or the puddle that made him slip, that fall caused his death. We may never know, but you're the reason for both. As some mercy, it appears that his death was instantaneous, as there was no sign of him struggling for help."

Blanche whimpered at that detail and buried her face on Dorothy's shoulder. Rose reached out to rub her back.

"That must have been sometime after Misia brought him his coffee but before we went up to meet with him," Blanche sobbed. "If it had had happened later one of you would have found his body."

Herman stood up from the table and began hyperventilating, and everyone stared at him until he composed himself again. "I was trying to protect him—and instead I killed him.

I will have to live with that for the rest of my life. But I'm no murderer!"

"That's for the justice system to decide," Dorothy said gravely. "You'll be arrested and face a trial. The police will investigate, and we will all share statements of what we've witnessed here. Isn't that right?"

Dorothy gave a stern glance around the room.

Blanche patted her eyes with a tissue, while Rose, Vee, and Akiko served up nearly identical dirty looks with narrowed eyes and pinched lips. Ralph's mouth hung open, and Luis had paused in his scribbling to stare at Herman, his pen dangling forgotten in his hand.

Misia strode to the window, silent tears coursing down her cheeks. When Vee joined her to pat her shoulder, Misia shook it off.

"There can't be a trial," Herman said. "My reputation will be ruined!"

"Your *reputation* is what you're worried about? You caused a great man's death!" Akiko said.

"Don't you see? I was protecting him!" Herman shouted, spittle flying from his lips.

"No one asked you to do that!" Misia cried. "I'm sure he wouldn't have wanted you to."

"And when we all went to view the scene of the crime, you quickly turned the blame on everyone but yourself," Akiko said, as she pointed an accusing finger at Herman.

"I didn't know what had happened! I was trying to

understand it myself," Herman said. "Because I knew that someone was after him, it made perfect sense to me that they had succeeded in their plan!"

"And when you saw him lying there in the mess you created, you didn't put two and two together?" Vee asked.

Herman refused to meet her eyes.

"Shame on you," Blanche said, her voice sounding husky and sore from crying. "You made everyone suspect one another of your horrible deeds. Then you zeroed in on Misia and treated her like a criminal."

Misia looked over to Herman with red-rimmed eyes. "What did I ever do to you?"

"Even though I knew you weren't guilty of the murder," Herman said, "I knew you were guilty of *something!*"

"But why pick on her?" Vee asked. "You could have framed any of us, since you'd uncovered so many probable motives."

"I visited one of the local galleries that had sold an early El Toro. The receptionist had met the mysterious buyer—and her description matched Misia to a tee," Herman said, counting the reasons off on his fingers. "Once he died, I knew she'd sell them for a massive profit. So I knew she must have been sending the notes and was planning to kill her boss! Didn't you all see Misia's vision board? It was made of cutout words just like the death threats. Not to mention that it showed her motive of wanting to eclipse El Toro as an artist in her own right!"

"That's not true!" said Misia.

"The paintings were in your room. We all saw them!" Herman said triumphantly.

"I had them because Declan told me to buy them!" Misia said. "He sent me to the mainland, told me which ones to purchase, and insisted I use a pseudonym."

Herman's eyes widened as he shook his head quickly from side to side, like a dog trying to get loose from its collar. "That makes no sense," he said.

"It makes perfect sense," Blanche said, waving Declan's diary in the air. "Because Declan was the one sending the threats."

Everyone stared at Blanche in amazement.

"Excuse me?" Herman said.

"What do you mean, he was behind the threats?" Vee asked.

"Do y'all remember the way the notes were made out of cutouts from newspapers and magazines?" Blanche said.

Everyone nodded.

"Something about some of the letters seemed familiar to me," Blanche said, striding over to Herman. "Hand them over."

"No," Herman said, covering the blazer pocket that held the notes. "It's not true."

"Fine," Blanche said. "Luis, do you have yours?"

Luis pulled his note from his blazer's breast pocket. Blanche unfolded it and pointed to a few of the letters.

"Here," she said, gesturing at a bubbly orange capital *A*

and a matching lowercase *n* with her fingernail. "This font reminded me of lazy mornings with Declan in New York. But I couldn't remember why."

Vee stepped in to take a closer peek at the letters and nodded as if she were beginning to understand.

"It took me a while to make the connection, but when I did, it was almost obvious. These are from *Little Orphan Annie*."

"Declan's favorite comic strip," Vee said. "And just the other night he told me how much he loved the musical."

"Exactly," Blanche said. "That's what gave me the idea that the letters could have come from him."

"But why would he threaten *himself*?" Herman asked in disbelief.

"We asked each other the same question," Blanche said, gesturing to her girlfriends. "We knew that Declan was desperate to return to the public eye in triumph and wanted to make sure his new painting made a splash. What better way to build intrigue about his work than threats against his life? When we found his diary, a lot of the details fell into place."

Akiko slapped her own forehead. "I should have known it was a publicity stunt," she groaned. "*That's* why he wasn't actually worried about the threats."

"Right," Blanche said. "He knew they were made up."

"He wanted to make sure his triumphant return was profitable," Dorothy added. "So he bought up some older works of his without anyone knowing."

"And he sent Misia as a screen," Vee said.

Misia wiped her eyes. "Declan told me which aliases to use, and Ralph and I went to the mainland together to buy the paintings."

"That's another piece of the puzzle," Dorothy said. "Ralph mentioned that he often birdwatched with El Toro in the villa's gardens. That's how they came up with the fake names—they're all based on types of birds."

"We loved birdwatching together." Ralph whimpered. "Oh no." He placed a hand over his mouth.

"What is it, darling?" Blanche asked.

"We'd been catching glimpses of what we thought was a Mangrove Cuckoo on the grounds over the past week." Ralph swallowed. "He wanted to see one so badly. Maybe he saw it—maybe that's . . . maybe *that's* why he went out on the lanai." He shoulders bounced as he sobbed.

"There's no way of knowing," Blanche said. "And if that's the case, then he was happy." She stepped around the table to where Ralph sat, and they hugged each other for a while, letting the tears out.

After they'd composed themselves, Misia continued, her voice full of sorrow. "When a forgery arrived in one of our orders, Declan had us continue to buy for him in case others turned up," she said. "He wanted to know who was making them. But I never suspected it was Herman. I guess you needed the money, huh?"

Herman scowled. "Even if I was guilty of forgery, who did that hurt? It's been decades since El Toro had new work to sell, and some of us have bills to pay!" He glanced at Akiko, who hung her head.

"Uh-oh," Ralph said, wringing his hands. "I just realized that I may have sent the threats. Declan instructed me to deliver a plain manila envelope to the *Herald*. That must have been one of them. And I always posted his mail, including letters to Akiko's offices. I just assumed it was regular correspondence. I had no idea what was inside. Am I in trouble now, too?"

"You didn't do anything wrong," Misia said. "Or maybe we *all* did." She looked to Blanche, to Dorothy, and then to Vee with worried eyes.

"I don't think there's such a thing as insider trading in the art world," Dorothy said. "Declan's plan was deceptive, but I'm not sure it was a crime."

"Listen to me," Herman interrupted. "We can still tell the authorities it was Misia. She's the youngest. And she's just an assistant—the most disposable of all of you. You should be thanking me for blaming her instead of any of you!"

"The most disposable?" Blanche said, her voice carrying more venom than a coral snake. "You are talking about a human being!"

She slapped Herman across the mouth.

Everyone gasped.

"I'm sorry, that wasn't very ladylike. I don't know *what* came over me," Blanche said, placing a delicate hand on her chest.

Vee started clapping, and Akiko joined in. Blanche flashed a hint of a smile to the two women.

"Not only did you commit murder, but you covered it up, and tampered with the evidence all while trying to frame an innocent person!" added Dorothy. "You're a shame to your so-called profession."

"You geronoconkin," Rose hissed.

"But, Rose, my intentions—" Herman said, trying to grasp at Rose's hands.

"Your intentions? Look at your actions," Rose said. She yanked her hands away and lifted her chin. "You're a fake and a phony—right down to your accent."

Dorothy looked at Rose in surprise as Herman tottered backward, his mouth opening and closing silently.

"He told us all that he was from Switzerland," Rose said. "But he's not from Europe. At first, I thought it was a little odd when he mentioned his fear of crocodiles. Anyone could have that fear, but he specifically mentioned a run-in with one as a child. And then over breakfast, he mentioned that he grew up an hour away from the ocean. And unless he meant by jet, the country of Switzerland isn't anywhere near the ocean."

"Color me impressed," Dorothy said, peering at Rose with newfound respect.

Rose smiled smugly. "I told you, I'm not as dumb as you all think I am. Sometimes I'm so busy listening that I don't always make sense when I'm talking."

"But I *am* from Switzerland!" Herman said. "That's the truth!"

"Technically, he's not lying about that," Rose agreed. "When I peeked at his driver's license, I saw his home address was listed as Switzerland, Florida."

"You took my wallet?" Herman cried.

"No, I only borrowed it," said Rose. "And if you hadn't kept trying to cuddle up to me, I wouldn't have been able to reach it."

She tossed the wallet back to Herman. He tried to catch it, but it slipped between his hands and fell to the floor.

"Luis, are you writing all of this down?" Blanche said. "Make sure you quote us accurately. And if you need any help with our physical descriptions, I'm about five four, and my measurements are . . ."

Luis pulled out the mini tape recorder from his shirt pocket and nodded. "This is going to be quite a story. . . ."

"Make sure you mention that I'm single," Blanche added.

"I'd love to get a peek at your notes," Dorothy said. "Maybe we can fill in a few missing pieces. But I'm not sure we'll ever know how Declan procured Akiko's financial records, or if he knew that Herman was behind the forgeries."

Luis bit his lip. "Actually, I can help you with that. I haven't been completely honest with you all, either."

"What now?" Blanche cried. "I can't take any more two-faced snakes in the grass. Declan was a wonderful person, and he didn't deserve all this dishonesty!"

"You're right. But he wasn't an angel," Vee whispered.

"No, he wasn't," Luis said. "He had a temper and wasn't the easiest person to work for. I should know—Declan hired me for my investigative chops and my writing skills, both of which he'd praise one day, and cruelly disparage the next. He paid me to dig into Akiko's financial records, to help trace the forgeries, and to track down the address for his long-lost Bianca so he could invite her to the villa, along with everyone else he felt he had unfinished business with. He was going to put all of this into a memoir that I was helping him write."

Dorothy turned to Luis, her jaw dropping. "So you knew about *all* of this?"

"Not all of it," Luis said. "And I had no idea he was behind his own death threats. I did know that he was planning to honor those who had helped him—and confront everyone about their transgressions against him. You guessed as much." He nodded at Dorothy and Blanche. "But what you didn't know is that he was planning to forgive everyone and delete their dirty dealings from his memoir if they came clean. He knew he'd made mistakes, too. Vee, he particularly regretted not being there for you when you really needed him. He told me that he wanted to approach this new chapter of his life like a fresh canvas."

Vee smiled sadly and continued weeping into a tissue as everyone else silently absorbed this new information.

Dorothy closed her eyes. The disparate pieces of their investigation were like multicolored dots in an Impressionist painting, finally coalescing into a coherent picture. "Do you have your research here?" she said. "Your notes and ours will be very helpful to the police when they arrive."

"Oh no," Herman said, shaking his finger at the rest of the group. "You will not do this to me."

"*We're* not doing anything to you," Dorothy said. "You did this."

"But I explained to you that it was an accident—I shared my sympathetic backstory!" Herman cried. "You're not taking me down for this!"

Blanche bristled. "A man we all love is dead. Of course we're going to tell the police what happened!"

"Then you can tell them it was Misia," Herman said, stepping close to Blanche with a menacing growl.

"Herman, I'm sorry, but this is just how it's going to be. Right, Ma?" Dorothy said, waiting for her mother to chime in with some Sicilian wisdom about standing up and facing the music.

After a beat of silence, Dorothy looked to her left, then her right. Blanche scanned the room for a cloud of white hair peeking over a high-backed sofa or a tall plant. But she was nowhere to be seen.

POKER FACE

28

"Dorothy, when's the last time you saw Sophia?" Blanche said, worry creeping into her gut like a kudzu vine.

"Maybe in the kitchen?" Dorothy said. She bit her lower lip. "Oh, I can't remember! Rose, have you seen her? Has anyone?"

Rose shook her head and bent down to peek underneath various pieces of furniture as if searching for a lost cat.

Blanche's stomach rumbled, reminding her that she hadn't had anything to eat yet today. The hunger pangs reminded her of her misguided attempts to fit back into her wedding dress by consuming only chalky shakes and one "sensible meal" per day. "She went looking for a candy drawer, remember?"

"We've got to find her," Dorothy said. "If she slips on one of these marble floors, or trips on the stairs—or god forbid, gets carried off by a pelican . . ."

Just then, a loud roar penetrated the stone walls of the villa. Dorothy's face went ashen, and everyone froze.

Whatever that was, it didn't sound good, Blanche thought.

"We have to find her!" Dorothy cried. "Everyone, please look for my mother. She might growl at you, but she's friendly, especially when offered a treat."

"Got it," said Luis, leaping up from his seat. "I'll check upstairs!"

"We can take the first floor, right, Akiko?" Vee said. Akiko nodded and the two women jogged out of the room.

"I'm worried she left the villa," Dorothy said. "Ralph, can you lead us through the gardens? She can't have gotten too far."

Blanche bit her lip. She knew that Sophia had a habit of slipping away unnoticed. *Who knows where she's gone or what she's gotten up to?* she thought.

"Don't go outside," Rose said. "The skunk ape!"

"I think that was a crocodile," Ralph said. "We should be careful."

"It—it sounded like a big one . . ." Herman said, backing away toward the fireplace. He grabbed an iron poker from an ornate stand and held it against his leg.

"What if Ma's outside?" Dorothy cried. "She could be in danger!"

"Then let's find her," Ralph said.

"I'll help," said Misia.

"But what are we going to do with Herman?" Rose said. "Shouldn't we tie him up or something?"

"Where's he going to go?" Dorothy called over her shoulder. "We're on an island."

Blanche wavered, taking a half step to follow Dorothy and then a half step toward Herman. Should she try to contain him somehow? Tie him up with tablecloths or bed linens? She briefly regretted leaving her personal handcuffs at home.

But while she dithered, Sophia could be wandering the island, cold and hungry, possibly disoriented or hurt. Blanche's head swam with horror stories about pets in Florida who were allowed outside and scampered too close to coastal waters without a leash. With her shuffling gait and small frame, Sophia could be as enticing to a gator as an elderly shih tzu.

She was just about to join Dorothy in the search when Herman rushed toward Blanche and snatched the diary from her hand. Then he whirled around and threw his forearm around Rose's neck, holding her close to his body.

"Now, Herman, I told you I'm not interested," said Rose mildly.

"You're coming with me, my dear," Herman said, all trace of his faux-European accent truly gone now. Without it, his voice sounded flat and foreboding.

"This really doesn't seem to be the time for dirty dancing," Rose said, a little more sternly. "I told you, I'm not interested."

"Rose . . ." Blanche said, feeling the atmosphere in the room suddenly become brittle.

Rose looked down and saw the heavy poker in Herman's hand. Her eyes grew round and saucerlike. "Mayonnaise," she whispered. "Mayonnaise!"

Blanche blinked, then realized that *mayonnaise* must have been the word Rose had chosen as her secret signal for help. She looked around the room for someone to do something. But everyone else had scattered to look for Sophia, and they were alone with a madman.

"You're going to be my insurance policy," Herman said. "No pun intended."

"What?" Rose said, trying to wriggle free. "Let me go!"

"No one is going to accuse me of any crimes," Herman said to Blanche. "Do you understand?" He brandished the poker as a beam of Florida sunshine illuminated its cruelly sharp tip. "When everyone returns, we'll explain that this is how it's going to be."

Blanche nodded frenetically. "Of course, yes—okay—" she said, praying that he wouldn't bring that poker any closer to Rose's face.

Herman backed up through the door to the dining room, dragging Rose roughly along with him. Blanche's mouth went dry, and she could hardly move. If only Ralph and Luis were here to help her, or even Dorothy, she thought. She hadn't felt this small and helpless since her relationship with Rex Huntington, when she'd tiptoed on eggshells just to avoid his ugly temper.

"Rose, I'm sorry," she whispered, near tears as she followed them down the hall. "I don't know what to do!"

"Just stay with us," Rose said, her voice quavering. "I'm sure Herman will let me go once he gets the reassurance he needs. Right, Herman?"

Herman grunted and tugged Rose into the living room and toward the back wall. The he unlocked the French doors with one hand while keeping his other arm tight around Rose's collarbone.

"Now, Herman," Blanche said, thinking as fast as she could in her frightened state. "We totally understand where you're coming from. You loved Declan like we all did. I understand you were only trying to protect him."

Herman kicked the French doors open with his foot and pushed his way through, dragging Rose along with him onto the patio.

"You could just let her go," Blanche said, pouring all the sweet tea in Georgia into her voice. "I promise, we won't follow you."

"You're hurting me," Rose whimpered, her mouth half buried under his tweedy sleeve.

Herman adjusted his arm so that it no longer pressed against her neck but sat lower across her collarbone. "I'm sorry, my dear."

Then he pulled Rose sideways to the edge of the patio so roughly that one of her shoes slipped off. Something about Rose's exposed foot with its pink toenail polish made her friend seem even more weak and vulnerable. Then an idea burst into Blanche's mind.

"Rose! Remember what you did when we protested at the docks? Do it now," Blanche urged.

Rose nodded. She turned her head so that her mouth was right next to Herman's ear and shouted "SAVE THE DOLPHINS!" at the top of her lungs.

"No, not that!" Blanche yelled. "The other thing, when that rent-a-cop tried to unlawfully disperse the crowd?"

"Aha!" Rose said, and let her body go limp. Herman struggled to hold her as she sagged in his arms. He dropped the diary and beads of sweat popped on his brow as he attempted to tilt Rose back onto her feet.

"Please, let her go. She'll only delay you," Blanche said, moving slowly closer to Herman as if approaching a rabid possum and deftly picked up the diary. Herman grunted as he tugged a very floppy Rose onto the wet grass, but Rose twisted around and managed to free one arm from Herman's viselike grip. Then she reached up and yanked hard on his mustache, which ripped away from his face in one clean motion.

Rose stared down at the furry adhesive strip in her hand and screamed.

Herman released the arm around Rose's neck and grabbed the mustache from her hand. He slapped it back onto his face, where it swung over his mouth like a broken windshield wiper.

Rose whirled around and pinched Herman anywhere she could connect with flesh.

"Ow!" he yelled, jerking his face away from Rose's flying fingernails while once again wrapping an arm around her.

"She'll take an eye out!" Blanche said. "Probably safer just to let her go once and for all."

"Maybe I can trust the two of you—but not the others," Herman wheezed in between Rose's swiping. "The only way to make sure everyone listens is if I have a hostage. As long as everyone keeps quiet until I can get off this island and out of the country—or Misia goes to jail."

Rose stopped swiping at Herman. "You're going to get caught eventually," she said. "If you let me go, I won't mention this little kidnapping attempt. I'll consider it water over the bridge."

Herman frowned. "You mean water under the bridge?"

"Oh, for heaven's sake," Blanche said. "It means she'll let this whole damn business wash away if you just leave us alone!"

Herman shook his head. He'd managed to drag Rose to the walled garden containing a maze of hedges and paused to catch his breath.

"What if we hatch a plan together to help you escape?" Blanche said. "You go hide somewhere on the island. When the police come, we'll tell them you fled on a boat or a raft or something. Then they'll leave, and you can make your real escape!"

"That's a great idea!" Rose said. "There are so many great places to hide in the house or the island—and you would know, since you have the blueprints!"

"An interesting idea," he said. "I'm listening."

"It'll be just like playing Ugel and Flugel, but we won't do the Flugel part," Rose added.

Herman looked at Blanche quizzically as he backed farther into the hedge maze.

"It's a St. Olaf thing. It means nobody will come to find you," Blanche explained.

"But how can I trust you? And how can I be sure you won't tell the police everything once you get home?" Herman wheezed, straining under Rose's weight.

"We could pinkie promise," Rose suggested as Herman tugged her sideways through a green archway. They were surrounded by boxwood hedges that had been pruned to make a narrow, woody corridor, completely invisible to anyone from the villa.

Herman shook his head. "Not good enough, my dear. Now back away, please." He lifted the iron poker higher, so that the point danced dangerously close to Rose's face.

Rose gulped.

"You'll just have to take our word for it," Blanche purred softly, remembering that Marilyn Monroe drew people toward her with her quiet, breathy voice. Herman leaned forward to hear her better as Blanche edged up a few more inches, so close that she could see the pores on Herman's ruddy face. If he wasn't trying to kidnap one of her best friends, she'd suggest a decent cold cream.

"We want to be in this situation even less than you do," she breathed, then quickly grabbed the poker out of his hand. As he reached for it, he released Rose, who staggered to her feet and hid behind Blanche.

Herman looked at Blanche, then looked at the poker, and then started running as fast as his legs could take him.

S.O.S. (SAVE OUR SOPHIA)

29

Dorothy dashed into the hallway, her heart pounding. Her mother had disappeared before and always returned unharmed. But that was back home in Miami, where Sophia knew the bus routes and had friends and neighbors all over the city—not on an unfamiliar island with crocodiles on the loose. What if her mother had gotten confused, and somehow gotten lost in the villa's series of hidden passageways? There were too many places for an elderly woman to disappear.

Dorothy quickly checked the most likely places Sophia

would be: the downstairs bathrooms, then up the three flights of stairs to their room. Finding nothing, she jogged back downstairs to check the other areas on the first floor, when she noticed that the front door was ajar. She raced through it, followed by a huffing and puffing Ralph. Though the ground was still wet from the recent rain, the sky had turned from gray to blue and sunshine illuminated the extensive gardens stretching beyond the villa.

"Where do you think she went?" Ralph asked.

"I don't know," Dorothy said, her voice cracking at the sudden thought of her mother falling into a decorative pool and drowning, or slipping on the wet grass and hitting her head, just like El Toro.

"She can't have gone far," Ralph said.

"You don't know my mother," Dorothy said, thinking of the time Sophia had run away in the middle of a hurricane, or the time she'd angrily wandered off at Disney World. Dorothy trotted next to Ralph as they raced through the gardens, scanning the area for Sophia. Under other circumstances, Dorothy would have admired the elegant stonework, Mediterranean architecture, and picturesque vines. Instead, she kept an eye on the damp ground for tiny footprints.

Soon they reached the sandy path that led to the dock and followed it until they saw the cerulean waters of the bay. Something glinted on the sand, and Dorothy's heart clenched when she realized that her mother's large round eyeglasses were catching the brilliant morning sunlight.

Dorothy picked up the glasses. Her hands shook when she saw that the slim gold chain that allowed her mother to wear them around her neck was broken. *Oh no*, she thought. Her mother could barely see without these. And why was the chain damaged? Had someone ripped it from her neck?

Dorothy clutched the glasses to her chest forced some deep breaths to steady herself. She reminded herself that mother was a tough cookie. Heck, Sophia had even lost her glasses before. Dorothy knew she had to remain calm and levelheaded to find her. The alternative was too terrible to even think about.

Dorothy heard feet pounding behind her. Vee and Akiko joined them on the narrow beach, slightly out of breath.

"We've looked everywhere," said Vee.

"We can't find her," said Akiko. "I'm sorry."

"Misia found the secret passageways and is checking them," Vee said. "And Luis is helping her."

Dorothy gazed out over the bay trying to put herself in her mother's orthopedic shoes and imagine where she might have gone. Fluffy white clouds scudded across the sky as a dark speck appeared halfway between Isla Sosiega and the mainland.

"Look," Dorothy cried, pointing at the speck. "What is that?"

"I'll get some binoculars," Ralph said.

"Don't bother," Dorothy said. "I think it's coming this way." She jumped up and down, waving her arms at the object bouncing over the waves. "MAYDAY! MAYDAY!" she yelled at the top of her lungs.

Vee, Akiko, and Ralph joined her in shouting. Then Ralph whipped off his shirt, revealing a hefty midsection with enough chest hair to make Tom Selleck jealous. He waved the shirt like a flag, drawing attention from the approaching watercraft.

Dorothy squinted until she was able to make out more details. A sizeable motorboat with a small figurehead at the prow jumped waves in a spray of white froth. But as the boat approached, Dorothy realized it wasn't a figurehead but a person in an orange life vest.

Dorothy felt a wave of relief cascade over her like a waterfall as the person's cloud of white hair came into view and she realized who it was. Then she tensed up again, hoping her mother wouldn't fall overboard into the turbulent waters.

Surely someone attached her to something, she thought.

Ralph gestured at the boat to veer right, so as to avoid the remnants of the damaged dock.

"They should be able to pull up on the sand," Ralph said. "At least, I hope so."

The foursome raced down the sandy pathway to the demolished dock, just as the boat slowed to approach the shore. Dorothy never thought she'd be so relieved to see the word POLICE painted in block letters along the hull. A tall woman in a Day-Glo jogging suit with a matching terry cloth headband placed a steadying hand on Sophia's shoulder as a uniformed policeman tossed a rope to Ralph.

Ralph pulled the idling craft in close to a partially intact section of dock. The policeman leapt to shore and secured the boat. Then the woman hefted Sophia in her arms and passed her across the deck to the groundskeeper as if she were unloading a sack of potatoes. When she stepped onto the dock, Dorothy realized that the woman in the jogging suit was Detective Silva and the policeman was Officer Pierno, whom she'd first met during their first murder investigation months earlier in downtown Miami.

"Thank goodness you're here!" Dorothy said. "We have a killer on the loose, inside the villa!" Then she enveloped her mother in a tight hug. "I was so worried, Ma. Don't you ever do that again!"

"I used to say that when you crossed Clinton Avenue without permission." Sophia winked. "How the tables have turned!"

Dorothy handed Sophia her glasses. "I was so scared when I found these, Ma. What were you thinking? And how did you—"

Meanwhile, Ralph began leading Silva and Pierno up the path to the villa, followed by Vee and Akiko. Sophia moved to follow, but Dorothy placed a heavy hand on her shoulder.

"Why are we stopping?" Sophia said. "They might need our help. Plus, I don't want to miss anything."

"Oh no," Dorothy said. "We're not going anywhere until I get a full explanation!"

"I'm sorry, but I did what I had to do," Sophia said casually.

"You could have told me you were going to run off somewhere, for starters!" Dorothy said. Her mother's nonchalance was infuriating. "How in heaven's name did you get off the island?"

"I snuck off to find some candy and went looking in the library. You know, some people keep candy in their desks. I like nonpareils, but I would have settled for anything—even a Chuckles. But when I saw how bright and sunny it was through those giant windows, I realized the fog had cleared and thought that maybe I could flag down someone out on the bay."

"Again, you might have mentioned this to me so that I didn't have a heart attack!"

"First of all, we didn't know when Herman would reappear. Second, I knew you wouldn't let me. You're too protective, too cautious. Third, I didn't want to spend any more time on this death trap of an island. Fourth, I was right, because Detective Silva's here now. And fifth, I'll plead the Fifth if we keep talking about this." Sophia held up five fingers and waved away her daughter's complaints.

Dorothy watched the wind rustle the leafy crowns of the mangroves at the edge of the beach and tried to quell her frustration. She knew her mother was right. But still . . . maybe they could have hatched a plan together. She also knew that once her mother decided to do something, stopping her was as pointless as trying to derail a Sicilian freight train. Better to just get out of the way.

"Okay, okay, but *how* did you do it?" Dorothy asked.

Sophia began charging up the path to the villa, and Dorothy had no choice but to follow. "Listen, I recognized an opportunity, and I went for it. I saw a young man on a Jet Ski out on the bay. I had to get his attention, so I used my glasses and the sunshine to signal to him in Morse code. I thought about taking off my top, but I didn't want to scare the poor boy off. That's also why I ditched the glasses once he pulled up. I was trying to look younger, so he'd think he was picking up some hot babe."

Dorothy shook her head in amazement.

"Turns out he was a lifeguard on his day off. He dropped me off at Morningside Park, and guess who jogged right by the lifeguard station? Detective Silva! I almost didn't recognize her without her uniform, but she'd clocked me and was looking at me funny. Then she asked me if I was lost, if I knew my full name, what year it was, et cetera. I told her everything.

"I need to sit down," Sophia said once they reached the garden. She pointed to a curving stone bench. As they sat down, somebody's knees popped—Dorothy wasn't sure whose. From this location, she could see Silva and Pierno approaching the front door of the villa with Akiko and Vee.

Suddenly, a man emerged from a nearby row of hedges and ran by, kicking up gravel from the walkway as he sped past them.

"That's him!" Dorothy cried, just as Blanche and Rose

raced by in bare feet, huffing and puffing to catch up with Herman. Blanche held her shoes in one hand, El Toro's diary in the other.

As they sped past, Sophia stood up and clapped. Blanche dropped the diary but kept on going.

"Fifty bucks on Rose!" Sophia shouted.

Then Dorothy took off after her friends, picking up the diary along the way. After a few yards she kicked off her party shoes so that she could actually run. Herman had the advantage, wearing flat men's shoes as the three women pursued him in their bare feet over gravel pathways, patches of grass, and concrete walkways. With Dorothy's long legs, she soon caught up to her friends. Just as Herman leapt over a low shrub, Rose dove for his legs. She missed him by a few inches and landed in a nearby rose bush in an explosion of pink blooms.

"Are you okay?" Dorothy paused, offering a rose-covered Rose her hand. If she weren't so worried about her friend getting hurt, she would have laughed.

"I'm all right," Rose said, wiping dirt from her hands and pulling petals from her hair. "Go on, get him!"

Dorothy stepped over the line of shrubs and pounded down a concrete walkway lined with trees in the direction Herman and Blanche had gone. Her peripheral vision was a blur of greenery as she panted hard with every step, trying to ignore the pain in her heels and the tiredness in her legs as Herman got closer and closer to the edge of the gardens. Once he made it to the wilds surrounding the estate, it would be harder to catch him, Dorothy realized.

"Stand aside!" Detective Silva called, pounding up behind Dorothy, with Officer Pierno huffing along at her heels. Dorothy pointed ahead. Herman was sprinting alongside a deep, decorative pool lined with reproductions of Renaissance statuary, with Blanche gaining ground behind him. Dorothy hadn't seen Blanche this red-faced since the time she'd found out that her fiancé Harry had been, in fact, concurrently married to six other women.

Dorothy watched the detective narrow the distance to Blanche, who was clearly flagging. Dorothy cheered her on as she hobbled on bruised feet. But when she reached the pool, she saw something that stopped her dead in her tracks.

THE JAWS OF DEFEAT

30

With a last gasp of energy, Blanche flung a slingback at Herman and it bounced off the back of his head. He turned, still running, and she nabbed him with her second shoe, causing him to nearly trip into the pool. Her old boyfriend Stevie, who played baseball professionally, would have been proud of her aim. Then Silva and Pierno lunged to grab at Herman, who jumped into the water to evade their grasp.

"Stop!" cried Dorothy from somewhere behind her, just as Blanche was about to dive in after him. She paused and did a double-take as she noticed Detective Silva and Officer Pierno teetering at the edge of the pool. Herman dog-paddled away as a dark shape appeared behind him. Two bulbous eyes emerged from the water, and Blanche watched in horror as they were joined by a long, scaly snout.

The crocodile's head swung left and right as if searching for a scent, its body and tail writhing powerfully behind. Blanche estimated that it was at least seven feet long. Her whole body shook as she realized the danger Herman was in. She didn't like the man, but she certainly didn't want to see anyone else die.

"H-Herman?" Blanche quavered.

"You'll never catch me!" he turned his head to yell as he continued to paddle. Then his face went white as he saw what swam just a few yards behind him. He panicked, slapping the water into a froth as he tried to quickly swim away from the massive reptile.

The animal followed him, drawn by the motion and the sound of Herman's fearful squeals. Blanche clenched her hands together as Herman made it to the other side of the pool, just as the crocodile lunged for him. He climbed up a marble plinth and then shimmied up a statue to evade the creature's snapping jaws.

Detective Silva called for backup on her walkie-talkie as they ran around to the other side of the pool. Both she and Officer Pierno gave the statue and the croc a wide berth as the rest of the group arrived, watching the scene unfold at a safe distance.

"Elizabeth, no!" Ralph shouted. "Elizabeth!"

The crocodile turned her huge head toward the sound of Ralph's voice.

"What are you doing?" Blanche hissed. "Be careful!"

"Elizabeth," Ralph said in a calm, smooth voice. "Come to Uncle Ralph." He stepped away from the group and slowly approached the animal.

Elizabeth grunted, a deep, prehistoric sound that Blanche recognized from the shrieks they'd heard the past two nights. The croc looked to Herman, then back to Ralph.

"He won't taste good," Ralph said. "I promise. Even if you peel off the tweed."

Elizabeth dropped her head. She slowly turned on her thick, scaly legs toward Ralph. She opened her mouth, revealing sharp yellowish teeth and a pink tongue.

It almost looks like she's smiling at him, Blanche thought.

Ralph reached into his pocket and opened a strip of something that looked like beef jerky. He broke off small pieces of the treat and tossed them to Elizabeth, who caught them in her powerful jaws. He walked slowly, leading Elizabeth away from the gardens until they disappeared into the mangroves.

Herman scrambled for purchase on the statue, which Blanche now recognized as a replica of Michelangelo's *David*. Silva and Pierno closed in, calling to Herman to come down.

He pushed himself higher, but his foot slipped on a surprisingly petite member of David's anatomy and he tumbled to the ground.

"You are under arrest," Detective Silva said as she cuffed him. He sobbed while she read him his Miranda rights. Blanche walked up and offered him a tissue from Sophia's purse. Even though she was livid with the man, she saw how broken he was by what he'd done, and what he was about to face.

"I know you didn't mean to kill him," Blanche said in a voice heavy with emotion. "But why so many lies? Why lie about who you are? Why not come clean sooner? Why try to hurt Rose—you liked her!"

Herman batted the tissue away, letting it fall on the ground. "None of you people understand what it's like to come from nothing and try to break into the art world!" he snarled from where he lay on the ground, looking like a turtle that couldn't right itself. "We had no museum where I grew up. I had to pull myself up by my own shoestrings! But El Toro knew the real me. When we were both starting out, he encouraged me to create a new life for myself—to paint a version of the man I wanted to be—a combination of brilliant, mustachioed men like Poirot, Conan Doyle, Rubens, and Caravaggio. Over the years I hid my humble roots, perfected my accent, and worked my way up. I evaluated and insured pieces all over the world, in the finest museums and collections. I worked harder than anyone. I have—"

Akiko let out a throaty laugh as Vee scoffed.

"Do you think no one else had to work hard and reinvent themselves to be taken seriously in this business?" Akiko said. "Look around you!"

"I grew up as Verna Sheldon in Akron, Ohio. My parents wanted me to be an accountant," Vee said. "They never encouraged my interest in art, so I chose my new name and forged my own path."

"I didn't give myself a new name, but my father wanted me to stay in Kyoto and get married," Akiko said. "I didn't know *anyone* when I moved to the States. Do you think the world just handed me opportunities? That the galleries uptown welcomed me with open arms? Do you think it was easy for me?"

Blanche reflected on her own struggles early on, trying to follow her dreams in New York. She'd practiced her high kicks for hours, until her hamstrings screamed and her heels were bruised. Why, she'd even sacrificed a few toenails to the rigors of rehearsing with the Rockettes.

Herman just stared at Akiko as Detective Silva shook her head. Blanche wondered if he'd truly never before imagined anyone else having to struggle as hard as—or harder than—he had.

"We all make up stories from time to time," Blanche said. "I was Bianca Holloway for a while. But you don't use them to do wrong or to put innocent people in jail!"

"I don't really even need these glasses," Luis said, removing his aviators. "I thought they'd help people take me more seriously as a journalist, especially since I'm the youngest person in the newsroom, and the secretaries keep hitting on me. I've won awards for my reporting—I'm not some one-dimensional sex object!"

At that, Dorothy gave Blanche a deliberate glance.

"And I didn't really wet my pants the other day," Sophia said. When Detective Silva looked at her strangely, she added, "That was all made up. No, really!"

"All of my stories are true," Rose said. "Especially the St. Olaf ones. But I agree with Blanche's sentiment."

"How about you, Misia?" Dorothy said. "Do you have anything to share?"

Misia shifted uncomfortably on her feet. "Am I still a suspect?" she said hoarsely.

"Not according to us," Dorothy said. "Or this." She held up the diary.

Misia shot a glance at Vee, then back down to her toes. "I'm not just El Toro's assistant."

"She's his daughter," Vee interjected. "And mine."

Everyone except for the two cops audibly gasped.

"He didn't know I was his daughter." Misia smiled ruefully as Vee slung an arm around her shoulders and hugged her tight.

"I should have known this, too!" Akiko said.

"I kept her from Declan when he didn't follow me to California," Vee admitted. "When I got pregnant, he chose to focus on his career." She swallowed back tears and looked up at the sky. "I couldn't have a baby and an unsupportive partner, so I cut all ties over twenty years ago. I wish I had done things differently."

"I wanted to be a great artist like him," Misia said. "I applied for this job because I wanted it—I wanted to get it on my own merits, but I wanted to learn from the *best*, too. So I never told him who I really was. And I'll never get the chance to now."

As the young woman dissolved in sobs, Akiko, Vee, and Sophia, who was standing the closest to her, enveloped her in a hug.

Dorothy tried to reach through the comforting tangle of arms to tap Misia on the shoulder. "I have something you might like to hear."

Misia poked her head out from under the older women's embrace and sniffled.

Dorothy read aloud from the beginning of the diary. "'Today, a young woman showed up on my doorstep with her portfolio and résumé. Her talent blows all the other candidates away. Of course, I could be biased—she's my daughter. It was obvious as soon as I met her—she's a perfect blend of myself and Vee. And how many girls these days are named after Artemisia Gentileschi, the famous female artist of the 1600s? For now, I'll respect her privacy and not let on that I know her true identity.'"

Misia listened and sobbed, her face a jumble of emotions. Blanche finally recognized pieces of Declan in the planes of

Misia's face, her strong eyebrows, and her powerful emotions.

Dorothy continued. "'I'm hard on her because she's talented, and I don't want her to waste one bit of her gift. Sometimes it's hard not to treat her as a father would, but I must keep up the charade. Her suggestion to incorporate miniature portraits in my masterpiece was a stroke of genius. Perhaps, when I finish this canvas, I'll tell her how proud I am of her. And how much I love her.'"

By now, almost everyone was crying—including the cops.

"That's why someone took the will," Blanche said. "We suspect Misia is named as Declan's sole heir."

Vee cleared her throat. "I took it," she said. "When Herman began talking about blaming whoever would benefit from Declan's death, I knew I had to check the will and protect Misia in case he'd found out who she was and named her as his heir. It's hidden up in my room."

Blanche spun to glare at Herman. "And *you* didn't figure any of that out, did you? *Quite* the investigator! Maybe you should apologize to all of us—and especially to Misia!"

Herman looked at Misia, then back down to his cuffed wrists. All he could do was hang his head.

A pitiful example of a man, Blanche thought. Nothing like the rest of them, who had come together to unravel the mystery in the face of their grief and Herman's meddling lies.

"None of you understand! I was trying to make my mark in the world by helping El Toro! He had all the fame, all the money, all the women . . ." He gulped. "It's rather horrible when no one loves you, you know?"

"That's enough, Herman," Dorothy groaned. "You've been misquoting Poirot all weekend! If he's your idol, at least get it right!"

"We'll take it from here," Detective Silva said. "Officer Pierno will take your statements."

As the detective led Herman away, Dorothy and Rose stood on either side of Blanche.

"You've got quite an arm," Rose said to Blanche. "I'm proud of you!"

"*And* you figured out why the will was missing," Dorothy said. "Well done. I'm sure El Toro would be happy to know that Herman won't be getting away with his schemes."

Sophia tottered over, leaving Misia to be comforted by her mother and Akiko, as Blanche sagged against Dorothy and Rose, momentarily unable to support her own weight after the heated chase, not to mention the revelations and the emotions of the day. Thank goodness for her friends, she thought. It hadn't been easy, but they saved the day—together.

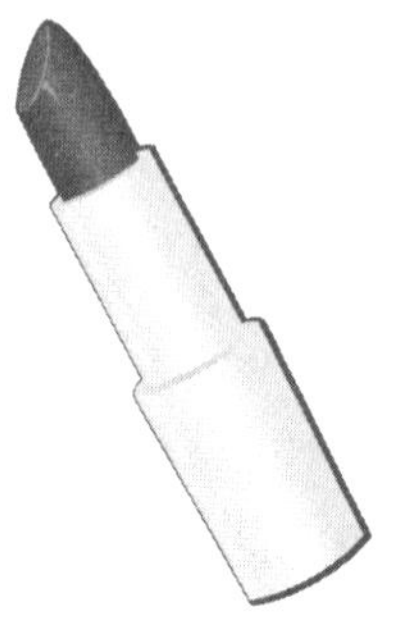

EPILOGUE
LIFE OF THE PARTY

.... *Six months later* ....

The windows of the ranch-style house at 6151 Richmond Street glowed a warm yellow against the encroaching darkness of the evening. Inside, Blanche pawed through her closet and pulled out a garment bag. Immediately after the stress of her weekend at Villa Velado she'd indulged in some retail therapy at Jordan Marsh to settle her nerves, and she'd been saving this outfit for months. She slipped into the white skirt suit with exaggerated padded shoulders and a nipped-in waist. Blanche turned this way and that in the mirror, satisfied that the jacket allowed a generous peek of the lacy camisole beneath. She'd nailed the look: professional, with plenty of sex appeal. After all, she had important roles to play at this upcoming gala: first, as Declan's muse, former lover, and friend, and second, as a representative for the Center for the Fine Arts in her newly created role of director of community relations.

Her role was a part-time position, the work taking place over long lunches and even longer dinners with potential museum donors. Blanche's strategy of focusing on wealthy businessmen and the recently widowed had paid off handsomely for the museum's coffers and for Blanche's social life. But another, equally rewarding part of her job was working with the local community to identify new artistic talent. And she'd found a wealth of it in Misia Toro, who had founded Miami's newest artistic organization: the Declan Toro Art Institute. The museum was cosponsoring the grand opening and fundraising gala for the center, and Blanche had advised Misia on the guest list, which included most of Miami's single men and everyone who was anyone in the art world, plus reporters and photographers from all local and national media.

Knowing she was likely to be photographed, Blanche checked her reflection one more time and realized she'd forgotten one small thing. She removed the butterfly brooch from her jewelry box and pinned it to her lapel, letting her hand rest over her heart for a moment as she thought of Declan. She knew he'd love what the villa was becoming under Misia's artistic vision and she couldn't wait to see what changes she'd made to the island in the past six months.

Checking her watch, Blanche realized it was almost time to

leave. She swiped on a little more lipstick and blew herself a kiss before stepping out into the living room, where Dorothy and Rose waited for her on the coral rattan couch.

Dorothy stood up, showing off her aquamarine velvet ensemble, complete with an ivory satin shirt and matching bow tie. "What do you think?" Dorothy said, gesturing to herself and Rose's periwinkle lace dress. "Are we dressed to kill?"

Blanche pouted. "Not funny, Dorothy. I'm ashamed of you!"

Rose giggled. "It was a little funny!"

Blanche forced a smile. Though they'd been through so much, this evening she'd been trying to avoid any thoughts of murder. If she could just keep her sadness about Declan pinned down tight like cellulite under a girdle, she would be able to enjoy the evening and celebrate the future. Then she looked Dorothy up and down, taking in the clashing textures of the brighter-than-her-usual colors that her friend was wearing.

"Let me fix that for you," Blanche said, reaching for Dorothy's collar. Though her friend looked stunning, Dorothy's high, buttoned-up neckline was a travesty against the type of femininity Blanche had been raised to uphold. She tugged on the bow tie, loosened it, and tossed it onto their rattan coffee table. She unbuttoned the top three buttons of Dorothy's shirt and popped the collar.

"Blanche, what are you doing!" Dorothy grumbled. "It's supposed to look like a tuxedo."

Blanche stepped back and admired her handiwork. Then

she leaned forward and unfastened one more button, revealing just a few inches south of Dorothy's clavicle, stopping short of showing actual cleavage.

"I'm helping you merchandise your goods," Blanche said. "Isn't that better?"

Dorothy looked down at herself. "I guess it does look a little more . . . *avant-garde* this way."

Blanche picked up the bow tie and swung it around her fingers. "And can I borrow this tonight? You never know when you might need to form a new attachment," she said with a naughty twinkle in her eye.

"You know what?" Dorothy said, grabbing the tie from Blanche's hand. "I think I'll hang on to it, just in case *I* meet someone tonight." She tucked the silky strip of fabric into her beaded evening bag.

Blanche opened her mouth to say that it was obvious that out of all of girls she'd be the one finding herself in flagrante delicto this evening, but she thought better of it. Now that she'd fixed Dorothy's outfit, her friend had more than a fighting chance.

"I'm not even worried about finding a man tonight," Blanche said airily.

"That sounds like real personal growth," Rose said. "I regret the time I called you a nautical toil—"

Dorothy cut her off with a sharp look.

"I meant that there'll be plenty of them at this event—more than enough to go around," Blanche said, completely ignoring

Rose's crack at her sexuality. She knew that St. Olafians were pathologically uptight, due to having been raised in layers upon layers of wool sweaters, so she wasn't offended by Rose's puritanical views.

"Plus, there are going to be so many VIPs at this party," she continued. "Elizabeth Taylor might even show!"

"Oh no," said Rose, wringing her hands. "Let's hope not!"

"The actress, not the croc, silly," Blanche said. "Though with the nature preserve aspect of the center that Ralph is spearheading, I suppose we can't rule her out."

Just then, Sophia emerged from her room in a gold floor-length skirt and matching twinset, as shiny as a life-size Emmy Award. She dragged along a large bamboo suitcase that perfectly matched her ever-present purse.

"Ma, what's all this?" Dorothy said.

"Last time we went to a party at this villa we got stuck for an entire weekend. I'm not taking any chances!" Sophia clicked open the suitcase, pointing to a tightly packed array of items. "Multiple pairs of underwear, three additional outfits, pajamas, toiletries, a stun gun, a two-way radio, some emergency flares, and a packet of Ding Dongs in case we run out of food."

"Where in heaven's name did you get all that?" Blanche gasped, placing her hands on her hips.

"You'd be amazed what you can get on the black market. I got these Ding Dongs at half price in the Winn-Dixie parking lot."

"She's talking about the stun gun, Ma," Dorothy said.

"Never mind that," Sophia said, snapping the suitcase shut. "I know people, okay?"

"Do you have room for Fernando in there?" Rose asked.

"Way ahead of you. I already packed your teddy bear." Sophia smiled, tapping the top of the suitcase. "Prophylactics for Blanche, a crossword puzzle for Dorothy."

"We're not going to get stuck overnight," Blanche said. "I've worked very hard to make sure nothing will go wrong at this party."

"Famous last words," Dorothy joked.

"I just want to do right by Declan's memory," Blanche said. Her voice wavered and she looked down at her hands until she was able to compose herself.

"I'm sure he would be proud to see what you and Misia have cooked up," Dorothy said kindly. "Come on, let's celebrate."

Dorothy pulled into the bayside parking lot where their adventure had begun six months ago. A dark-haired woman in her thirties emerged from a squad car in a slinky, off-the shoulder black dress.

"I hope you don't mind that I invited someone very special to make sure that nothing bad happens here," Blanche said.

"Detective Silva," Dorothy said, relieved to see her again.

"Hello, ladies," Detective Silva said. "But please, call me Carmen."

"If we're all buddy-buddy now, you can call me Rose," Rose said. "As in *to the occasion*."

"You must be working deep undercover," Sophia said. "I don't see any room in that dress for a badge."

"I'm here in an unofficial capacity, at Blanche's invitation," the detective said with a smile. "But don't worry, I'll do my best to prevent any murders or crocodile attacks."

The five women waited to be ferried to Isla Sosiega as evening fell. Sophia expressed her strong preference for a craft with a motor, but Blanche explained that went against the center's new ecological focus.

A muscular young man wearing a whistle around his neck piloted a glossy wood gondola to the pier and flashed a brilliant smile to the five women.

"It was my idea to hire lifeguards to row the guests to and from the gala," Blanche boasted. "Like I said, safety first!"

The lifeguard/gondolier extended a hand to Dorothy as she stepped into the boat. Was it her imagination, or did his hand linger on the small of her back as he helped settle her into her seat? Unlike the first time they made this journey, this ride was smooth, with a noticeable lack of grunting from the gondolier, who instead regaled them with stories about rollerblading in South Beach.

As they bobbed over the waves, Sophia tugged at Dorothy's

arm. "Returning here is making me think. Remember when everyone shared the stories they made up about themselves? Unlike most of us, you're not living a lie, not even a harmless one," she said. "I think it's because you're an original. You know who you are, pussycat, and it's wonderful."

Dorothy felt her eyes prickle as her mother's words sank in. She'd been feeling like her life was a washed-out pencil sketch compared to the vibrant mural of El Toro's cultural impact, Blanche's colorful love life, and Vee's and Akiko's professional accomplishments. The fateful weekend at Villa Velado had shown her that everyone—even El Toro—had their reasons for the stories they told the world.

But what about the stories we tell ourselves? Dorothy wondered.

Perhaps she needed to remind herself that she was an original, as her mother had said—not a copy of anyone else. Someone authentic who had raised a family and then built another with her friends, full of teaching, laughter, good books, midnight cheesecake, joy, and tears—a life just as big and meaningful as anyone else's.

Dorothy patted the corner of her eye with her sleeve. She didn't want to let on how much her mother's words had touched her.

When they reached the island, they found it transformed. The dock had been rebuilt and colorful banners hung from the trees, featuring the names and faces of the first cohort of students at the Declan Toro Art Institute.

The crowd spilled out of the villa and into the gardens, which were alight with twinkling votives, and the exuberant sounds of a live jazz band danced through the air. Misia greeted them at the entrance to the villa in a simple black dress with a bell-shaped skirt.

"Doesn't she look stunning?" Blanche said. "She's in Vivienne Westwood."

"Thank you all for coming," Misia said. "It's a bittersweet night, and it means a lot that you all are here."

"Where's your mother?" Dorothy asked.

"She's leading tours of her newest installation in the gardens," Misia said, taking them inside the villa. "This one's called *Veneration*, and it's in honor of my dad."

Dorothy smiled as they entered the party. Even though it was El Toro's death that had brought them all together, his bold, artistic spirit was very much alive this evening. His final masterpiece hung in the foyer, where every guest could stop and stare at El Toro looking down at them. He had captured his unique blend of pride, charisma, insecurity, and humanity so vividly in paint, and the unfinished corner added a raw, authentic feeling to the piece. Dorothy squinted to take in the myriad tiny portraits that made up the whole, including the faces she'd gotten to know in this very villa. As she relaxed her eyes again, she realized that El Toro's expression subtly changed depending on where the viewer stood.

Blanche dabbed at her eyes, and Dorothy slung an arm

around her waist as they gazed at the painting for a few more minutes before heading into the dining room, where the party was in full swing. While her mother made a beeline for the restroom and Rose made one to the buffet table, Dorothy leaned in a corner of the room, watching Blanche work the crowd of artists, donors, and Miami's glitterati.

"I hear you solved the murder with only your instincts and some lipstick," Detective Silva said, carrying over two champagne flutes. "That's some pretty good detective work."

"Oh, it was a group effort," Dorothy said. "Blanche figured out a lot of it. Even Rose helped. And if it weren't for my mother, you'd never have come to save us."

"Don't downplay your achievements," the detective said. "You worked together as a team and got it right. That's the hardest part, and I should know."

Dorothy allowed the compliment to sink in. She had kept their investigation on track, and they were all still standing at the end of it.

"To getting it right," she said, raising her glass.

As she sipped her champagne, she realized that a striking man across the dining room was looking their way. He was tall and silver-haired, with more than a passing resemblance to Richard Gere. Something about his eyes made Dorothy feel a little warm under her velvet tuxedo. She mentally shoved the feeling away, since he was obviously looking at Detective

Silva. But when the younger woman drifted off into the crowd, his gaze remained fixed on Dorothy.

He walked across the room sipping from a martini glass in a way that made her feel even warmer. Dorothy gulped her champagne, trying to work up the courage to say hello. Just as she was about to introduce herself, Sophia stepped right between her and Mr. Dreamboat. *Just my luck*, Dorothy thought.

"Have you met my daughter?" Sophia asked. "Isn't she beautiful?"

Dorothy coughed on her mouthful of champagne. Her mother had never spoken this way about her in front of other people, and she felt secondhand embarrassment for this man who was probably just trying to get to the cheese puffs.

"I'd like to," the man said in a deep, velvety voice. "And she certainly is."

"Well, you better watch out, because she's smart, too. She solved a murder right here in this villa, and she demolishes the crossword every Sunday. In *ink*," Sophia said proudly.

"As you can see, my mother doesn't hold back. If only I could make a decent lasagna—then she'd really be proud," Dorothy joked. She extended her hand and introduced herself. Then she turned to her mother. "Ma, why don't you check out the pie," she said sternly.

"Your mother is charming." The man chuckled as Sophia walked away.

"That's one word for it," Dorothy quipped.

His name was Vincenzo, and they talked about everything from their favorite artists to his business arranging food and wine tours throughout Europe. Unlike Stan and many other men she'd dated, he asked her as many questions as she asked him, and she felt the rest of the party fade away as they got to know each other. The conversation flowed so easily that Dorothy had the distinct feeling that he was going to ask her to come home with him. Vincenzo was so captivating and handsome, she doubted she would say anything but yes.

As the clock inched closer to midnight, Dorothy realized that the jazz band had packed up and a DJ playing current hits had taken over. Most of the crowd had gone home, except for the twentysomething students and their friends. Ralph cleared most of the empty platters and glasses from the dining room and returned with a fresh "off-key" lime pie in his hands. As he sliced it and served it to her friends and her mother, they stole glances and shot encouraging smiles at Dorothy, clearly not wanting to interrupt her flirtation. Dorothy realized that they were giving her plenty of space to explore this new connection—even Blanche wasn't inserting herself into the conversation. She felt a rush of appreciation for her friends, who knew how hard it was for her to open herself up to any man after what felt like a lifetime of bad dates.

After several minutes, Blanche apparently couldn't hold

back any longer. She strutted over to Dorothy. "I'm just going to borrow her for one minute," she called to Vincenzo as she pulled Dorothy to a corner of the room. "Don't you go anywhere!"

Blanche peeked at Vincenzo over Dorothy's shoulder. "You've got him, honey," she squealed. "We're all plumb tuckered out and we're going to take the next gondola back. Ralph even wrapped up some pie for us to take home, wasn't that sweet? We'll leave the porch light on for you."

Dorothy imagined Blanche, Rose, and Sophia at their kitchen table at home, giggling and gossiping about the night in their pajamas over sweet slices of pie. Her heart twinged, and she realized where she really wanted to be tonight. If Vincenzo was half as wonderful as he seemed to be, he'd wait for her and he'd understand.

Dorothy wrote out her phone number on a slip of paper from her purse and handed it to Vincenzo.

"I'll call you tomorrow," he said, and kissed her hand as if they were in an old movie.

Dorothy turned to join her friends. They linked arms and left the villa—and all of its memories—behind them. The night turned chilly as a strapping lifeguard ferried Dorothy, Blanche, Sophia, and Rose back to the mainland, and the four women huddled close together with their arms around one another. Dorothy basked in their shared warmth. Nothing felt better than their friendship.

ACKNOWLEDGMENTS

Thank you—always—to the creators of *The Golden Girls*, and to Bea Arthur, Rue McClanahan, Estelle Getty, and Betty White for inspiring me and for bringing joy and laughter to so many.

A huge, golden thank-you to my husband Nick Courage for his heroic support. Many thanks to my wonderful parents, and to Adrienne, Maria, and Danny for their Miami knowledge.

I am so grateful for my brilliant editor, Adam Wilson, my amazing agent, Andrea Somberg, and the team at the Harvey Klinger Literary Agency. Additionally to Tonya Agurto, Jennfier Levesque, Amy King, Olivia Zavitson, Crystal McCoy, Daniela Escobar, Matt Schweitzer, Daneen Goodwin, Greta Shull, Sara Liebling, Guy Cunningham, Sylvia Davis, Karen Krumpak, Jerry Gonzalez, Pearl Boonyawan, Jennifer Menjivar, and the audio team at Audible.

Thank you to my dear friends Emily Askin, Melissa Bramowitz, Allison Carey, Danielle Chiotti, Erin Craig, Annie Colvin, Alisa Drooker, Michelle Elsner, Emily Erstling, Katy Hershberger, James Meader, Hector DeJean, Janine Jelks-Seale, T. Kamara, Michael Lotenero, Lindsay Patross, Bronwyn Roantree, Tamar Krishnamurti, Bess Newman, Abby Wilson, Moira McGinley, Robin Carroll, and Katie Kurtzman, and to H. Alan Scott, Kerri Doherty, Albert Pellechia, Rhys Bowen, Elle Cosimano, Christina Lauren, Nancy Martin, and Julia Spencer-Fleming, for their kind support of this series.

To booksellers and librarians everywhere, and especially Susan Hans O'Connor and Penguin Bookshop, Barbara Jeremiah and Riverstone Books, Mike and Amy O'Brien at the Book Cellar, Andrew Medlar and friends at the Carnegie Library of Pittsburgh, and Ryan Labay at the Akron-Summit County Public Library.

"OFF-KEY" LIME PIE

For the Crust:

1 ½ cups crushed graham crackers
6 tablespoons melted butter

For the Filling:

3 egg yolks
28 oz sweetened condensed milk
1 teaspoon vanilla
½ cup sour cream
1–2 teaspoons lime zest (optional)
¾ cup lime juice

Crust

Mix graham crackers and butter. Press into a 10-inch pie plate.

Bake 8–10 minutes at 350 degrees.

Let cool.

Filling

Whisk eggs and add condensed milk, vanilla, sour cream, and lime zest (optional). Whisk thoroughly again. Then mix in lime juice and pour into cooled crust.

It you prefer a stronger lime flavor, reduce vanilla and add lime zest to taste.

Bake at 350 degrees for 10–15 minutes, watching carefully.

Decorate with whipped cream and lime slices as desired.

Recipe developed by Sandra Ekstrom and Rachel Ekstrom Courage

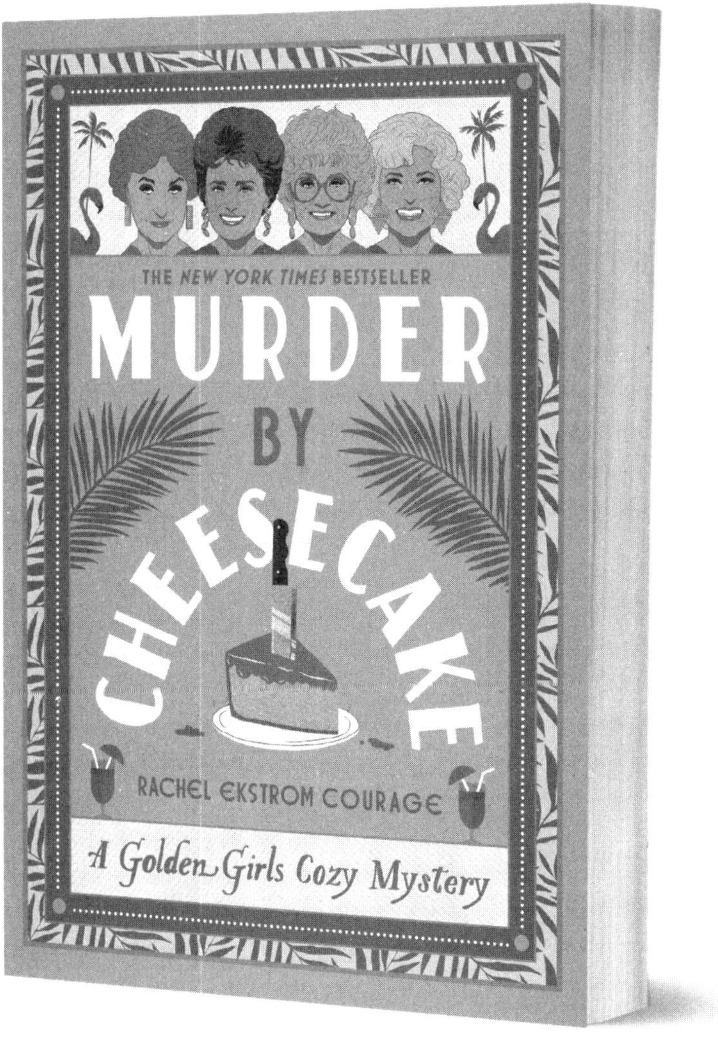